IN A HARD WIND

ALSO BY DAVID HOUSEWRIGHT

Featuring Holland Taylor

Penance

Practice to Deceive

Dearly Departed

Darkness, Sing Me a Song

First, Kill the Lawyers

Featuring Rushmore McKenzie

A Hard Ticket Home

Tin City

Pretty Girl Gone

Dead Boyfriends

Madman on a Drum

Jelly's Gold

The Taking of Libbie, SD

Highway 61

Curse of the Jade Lily

The Last Kind Word

The Devil May Care

Unidentified Woman #15

Stealing the Countess

What the Dead Leave Behind

Like to Die

Dead Man's Mistress

From the Grave

What Doesn't Kill Us

Something Wicked

Other Novels

The Devil and the Diva
(with Renée Valois)

Finders Keepers

IN A HARD WIND

David Housewright

MINOTAUR BOOKS
NEW YORK

First published in the United States by Minotaur Books, an imprint of St. Martin's Publishing Group

IN A HARD WIND. Copyright © 2023 by David Housewright. All rights reserved. Printed in the United States of America. For information, address St. Martin's Publishing Group, 120 Broadway, New York, NY 10271.

www.minotaurbooks.com

Library of Congress Cataloging-in-Publication Data

Names: Housewright, David, 1955– author.
Title: In a hard wind / David Housewright.
Description: First edition. | New York : Minotaur Books, 2023. |
  Series: Twin Cities P.I. Mac McKenzie novels ; 20 |
Identifiers: LCCN 2023004515 | ISBN 9781250863584 (hardcover) |
  ISBN 9781250863591 (ebook)
Subjects: LCGFT: Detective and mystery fiction. | Novels.
Classification: LCC PS3558.O8668 I6 2023 | DDC 813/.54-dc23/
  eng/20230202
LC record available at https://lccn.loc.gov/2023004515

Our books may be purchased in bulk for promotional, educational, or business use. Please contact your local bookseller or the Macmillan Corporate and Premium Sales Department at 1-800-221-7945, extension 5442, or by email at MacmillanSpecialMarkets@macmillan.com.

First Edition: 2023

10   9   8   7   6   5   4   3   2   1

FOR RENÉE
TIME AND TIME AGAIN

ACKNOWLEDGMENTS

Allow me to acknowledge my debt to John Brand, Vienna Crosby, Grace Gay, Moose Giannetti, Kayla Janas, Keith Kahla, Alice Pfeifer, Alison Picard, Daniel Polachek, Emily Polachek, Serena Soares Roberts, and Renée Valois for their assistance in writing this book.

I would also like to give a shout-out to the "Plot Whores Book Club," who really should find a better name: Jeanette Carrell, Bethany Gilman-Ryder, Ruth Krider, Amy DeVries Linabery, LuAnne Kinney Pederson, Rebecca Westerman Sauer, Sara Vaneps Smith, Jenny Carlson Wagenman, and Rachel Westerman Wright.

IN A HARD WIND

ONE

The alleged murderer seemed hesitant to shake my hand when we were introduced on the front steps of her suburban home. Truth be told, she gave off an aloof, if not haughty vibe that made me think she'd be reluctant to shake anyone's hand even under the best of circumstances. Only Sara Vaneps, the woman who had insisted on the introduction in the first place, assured her that I was a friend, so she placed her hand in mine. Her fingers were long and delicate and her grip wasn't particularly firm.

It must have taken some effort for her to bludgeon a guy to death, my inner voice told me.

"May we come in?" Sara asked.

The alleged murderer glanced quickly behind her as if she were afraid that something back there might escape and, after a moment, opened the door wider, giving us room to pass across the threshold.

"Where are my manners?" she asked. "Of course, of course, please."

After we entered, she closed the door and led us deeper into her house, gesturing at the sofa in the living room where she expected both of us to sit. None of us were wearing a mask despite the most recent COVID onslaught. 'Course by then most of us were so tired of it, we were more than willing to roll the dice.

"I must say, this has been one of the warmest autumns that I can recall," she said. "A warmer than average autumn after a warmer than average summer after a warmer than average spring. I'm wondering if this is the new normal. If it is, we might as well leave Minnesota and move to Arizona."

The alleged murderer smiled while she waited for us to agree with her.

"It certainly has been warm," Sara said.

I don't know what I had been expecting, but it wasn't Jeanette Carrell. She was tall and attractive, almost statuesque, with brown eyes, short blond hair, and a dignity that seemed to transcend the simple blue shirtdress that she wore. She found a wingback chair across from us and sat. When she crossed her legs, I noticed the black electronic GPS monitor strapped to her ankle. She noticed me noticing.

"Court ordered," Carrell said. "I was released on bail, yet only if I remain attached to this ornament. Do you realize that it costs me ten dollars a day to wear this thing? And unlike the cash bail I paid to the court, that money will not be returned to me when I appear for trial. Outrageous."

"You posted your bail in cash?" I asked.

"Certainly more fiscally responsible than paying a bail bondsman ten percent off the top merely to handle the transaction, wouldn't you agree?"

"Most people don't have a half million dollars lying around."

"I've always been good with money. In any case, my bail was set at two hundred and fifty thousand."

"Oh?"

That surprised me. In Minnesota, a charge of second-degree murder with intent is usually worth double that amount, if not considerably more.

"Apparently, the judge thought at my age I was a low flight risk." The alleged murderer held her leg straight out toward me. "And, of course, there's the anklet."

Carrell studied me for a few beats and smiled some more.

"I gave you a lead, yet you didn't follow it," she said.

"Lead?"

"When I said 'at my age' you were expected to ask 'how old are you?' I would answer 'I'll be sixty-five on December fourth' and you would say 'you don't look a day over sixty' and I'd say 'Oh, you charmer, you.'"

"My mistake," I said. "I'll try to do better next time."

"It usually takes me five minutes to decide if I'm going to like or dislike someone. With you it might take a bit longer."

"Stop it," Sara said. "Both of you."

The alleged murderer gazed deep into my eyes as if she was searching for something, a clue perhaps, that might tell her if I could be trusted. I stared back for the same reason.

"So, Mr. McKenzie," she said. "Why are you here?"

Good question.

The answer began for me with a phone call from Shelby Dunston's older sister Evangeline. I had known Evan almost as long as I had known her sister; Shelby had introduced us when we were all in college. Back then, Evan didn't care for me even a little bit. In fact, she was actively unpleasant. 'Course, in those days I still harbored designs on Shelby; I still thought I could win her away from that loser Bobby Dunston who, by the way, is my best friend and has been since we were about five years old. Finally, Shelby made it clear in no uncertain terms that she had made her choice and had simply become my friend, too. Afterward, Evan became much more agreeable. She even enlisted me as her plus one on a number of occasions when an "acceptable escort" was required.

The last time I had seen her was at the reception that Nina and I threw to celebrate our wedding. She arrived alone, which came as a surprise. Shelby had told me that her family had high hopes for Evan's third husband. I thought that might be the reason she had called me on her cell phone, because of her ex. Instead, she told me that she needed a favor for a friend.

"Actually, it's not for her, but for a friend of hers," Evan said.

"You want me to do a favor for a friend of a friend of my friend," I said.

"Yes."

"Uh-huh. What would that favor be?"

"Not much. Just help her get away with murder."

That caused me to pause for a few beats.

"McKenzie, are you still there?" she asked.

"I'm here. Evan, I'm not sure I'd help you get away with murder and I actually like you, so . . ."

"Well, my friend claims she didn't do it; that she's innocent."

"Who is she?"

"My friend?"

"No, her friend."

"McKenzie, you're confusing me."

"Look at it from my point of view."

"My friend is named Sara Vaneps and she's just a sweet-heart. You'll like her when you meet her. Her friend is Jeanette Carrell, who's not nearly as sweet. Anyway, Carrell was arrested for killing this guy and burying him in her backyard. She's out on bail now and awaiting trial which starts, I don't know when it starts. On TV the trial always begins like the day after the arrest, but in real life . . . She was arrested in May, if that makes any difference. That's what, six months ago?"

"I don't know, Evan. Murder?"

"Have I ever asked you for a favor before?"

"Frequently. How 'bout that wedding when you made me pretend to be your boyfriend to make two—count 'em—two ex-boyfriends jealous? I must have danced with you thirty times and I don't even like to dance."

"That was fifteen years ago and you got a couple of hugs and kisses out of it. What more do you want?"

"The hugs and kisses were just for show."

"McKenzie . . ."

"All right. I'll meet with your friend, but no promises. Just so we're on the same page, though, I'm doing this for you, not her, and not for her friend whatshername, the murderer."

"Thank you. Who knows, you might get another hug and kiss out of it."

"Promises, promises."

I followed Evan's directions to her home in Shoreview, a second-ring suburb located north of St. Paul that a now-defunct national magazine had once named the fourth–Best Family Town in America. I asked when she had moved there; the last I heard, Evan lived in Minneapolis.

"I bought this place in March," she said. "Right after I divorced husband number three. My family keeps telling me that I marry very poorly and they're right. On the other hand . . ."

"You divorce very well."

"We all have our special talents."

There were very few sidewalks in Shoreview, so we walked along the lightly traveled street four houses down to where Sara Vaneps lived. The house was covered in tan stucco with brown wood trim and looked at least two decades older and twice as large as the houses surrounding it. At the end of a cobblestone path we found an enormous rounded-top front door with an antique knocker. Evan didn't use the knocker, though. Instead, she pressed a doorbell. A few moments later, the door was pulled open by a young woman dressed in baggy sweatpants and a sweatshirt that didn't match. Her hair was unkempt and her eyes looked tired.

"Hi," she said.

Evan's response was to wrap the woman in her arms and hug tight.

"How are you, Sara?" she asked.

"I've seen better days. What else is new?"

"Your grandfather?"

"He's not here."

Evan released the woman and stepped back, an expression of genuine concern on her face.

"Where is he?" she asked.

"My sister took him; I'm not sure where they went."

"She did?"

"I've been begging my family for help. For months I've been doing this alone and it's so exhausting, only my parents, aunts, uncles, brothers, sisters, cousins—they're all too busy, or so they say. I'm the one without a job, they also say; without a husband. I'm the one who should be taking care of my grandfather. How hard can it be? Except my sister came over to drop something off and took one look at me and—and I guess she didn't like what she saw because she apologized and said from now on she'll do more to help out; that she'll make the rest of the family help out, too."

"Good for her."

"We'll see. You must be McKenzie." Sara stepped away from the door and Evan and I entered her house. "I've been told a lot about you."

"Don't believe everything you hear."

"Not even that you saved that woman from kidnappers? What was her name? She was, like, a billionaire."

"Idle gossip," I said.

"It was in the newspaper."

"They'll print anything these days."

"I met her at your wedding reception," Evan said. "Riley Muehlenhaus Brodin-Mulally. She thinks you walk on water."

"You've known me for twenty-five years. Do you think I walk on water?"

"Honestly?" Evan did something I didn't expect. She rested her hand on my wrist and smiled in a way that made me think that those long-ago hugs and kisses hadn't been entirely for show after all. "You've had your moments."

It seemed like a good time to turn my full attention on Sara.

"You said you're taking care of your grandfather?" I asked.

"What did Evan tell you?"

"Almost nothing."

Sara nodded as if that was the way she wanted it.

"I suppose you could argue that everything that's happened, happened because of him," she said.

The gazebo on the hill was large enough to shelter the University of Minnesota Alumni Band. It had eight sides, a concrete floor with brick steps leading up to it, a two-foot-high wooden railing, arched walls, and a roof that resembled the hat the Wicked Witch of the West wore in *The Wizard of Oz*. It was surrounded on each side by a football field's worth of carefully mowed, gently sloping lawn. A thick circle of black oak, white cedar, red maple, Scots pine, butternut, and American elm trees began where the lawn ended. Beyond the trees, I could see only the rooftops of the dozen or so houses that surrounded the park.

The gazebo was furnished with plenty of comfortable mismatched lawn furniture. We sat on some of it and drank red wine from the bottles Sara had stowed in a picnic basket. Apparently, a wine, cheese, and French bread lunch was not uncommon at the gazebo.

"I remember when my grandfather built it," she said. "That was what? Twenty-seven years ago? I think I was four or five at the time."

"Your grandfather built all of this?" I asked.

"Yes. Him and"—she gestured at a roof on our left—"Jeanette Carrell, too. Over there"—she gestured at a small shack erected on a cement slab near the trees overlooking Carrell's roof—"they also built a shed. There are lawn mowers, shovels, axes; all kinds of stuff in there that neighbors can use. You can't see it from here, but there's also a brick fire ring. They did that, as well. The fire ring is on Jeanette's property, all of the rest of this belonged to my grandfather. Everyone calls it the Circle."

"Belonged?"

"You get to the point, McKenzie. I like that. Yes, 'belonged.' What happened was, my grandfather bought the lot where his house sits now, I don't know, fifty-some years ago? Shoreview wasn't even incorporated until 1957 and hardly anyone lived out here back in those days; only about five thousand people. It was all open fields, which was why my grandfather moved here. He said it was like living in the country. There was his house and J. C.'s and Ruth Krider's and that was about it. In the early nineties, this was, like, two decades or more after grandfather had moved here, they started to get serious about developing the place. One of the developers who was active back then, a guy named Charles Sainsbury who built a house—do you see the roof over there with the charcoal-colored tiles?"

I did.

"That's his place," Sara said. "Anyway, one day he was chatting with my grandfather and J. C.—she had just moved in with her husband; moved into the house where she lives now—and he was telling them about his grand plan to develop the neighborhood, this neighborhood. I think he even had a name for it, for his development, only I don't remember what it was. Shoreview something. Instead of being impressed, though, my grandfather and J. C., they're like, oh no. So they got together without telling Sainsbury—my grandfather had done very well for himself. His name is Carson Vaneps. He was a bigwig at General Mills. You know Bugles, the corn chip shaped like a horn? That was him.

"Anyway, he and J. C. bought the entire hill. Grandfather bought about four-fifths of it and Jeanette the other fifth. The thing is, though, and this is important—Sainsbury didn't seem to care. Not at the time, anyway. Back then there was plenty of other property around here that he could work with, not like today, when there's a serious shortage of affordable housing and places to build it. So everybody remained friends. I mean, Sainsbury and his family spent as much time in the Circle, enjoying the gazebo and fire ring, as anyone. My grandfather made sure that everyone who lived around it was welcome. J. C. did, too. It was like a private park. Families would hold picnics. One family—the Westermeyers—actually held a small wedding reception right here in the gazebo. Kids would play here; camp out, even. We have a book club that gathers around the fire ring. During the height of COVID, neighbors would congregate in the gazebo, sitting six feet apart, you know? People sang songs. It was wonderful.

"Then about eight months ago, right after the snow started melting, neighbors found surveyors on the hill who claimed they were charting property lines. That's when we found out that my grandfather had sold the rights to the Circle to Charles Sainsbury's company. Everyone was appalled. They went to my grandfather and asked him about it, but he claimed he didn't sell the property; he didn't know what they were talking about. Only Sainsbury's son, William, had a signed contract that said he did. That pretty much confirmed what some of us in the family had suspected but ignored for a long time, that Granddad was having memory issues. My parents brought him in and had him tested and yeah, he had Alzheimer's. So, now we're in court fighting the contract, citing diminished capacity, arguing that Granddad was not of sound mind when he signed. Well, not 'we' exactly. The contract—it's actually a pretty lucrative deal the lawyer said, and half the family would be happy to see the court enforce it if it meant they'd get a cut when Granddad passes."

Sara sighed deeply and covered her face with her hands. For a moment, I thought she might begin weeping; only she resisted the impulse. After a moment, she uncovered her face and took a long pull of her wine.

"Which brings me to the favor," Sara said. "As angry as my family was, as Grandfather was when it was explained to him what happened, Jeanette Carrell was even angrier. I mean, she gave new definition to the word furious. At one point, Sainsbury came up on the hill to explain himself; J. C. wouldn't even let him speak. She just blew up at him. It was one of those moments like on TV comedies when mothers used their hands to cover the ears of their children. She threatened to kill him in front of a lot of witnesses. She threatened a lot of things. That was in April, the middle of April. Then Sainsbury disappeared. Two weeks later, they found his body buried in a shallow grave on J. C.'s property. They arrested her for murder. And here we are."

"The favor?" I asked.

"Help her," Sara said. "Help J. C. She didn't do it, McKenzie.

I know she didn't. She's one of the kindest, most generous people I've ever known. She was always looking out for me when I was a little girl, looking out for all the little girls; one of the few people who spoke to us like we were adults. Who told us things we needed to know, mostly about men. One of the few people today who seem to understand how difficult it is for me to take care of my grandfather. I'm happy to do it; please don't get me wrong, McKenzie. I love my grandfather. It's so hard, though. J. C. is one of the few people who have actually offered to help, sitting with him sometimes while I run errands. I just can't—I can't lose her, too. McKenzie, I used to work in the fashion industry before COVID and my bosses closed the shop. I was very chic and very pretty and I could get men to do my bidding with a smile. All that's changed . . ."

"Oh, I don't know," Evan said. She was gazing at me and grinning when she added, "Give it a try, girl."

Sara hesitated for a moment before she looked at me, too.

"Please," she said.

"Let's go talk to your friend," I said.

Ten minutes later, I was sitting next to Sara Vaneps on a sofa in Jeanette Carrell's spacious living room. Evangeline had declined to accompany us.

"It'll be hard enough to get Carrell to speak to McKenzie without having me standing there," she said.

"She likes you," Sara said.

"No, she doesn't. I haven't been a member of the Circle long enough for her to like me. At best she tolerates me."

Now Carrell was barely tolerating me.

"Sara said she might bring a friend by to meet me," she said. "Are you that friend?"

"Yes."

"You know I'm sitting right here," Sara said.

"Sara, I meant to inquire—how is your family's court case going?" Carrell asked.

"Like yours. It just seems to drag on and on. Our lawyer says we're in"—Sara quoted the air—"the disclosure and discovery phase, although I don't know what more needs to be disclosed or discovered in order to rescind a contract. I think trials take this long because all the lawyers want it to take this long. More billable hours for them."

"You'll let me know immediately if there are any developments, won't you?"

"Of course."

Carrell turned her attention back to me.

"McKenzie, I thought you'd be taller," she said.

"How tall do I need to be?"

"Why did Sara insist we meet?"

"She thinks I might be able to help you."

"Help me what?"

"Escape what could very well be a life sentence in prison, I mean for a woman who's fast approaching sixty-five but looks fifty."

"Fifty?" Carrell chuckled. "Nice try, McKenzie. I have the situation under control, though."

"If you say so."

I stood. Carrell stood. Sara leaned back against the sofa and folded her arms over her sweatshirt.

"Dammit," she said.

"Sara . . ." Carrell said.

"Sit down, Jeanette, and listen just this once. And you . . ."

"Excuse me," I replied. "May I use your restroom?"

Carrell gestured more or less toward the front door.

"Down the corridor on your right," she said.

I left the living room in a hurry. The wine I drank was starting to work on me, only that wasn't the reason for my retreat. I just wanted to get out of the way of what I expected to be an animated heart-to-heart discussion.

I found the bathroom, entered, and closed the door behind me. I noted that the toilet seat was up. Nine months ago that wouldn't have affected me whatsoever, but now I could hear my wife's voice in my head. "Put the damn seat down." I try to remember, yet old habits are hard to break.

I finished my business and cautiously made my way back down the corridor. I heard voices.

"I'm serious, J. C."

"Oh, I'm J. C. now. Do you think you're old enough to call me that, little girl?"

"You know I am."

"Only my dearest friends call me that."

"So you've often said, J. C."

"Just tell me—do you trust this man?"

"Yes."

"Why?"

"Look at me. Look at how I'm dressed. My hair. This man has seen me at my very worst, and yet he's still willing to help. I haven't had a lot of experience with men who are like that."

"He's seen me at my worst, too."

"I've noticed and I keep wondering why you're behaving so . . ."

"Bitchy?"

"Yes."

"Where did you find him?"

"He's Evangeline's friend."

"That's not necessarily an endorsement."

"I think it is."

"All right, I'll let him help—if it'll please you and Evan. I don't know what he can do, though."

That's when I reentered the room. Both women watched me do it.

"Tell me, Ms. Carrell," I said. "Do you live alone?"

For the briefest of moments, I thought I saw a flash of alarm in her eyes.

"Yes, I do," she said. "Why do you ask?"

"What about your husband?"

Carrell leaned heavily against the back of her chair, closed her eyes, and blew a lung full of air out of her mouth.

"Well," she said. "Well, that's— McKenzie, Sara told me that you used to be a police officer. She told me that you saved the Muehlenhaus girl from kidnappers and helped catch the man who murdered the beekeeper years ago and even found the gold hidden by Jelly Nash. I'm sure there are many other things you've been involved in that didn't reach the news media, as well."

"One or two."

"She told me that you've made a hobby out of helping people who don't necessarily have anywhere else to turn."

"I wouldn't call it a hobby but, yes, I suppose that's true."

"Tell me why."

"Because I can."

Carrell took a deep breath and released it slowly.

"My husband abandoned me twenty-seven years ago last June," she said. "He didn't even bother to say good-bye. I actually filed a missing person's complaint when he didn't come home from work. Three days later, the police found his car parked at the airport, only they never found him. I don't think they looked very hard. It was a domestic matter, they said. I haven't seen or heard from my husband since. I haven't remarried. I haven't been able to fully trust a man with the singular exception of Carson Vaneps. Now you want me to trust you."

Question is: Can I trust you? my inner voice asked.

"You need to trust someone," I said aloud.

"Tell me what you want to know," Carrell said. "Ask me anything."

"You said earlier that you had all this under control. What did you mean?"

Carrell took what seemed like a long time before she answered.

"I'm innocent," she claimed. "I have confidence that a jury of my peers will agree."

"That's very optimistic of you," I said.

"My lawyer says the state's case is circumstantial at best. That's why the county prosecutor keeps offering plea agreements."

"That you turn down?"

"That I turn down. I'm not naïve, McKenzie. I appreciate the immense danger I'm in. And, make no mistake, I despised Charles Sainsbury. I hated the ground he walked on and the air he breathed and I do not mourn his passing because of what he did to us; the way he betrayed us. Yet, as I continue to tell anyone who will listen, I did not commit this crime. If you can find a way to excuse my rude behavior, I would appreciate any help you can give that will prove my innocence."

"Well, for one thing, you should stop telling everyone how much you hated the victim."

"My attorney says the same thing. Everything will be fine, though. If things look bad—well, you'll see."

"See what?"

Carrell didn't answer.

"I would very much like to speak with your attorney," I said. "Please give me his name and cell number and then call and tell him that it's okay to discuss your case with me."

"I can tell you everything you need to know."

"No, you can't."

"McKenzie . . ."

"Do you have copies of the police reports?"

"As you wish. I'll contact my lawyer immediately."

"He probably won't like me kibitzing."

"He works for me, I don't work for him. Remind him of that if he gives you any trouble."

"All right."

"Tell me, though, this desire to examine the evidence compiled against me—is it to assure yourself that I am, in fact, not guilty?"

"I'll call you later."

"I'll understand if you don't."

I gathered the information I required and Sara and I left Carrell's house through the rear exit. Carrell walked us out. Clearly, she was an avid gardener. She had twelve raised gardens in her backyard, each in the dimensions of a small car, separated in three rows of four. The gardens had once held assorted flowers, vegetables, and herbs but were now covered with mulch in preparation for a hard Minnesota winter. However, there was a wide strip of fading white, white and pink, yellow, orange, and purple wildflowers that had yet to succumb to an early frost spanning the width of the backyard and the red and orange flowers of trumpet vines growing along the five-foot-high wooden wall that separated Carrell's backyard from her neighbor's.

"I'm surprised that they're still blooming," Carrell said of the flowers. "Usually this time of year—of course, it's been so warm."

"Where was Sainsbury's body found?" I asked.

"Not here," Carrell said. "I would have known if someone had been in my backyard, don't you think? No, it was up there."

She pointed at a spot, not above her own yard, but her neighbor's, just past the trees that circled the hill.

"My property goes this way." Carrell pushed two hands directly in front of her. "It goes up the hill until it reaches the trees, and then this way across the hill." She pushed both hands apart. "Like a T. Charles's body was found on the left side of the T at the edge of my property near the trees where we have the fire ring."

"That's what?" I asked. "Sixty, seventy yards away from where we're standing?"

"How can people say they found Sainsbury in my backyard? It's not my backyard."

"No, it isn't."

Once again I told Carrell that I would call her. She returned to her house while Sara and I crossed her yard, passed through the circle of trees, and climbed the hill. We veered to the left to look at the spot where the body had been discovered. The fire ring was basically a shallow six-foot circle surrounded by gray and brown paver brick that looked as if it had been carved from the same quarries as the blocks they had used to build the pyramids. There was a pile of wood, some cut with a chain saw and some split with an axe, along with branches from the trees that residents had just dragged up there. Near the brush pile was a hole the length and width of a man and about two-and-a-half-feet deep. It was partially covered with leaves.

"This is where they found him?" I asked.

Sara stood on the far side of the fire ring as if she was reluctant to move any closer.

"Yes," she said. "There had been some yellow tape and wooden stakes posted, but that all came down a few months ago."

I stood next to the hole and looked around. I was impressed by how secluded it seemed, even knowing there were a dozen houses nearby and streets with traffic. I couldn't see Jeanette Carrell's house, much less her backyard. It wasn't the worst spot to hide a body, I decided, if the killer had done it right; had dug the hole deeper.

"How did they find the body?" I asked.

"I think they call them cadaver dogs," Sara answered.

Which meant the authorities had already suspected that Sainsbury had been killed when they began looking for him, my inner voice told me.

"Okay," I said aloud.

Sara and I left the fire ring and hiked to the gazebo. I didn't know if Evangeline had left and come back, or if she had been waiting for us the entire time, yet she was sitting in a comfy chair and drinking wine when we arrived. Sara moved to the picnic basket and retrieved a bottle. She waved it at me. Because I nodded my head, she poured a glass and handed it to me. I took a sip and sat near Evangeline. Sara did the same.

"McKenzie," Sara said. "Tell me what you're thinking."

"I'm thinking that I have many questions that have yet to be answered before I decide what I'm going to do."

"If it was me, I'd be climbing the walls," Evan said. "Only, from what I've seen, Jeanette doesn't seem particularly worried. I wonder why."

"That's one of them."

"She didn't do it," Sara said. "J. C. couldn't have done it."

I nodded my head just to be polite. Truth was I hadn't formed an opinion although, as was usually the case, I was leaning heavily toward the cops.

"I have a question," Evan said. "If Jeanette didn't do it, if she didn't kill Sainsbury and bury his body, who did?"

"Off the top of my head, with almost no evidence to support it, I'd say it was done by someone who lived on the Circle," I said.

Evan and Sara immediately glanced at each other as if to ask, Was it you? and quickly glanced away. They continued to sip their wine in silence, yet I knew what each was thinking, what they were asking themselves—who among their friends and neighbors was most likely to commit murder?

TWO

Alexander Brandt was wearing a dress shirt with the sleeves rolled up and his top two buttons undone. His suit jacket was hanging from a hook attached to the door of his office; if there was a tie, it was stashed somewhere out of sight. His mask was lying on his desktop; mine was in my pocket. He smiled at me as he swiveled back and forth in the chair behind the desk in his office.

"How did Jeanette Carrell come to hire you?" I asked.

"I'd like to think it's because I'm very good at my job; because *Mpls.St.Paul Magazine* named me one of the Top Criminal Lawyers in the Twin Cities. But mostly it was because of the first result she found when she surfed the internet; a website listing the top thirty Twin Cities criminal attorneys. Carrey-Brandt was third. The first two firms were located in downtown Minneapolis, however. We're the first with a downtown St. Paul address. Apparently, Ms. Carrell wanted someone who was close to the Ramsey County Adult Detention Center. That's where she called us from."

"You did a good job getting her bail reduced," I said.

Brandt raised his hand and let it fall as if the achievement was barely worth mentioning.

"Mr. Brandt," I said.

"Alex. Call me Alex."

"Alex, what do you think Carrell's chances are?"

Brandt smiled.

"I like that you didn't ask me if she was guilty or not," he said.

"I've been in this business for a long time, first as a cop with the St. Paul Police Department and now as a kind of unlicensed private investigator. I know how it works. Most people believe the criminal justice system is designed to favor the guilty. Defense attorneys are routinely blamed for helping bad and dangerous people go free and, let's face it, sometimes you do help bad and dangerous people go free. But it's the system we live by. Without it—I suppose we'd have the chaos that Shakespeare predicted in *Henry VI* when Dick the Butcher told the pretenders to the throne that if they wanted to take over England, *The first thing we do, let's kill all the lawyers*."

Brandt smiled some more.

"All right, all right," he said. "There's no need to suck up."

"Just wanted you to know that we're on the same page."

Brandt held his hand straight out and gave it a little wag.

"About fifty-fifty," he said. "Carrell's chances depend on how well the evidence against her is presented. The assistant county attorney is a young guy named Ted Kaplan; at least he's younger than I am. It's been my experience that he likes to present a case in chronological order. This happened, then this happened, then that happened. He tries to simplify it; dumb it down. He figures if he walks the jury through the particulars one by one, they'll come to believe that they would have reached the exact same conclusion that he had. It's not a bad strategy."

"Carrell told me that the evidence against her was circumstantial."

"The ACA might agree. At least, he doesn't seem overly confident in his case. He made what he said was a 'courtesy call' when I demanded disclosure under Rule 9. At the time, Carrell had been charged with murder in the first. He offered to amend the charge to murder two if we accepted a plea deal. We refused and yet he reduced the charge, anyway. Two weeks ago, he offered manslaughter in the first. We turned that down, too. I thought he might make another offer when we had a remote meeting with the judge last week; everything is remote because of COVID. Only he didn't. 'Course, we don't have a trial date, yet. Once that's set, negotiations will escalate and I expect that to be soon; possibly this week."

"Carrell also gave me the impression that she has a secret weapon," I told him.

Brandt lifted and dropped his hand again, making me think that was something he did a lot.

"Me, too," he said. "I've asked her if she can prove she's innocent. I even gave her a lecture; quoted the law at her. In a criminal trial, the defense must provide the prosecution with a list of witnesses who may testify and all the evidence it might present. The prosecution will then have the opportunity to interview those witnesses and examine the evidence. This includes any alibi she might think she has, what they call an alibi defense. She must explain in detail where she was at the time the crime was committed and what witnesses will be called or evidence that will be presented to support the alibi. If she doesn't do this before the trial, she might be prevented by the court from doing it at all."

"What did she say?"

"She said she wasn't a martyr. She said she wasn't going to pour kerosene over her head and set herself on fire; that when the time came, she would do what she had to do to save herself just like everybody else. McKenzie, should I tell you why I'm glad you're here?"

"I didn't know you were."

"I checked you out; that shouldn't come as a surprise. Turns out we have friends in common. Genevieve Bonalay, for one."

"You know G. K.? She's my attorney."

"For what it's worth, she said that half the fun she gets out of her practice is when you call her. So, yeah, I'm glad you're here and I'm going to answer any questions you might have and in exchange, you're going to tell me what Jeanette Carrell is holding back before it's too late."

"Just as long as you know I'm not a lawyer, Alex. I am not bound by the ethics of your profession. If I decide that she's guilty, I'm not going to help defend her, anyway. At the very least, I'll just walk away."

"Fair enough."

Brandt swiveled his chair toward the credenza directly behind him. On top of the credenza was a file folder. He picked up the folder, spun back around, and set the file on his desk directly in front of me.

"I have a meeting," he said. "I'm already late. Why don't you read this? When I get back, we'll talk some more."

The first page in the file came from the State of Minnesota, County of Ramsey, District Court, 2nd Judicial District, in the matter of the State of Minnesota (Plaintiff) vs. Jeanette Lee Carrell (Defendant) and stated:

The Complainant submits this complaint to the Court and states that there is probable cause to believe Defendant committed the following offense(s):

COUNT 1

Charge: Murder—2nd Degree—With Intent—Not Premeditated
Minnesota Statute: 609.19.1(1)

Maximum Sentence: 40 years

Charge Description: On or about April 19, 2022 in the County of Ramsey, Minnesota, the defendant, Jeanette Lee Carrell, did cause the death of Charles Sainsbury with intent to affect the death of Charles Sainsbury.

STATEMENT OF PROBABLE CAUSE

At around 8:30 PM on April 19, 2022, William Sainsbury called 911 and asked police to perform a welfare check on Charles Sainsbury, age 83, at his address in the City of Shoreview, Ramsey County. William Sainsbury said he had not seen Charles Sainsbury that day as expected and that Charles had not answered his phone when called. William Sainsbury said that he usually hears or sees Charles a few times a week, if not daily.

Deputies from the Ramsey County Sheriff's Department, which provides police services to the City of Shoreview, went to the Shoreview address and found the house lights on. However, Charles Sainsbury did not answer when the deputies attempted to contact him. The house was unlocked and the deputies entered the premises. A search revealed the house to be empty. Deputies conducted a search of the surrounding neighborhood including a private park located directly behind the house but were unable to locate Charles.

William Sainsbury was contacted by deputies. A Minnesota Missing Persons Bulletin Information and Release Form was subsequently filed and forwarded along with appropriate photographs to the Bureau of Criminal Apprehension Minnesota Missing & Unidentified Persons Clearinghouse. Charles Sainsbury was listed as endangered because of his age, although William Sainsbury said Charles did not present any cognitive disorders associated with Alzheimer's or dementia.

After the missing persons report was filed, deputies reached out to William Sainsbury, as well as family, friends, and neighbors of Charles. It was determined that Charles Sainsbury was working as a semi-retired property developer for the company he founded, Sainsbury Construction, Inc. The company is now operated by his son, William Sainsbury. Charles Sainsbury was expected to arrive at the office in the early afternoon of Tuesday, April 19, 2022. When he did not, efforts were made to contact him. Charles lived alone.

On April 20, deputies interviewed Charles Sainsbury's next door neighbor, Ruth Krider. Krider said that she thought she saw Charles leave his house and walk up the hill to the park that bordered both his and Krider's property, but that she could not be sure of the time except to say it was in the late morning. She also said that neighbors were very angry at Charles because of his plans to raze the park and turn it into a housing development.

Interviews with other neighbors confirmed Krider's statement. Jennifer Carlson told deputies that the anger was so great that an additional neighbor—Jeanette Lee Carrell—threatened to kill Charles in front of numerous witnesses.

At around 4 PM on April 20, deputies working out of the Criminal Investigations Unit interviewed Jeanette Lee Carrell in her home located at 541 East Glendale Road. She said she had not seen Charles Sainsbury for several days and did not know that he was missing. She confirmed that she did threaten Charles when she learned of his plans to develop the private park, of which, she claimed, she was part owner. She said the threats were "the mere utterances of an angry suburban housewife."

At around 5 PM on April 20, deputies spoke with Sara Vaneps, another neighbor. Like the other neighbors, she confirmed the threats made by Jeanette Lee Carrell against Charles Sainsbury. She said that a lot of the neighbors made similar statements. She also told deputies that a civil suit had been filed in Ramsey County Court on behalf of her grandfather, Carson Vaneps, to halt Charles Sainsbury's housing development, but that the outcome was still pending.

At around 10 AM on April 28, 2022, Jennifer Carlson called Deputies from the Ramsey County Sheriff's Department. She said that she had noticed what she called "a terrible smell" coming from an area in the private park near a fire ring. She said she had first noticed it a few days earlier but thought little of it. It smelled like someone had dumped their garbage, she said. She said the smell now is "horrendous." She said, because she knew that Charles Sainsbury had been missing for nine days, that she "feared the worst."

On April 29, deputies executed a cadaver dog search warrant in the private park. The cadaver dog searched the park and indicated an interest in an area along the tree line near the fire ring. The handler said it was a strong indication and showed that there was sign of decomposition or blood present.

Deputies later determined that the property was owned by Jeanette Lee Carrell, that it was part of her backyard.

On April 30, 2022, the Minnesota Bureau of Criminal Apprehension crime scene response team excavated the area. The team uncovered a human body. The body was turned over to the Ramsey County Medical Examiner's Office.

The crime team also uncovered a gold and diamond pin very near the crime scene, but not actually in the grave, specifically a brooch approximately one and a half inch by one and three-quarter inch in size, with the initials J. C. in gold in the center surrounded by twelve small diamonds.

Many neighbors had gathered in the private park as the body was uncovered. One neighbor, Katherine Hixson, told deputies that she had seen Jeannette Lee Carrell digging in the area at about 11 PM the night that Charles Sainsbury had disappeared. Deputies asked where she had been when she witnessed Carrell digging, and Hixson said looking out her upstairs window. She lived next door to Carrell. Deputies quickly determined that because of the trees, distance, and lack of light it would have been extremely difficult for Hixson to identify Carrell. Hixson said that she didn't know it was Carrell until she saw Carrell emerge from the tree line and walk to her property. Hixson said Carrell was carrying a spade shovel that she set next to a compost pile that was located against a five-foot-high wooden wall that Hixson and Carrell shared. She said the light shining from above both her and Carrell's back doors made Carrell easy to identify.

On May 2, 2022, the Ramsey County Medical Examiner completed an autopsy on a body recovered from the backyard of Jeanette Lee Carrell. The body was identified as Charles Sainsbury. Sainsbury's body had two blunt force injuries to the back of the head. The cause of Sainsbury's death is cerebral laceration and destruction due to the two blunt force injuries to the head; the manner of Sainsbury's death is homicide. The time of death was placed at between 9 AM and 11 AM on April 19, 2022.

On May 3, 2022, deputies interviewed Jeanette Lee Carrell in her home. Sergeant Michael Swenson told Carrell that a cadaver dog had been alerted to the smell of a dead body in her backyard. Carrell was repeatedly asked if Charles Sainsbury's body was buried in her backyard. Finally, Carrell gave deputies permission to dig in her backyard to their heart's content.

Sergeant Swenson told Carrell that they had dug up her yard and had discovered Sainsbury's body. Carrell repeatedly asked "Where, where?" Sergeant Swenson said it was up near the fire ring. Carrell told him that anybody and everybody goes up there. Carrell wanted to know why he was bothering her.

Sergeant Swenson displayed a photograph of the gold and diamond brooch with the initials J. C. Carrell wanted to know where the brooch was found. She indicated that she had lost the brooch "weeks ago" and had wondered what became of it. Sergeant Swenson said that the brooch was found near where the body was discovered. Sergeant Swenson said that an eyewitness said Carrell was digging in the area near the time that Sainsbury disappeared.

Carrell refused to answer any more questions. Carrell was arrested and advised of her constitutional rights. As she was being led away, she asked Sergeant Swenson when exactly Sainsbury had been killed. Sergeant Swenson answered honestly. Carrell replied, "It'll be okay, then. That's the least of my worries." Sergeant Swenson pressed Carrell to explain her meaning. She refused.

Complainant declares under penalty of perjury that everything stated in this document is true and correct. Minn. Stat. § 358.116; Minn. R. Crim. P. 2.01, subds.1, 2.

Complainant	Michael Swenson
	Sergeant
	425 Grove St.
	St. Paul, MN 55101
	Badge: 638

Hey, you know that guy, my inner voice reminded me. *Mike Swenson, you've worked with him in the past.*

Beneath the complaint was another court document that stated:

NOTICE BY PROSECUTING ATTORNEY
OF EVIDENCE AND IDENTIFICATION PROCEDURES
PURSUANT TO RULE 7.01

To the above-named Defendant and her attorney: Pursuant to Rule 7.01, Minnesota Rules of Criminal Procedure, you are advised that in the above-named case the prosecution has:

- Evidence against the Defendant obtained as a result of a search, search and seizure, wiretapping, or any form of electronic mechanical eavesdropping.
- Confessions, admissions, or statements made by the Defendant

At trial, the State may offer any of the items of physical evidence described in the attachments to the complaint, or to this Disclosure.

The evidence in question was the brooch found near the crime scene and the statement consisting of the words Jeanette Lee Carrell spoke to Sergeant Michael Swenson—"Where did you find that? I've been looking for it for weeks."

Next in the file Brandt had given to me was a transcript of a deposition that Katherine Hixson had given to Brandt. This surprised me. In Minnesota, if witnesses for the prosecution decide not to speak to a defense attorney, there's no legal way to compel them. They could easily say "See you in court, jerk" and that would be the end of it. Yet Hixson not only agreed to speak with Brandt, she agreed to do it in her own home while being recorded.

"All right, then, let's begin. First, can you please tell me your name?"

"Katherine Hixson."

"Where do you live?"

"At 539 East Glendale Road in Shoreview, Minnesota."

"Is your house adjacent to the house where Jeanette Carrell lives?"

"Right next door, yes."

"Right next door to 541 East Glendale Road?"

"Yes."

"Jeanette Carrell is your neighbor."

"Yes."

"How long have you lived here?"

"Three years. We moved in three years ago last September."

"We?"

"My boys and I. I have two sons. Tom and Mark. Tom is ten now and Mark is eight. They both go to St. Odilia Elementary."

"Your husband?"

"I'm a single parent."

"Have you had much opportunity to talk to Jeanette Carrell during the time you've lived here?"

"Oh, sure."

"Frequently?"

"I don't know. A couple times a month, anyway. Mostly up on the Circle."

"Would you say you know her well?"

"No. No, I don't think anyone knows her well, except maybe for old man Vaneps. She's not—well, she's not an easy person to know."

"Would you say you were friendly?"

"Neighborly, anyway."

"But not friendly?"

"It's not like we go shopping together; have girls' nights out. But we get along just fine."

"How would you describe her?"

"Aloof."

"I mean, physically."

"Physically? Why?"

"How tall would you say she was?"

"A little taller than me."

"How tall are you?"

"Five six."

"Would you be surprised if I told you that she's five nine?"

"No, not really."

"What color are her eyes?"

"Brown."

"Light brown, dark brown?"

"What's in the middle?"

"Ms. Hixson . . ."

"They're just your basic brown."

"How much does she weigh?"

"I have no idea."

"How much do you weigh?"

"One thirty."

"Is she as heavy as you?"

"I'm not heavy."

"I meant . . ."

"I would say about the same. Maybe a little less. One twenty-five."

"Would you describe her as thin?"

"Slender, I would say slender."

"What color is her hair?"

"Oh, I get it. You want to make sure that I can identify her in the dark. Well, I can. I've known her for three years and maybe we don't talk as much as neighbors should, but I see her all the time. Besides, it wasn't dark because of the lights in our backyards. Her hair is blond, by the way. A whitish blond. I think she dyes it, you know, to hide the gray."

"You told police that you saw Jeanette Carrell digging behind the trees on the hill behind your house."

"Not really, no."

"No? You didn't see her?"

"No. Well, I saw her, but . . ."

"Ms. Hixson, you saw Jeanette Carrell or you didn't see her."

"Stop trying to confuse me, okay? I don't even have to talk to you, you know? I'm doing you a favor."

"I appreciate that, Ms. Hixson . . ."

"And stop calling me Ms. Hixson. My name is Katherine. My friends call me Kate."

"Kate . . ."

"Listen, Alex—you said to call you Alex."

"Yes."

"I don't know what the cops told you, the deputies, whatever they are. What I said is that I saw someone up by the fire ring and it looked to me like that someone was digging, okay?"

"Where were you when you saw this?"

"I was in my bedroom. I was getting ready for bed. It was a school night and when you have kids as old as mine, morning comes awfully early. So, I was getting ready for bed and I looked out the window."

"What time was this?"

"Eleven o'clock. Well, maybe a little before eleven."

"Five minutes before?"

"I don't know, maybe."

"Ten minutes before?"

"No more than ten minutes before."

"Where is your bedroom?"

"Upstairs facing the back. Do you want to see it?"

"I would, thank you."

The recording was paused. When it resumed, Brandt made it clear that he and Katherine Hixson were standing in her bedroom and that the bedroom was facing the backyard.

"This is the window you were looking out?"

"Yes. I was taking off my clothes right here where you're standing now and I looked up and out the window and I saw someone moving behind the trees."

"Were the lights on in your bedroom?"

"That one was, over there in the corner next to the bed, but it's not very bright."

"But the light was on inside your bedroom?"

"Yes."

"There would have been a mirror effect, wouldn't there?"

"I could see through the window."

"The light would bounce off the window, making it difficult if not impossible to see out."

"The light wasn't that bright and, besides, when I noticed the movement I went close to the window like this, and I had my hands cupped along my face like this, and that blocked the light from the bedroom. I could see everything happening outside."

"What did you see?"

"I saw movement, like I said; what I told the cops, the deputies. You see a lot of people up on the Circle. At night you see them around the fire ring, roasting marshmallows or something. Only that night, it was a Tuesday night, a school night, and you don't usually see people that late, around eleven o'clock I mean, and, besides, there was no fire in the fire ring, just someone moving around and that's why I was watching when normally I would have just ignored it because I was curious, you know, wondering who it was."

"But you couldn't tell who it was, is that right?"

"That's right."

"You couldn't see that it was Jeanette Carrell."

"I didn't say that I did."

"The sheriff deputies reported . . ."

"Listen, I'm really glad you came here now because clearly the deputies got it wrong. I never said that I saw Jeanette digging in the trees. I said I saw someone digging in the trees."

"Someone?"

"Yes. I didn't know it was Jeanette until she came down the hill."

"You could see that it was Jeanette Carrell walking down the hill?"

"Yes."

"In the dark?"

"Look. You see that path there? Look out the window. You see that path there that kinda starts where the wooden wall is and curves up the hill and behind the trees? Do you see it?"

"Yes."

"So, I'm watching, my face pressed against the window glass like I showed you, okay? I'm watching the figure; I didn't say I *knew who it was. I watched the figure follow the path through the trees and down toward the wall and that's when I knew it was Jeanette, when she got close to our backyards. I could identify her because of the light she has above her back door and the light I have above my back door. I watched her, wondering what she was doing. She came down the path and then I noticed she was carrying a shovel. She went to the wall, the wooden wall. You can see over the wooden wall from my window, right? I watched her walk to the wall. There's a compost pile against the wall, her side of the wall. You can't see it from here, but it's there."*

"Okay."

"Jeanette set the shovel against the wall next to the compost pile. Well, you can't see the shovel now, either, because the deputies took it. Probably they thought it was evidence."

"I'll check."

"Then Jeanette walked toward her back door and I stopped watching."

"Ms. Hixson . . ."

"Oh, we're back to that, are we?"

"Why didn't you come forward right away?"

"What do you mean?"

"Why did you wait so long before telling the deputies what you saw?"

"I didn't know what I saw."

"You knew that Charles Sainsbury had gone missing."

"Not until the next day."

"Deputies interviewed you when you got home from work at—I think it was 5:30 P.M. on Wednesday, April 20."

"Yes."

"They told you that Sainsbury was missing."

"I didn't know he was dead, though. That he was buried on the Circle. Why would I even think that?"

"You didn't tell the deputies what you saw for eleven days."

"That's not fair. I didn't have any idea about what was going on until that Saturday . . ."

"Saturday, April 30?"

"Yeah. I mean, all these cops and guys dressed in white were up on the Circle so I went up there to see what was going on like everybody else. I mean, there were, like, two dozen people up there. And I watched what they were doing, the deputies and the guys doing the digging by the trees near the fire ring, and when they found Charles's body . . ."

"Kate . . ."

"'Course everyone on the Circle hates me now. I mean, not everyone, but Jeanette was mostly popular. I didn't see it myself, but I guess she did a lot for the people, helping to build the Circle and maintain it and let everyone use it and then when we heard what Charles was planning, I didn't like it, either. But God . . . God! I mean, I had to tell someone what I saw. Wouldn't you?"

"I'll kill you. I'll kill you, motherfucker, for what you're doing," I said.

Alexander Brandt had just returned from his meeting. He hung up his suit jacket and was removing his tie when he asked, "So, McKenzie, see anything interesting?"

I answered him, reading from the notes he took when he interviewed Carrell's neighbors.

Brandt reclaimed the chair behind his desk.

"When I first met her, I thought Jeanette Carrell was very prim and proper; almost Victorian in her bearing," he said. "To hear those words coming out of her mouth . . ."

"Surprised me, too."

"I can put twenty people on the stand all testifying to her

character; all stating that she was warm and loving, especially to the young girls who lived on the Circle. One of them, Sara Vaneps, actually said that an injured bird would bring tears to her eyes. Unfortunately, half of them would also be forced to testify that they heard Carrell threaten to gut Charles Sainsbury like a fish if the ACA questioned them and you know he'll question them. I asked Carrell about that. 'Gut you like a fish?' I asked. She told me that she had no idea where the words came from. She said she had never been fishing in her life and wasn't even sure what 'gut you like a fish' meant."

"I bet Sainsbury did, though," I said.

"You read the transcripts—Sainsbury was invited to go up to the gazebo and explain himself to his neighbors. He spoke about business opportunities and caring for his family but when he started going on about how tearing down the gazebo would actually be good for the community, Carrell just exploded. Fortunately, she wasn't the only one. Unfortunately, she was the loudest. Couple of days later, Sainsbury disappeared."

"It's interesting to me that everyone seemed to be angry with Sainsbury, but not Carson Vaneps," I said. "He's the one who sold the property to Sainsbury in the first place."

"The people I've spoken with believe that he was taken advantage of."

"I wonder if he was."

"My understanding, there's a civil suit winding its way through the court to decide just that. So, McKenzie—are you in or are you out?"

"I don't know what I could do to help."

"People say things, don't they, to their family and friends, to a guy on the street that they wouldn't necessarily repeat to law enforcement or prosecutors or a defense attorney. Sometimes it's because they don't want to be involved; sometimes it's because they're afraid they'll get in trouble themselves.

"Yeah, I get that."

"Go out and make a nuisance of yourself and see what turns up. Genevieve Bonalay said that's what you're best at, making a nuisance of yourself."

"I've had some experience. The thing is, I'm unlicensed, Alex. There are those who will tell you that I carry a lot of baggage, too. You don't necessarily want to put me on a witness stand."

"Give me something I can use; the rest will take care of itself."

"I have a question for you, though—all things considered, would you rather defend Jeanette Carrell or prosecute?"

"Oh, defend. There's more money in it and we always get paid whether we win or lose."

"And you wonder why defense attorneys get a bad rap?"

THREE

It had an official name—the Ramsey County-St. Paul Criminal Justice Campus—and it was located just northeast of downtown St. Paul in a neighborhood called Payne-Phalen that had originally been settled by transplanted slave owners from the south who named the roads after the flowers of their homeland. It consisted of the Ramsey County Sheriff's Department, St. Paul Police Department, Adult Detention Center, Second Judicial District courtrooms, and a regional training facility and did resemble a college campus, except for all the police cars. Deputy Sergeant Michael Swenson worked out of the comparatively new Law Enforcement Center, which I'm sure pleased him greatly. Back in the day, I had a desk in the SPPD's James Griffin Building on the corner of the campus, which apparently had been built before air-conditioning. On the other hand, the coffee was just as awful in both places.

Swenson and I chatted in the cafeteria. His "workspace," as he called it, was a desk in a room surrounded by a dozen other desks and manned by his colleagues in the Ramsey County's Criminal Investigations Unit. It was actually quieter and more private in the cafeteria. Ramsey County had a mandate—all visitors and employees were required to wear cloth face coverings regardless of whether they were vaccinated or not. We could remove our masks only while we talked. Given our current COVID infection rate, that was probably a good idea.

"How long has it been?" Swenson asked. "I haven't seen you since that joint task force thing that Bobby Dunston ran, what was it, five years ago?"

"No, I saw you at Kale's retirement bash . . ."

"That's right."

"And the fund-raiser they did for Scotty Holman's wife."

"When she was diagnosed with cancer. That was big of you, by the way. Stepping up like that. Except I know you, McKenzie. You're not a guy who makes social calls, so to what do I owe the pleasure?"

"Jeanette Lee Carrell."

"I should know that name, shouldn't I?" Swenson asked.

"Homicide in Shoreview. . . ."

"Yeah, yeah, yeah. Tall and blond; an older woman yet still a babe, am I right?"

"Some would certainly call her that," I said.

"She killed her neighbor and buried him in her backyard."

"Not her backyard."

"If memory serves, the grave was discovered by cadaver dogs on property she owned that was right behind her house. What would you call it?"

He had me there.

"That was what, April?" Swenson asked. "May?"

"You arrested her May third."

"There was something about that case, nothing pertinent or I would have included it in the complaint . . . What was it? Ah, I can't remember. It's probably in my notes, though. Anyway, what about it?"

"I've been asked to look into it," I said.

"You're telling me this because . . . ?"

"I don't want to piss you off by double-checking your work."

"What do I care?" Swenson asked. "I always know the defense attorney will involve someone to challenge the evidence, usually a PI, but why not you? You can't take it personally, you know that. You work the case as best you can, as diligently as you can, gather the evidence, present it to the ACA—after that, it's on him. I've already moved on. Well, not moved on. I still have to present the evidence in court if the suspect doesn't take a deal, still . . . May third, you say? Do you know how many cases I've worked since then, how many homicides?"

"Too many," I said.

"Way too many."

"You won't care if I involve myself?"

"No, I told you."

"What if I find something that proves she's innocent?"

"It's like I said, you can't take it personally," Swenson said. "You know, McKenzie, I wouldn't have signed the complaint if I didn't think she was guilty and I had the evidence to prove it. On the other hand, if I screwed up, if I missed something, by all means give it to the ACA; help set an innocent woman free. That's how it's supposed to work, the system. 'Course, if you find something that proves beyond a doubt that she's guilty, I'd expect you to give that up, too."

"I'm not an officer of the court," I said.

"You're not an asshole, either. Are you? You didn't become an asshole since the last time I saw you, did you, McKenzie?"

"I hope not."

"The other thing I remember about her, Carrell—besides being a babe, I mean—when I wound the cuffs on her, she said something cryptic that suggested she might have an alibi. I'd have to check my notes to remember exactly what. What I do remember is that I spent a lot of time reviewing everything I had on the case after that and I didn't find a thing. I even went to the ACA to get a search warrant to check the GPS coordinates on both her cell phone and her car. The car never left her garage. The cell was ten years old, a G3 for God's sake, and the GPS wasn't nearly as accurate as the newer models, especially around trees, and there are a lot of trees in the area. Yet it was good enough to place her within twenty, twenty-five yards of her house both when the murder took place and when a witness placed her at the grave site."

"Twenty yards puts Carrell in her house, not at the crime scene," I said.

"It places her phone in the house, not her. My point is—she can't claim she was shopping at Rosedale or eating a Dilly Bar at the Dairy Queen when it went down. Plus, it's been what, six months, and nothing's come out? I'm confident we got the right girl."

What bugged me is that I thought he might be right.

I called Jeanette Carrell.

She seemed surprised to hear my voice, although she didn't say so.

"Let's talk," I said.

"Okay, talk."

"In person."

"Why? So you can watch my eyes; see what I do with my hands?"

She understands body language, my inner voice told me.

"You're a smart woman," I said aloud.

"Smart enough not to bury a man in a shallow grave in my backyard. You believe that, don't you?"

"Let's talk," I repeated.

She sighed her reply—"How aboat the gazebo?"

Aboat?

"In fifteen minutes?" I asked.

"I'll be waiting."

She was, too. I had driven around the area twice looking for a path that led to the Circle and didn't find one. The only way to gain access to the park was to cut through someone's yard. I cut through Evangeline's. I found Jeanette Carrell sitting on the steps of the gazebo and staring at nothing in particular.

She waved her leg at me as I approached.

"I'm legally allowed to go anywhere I like within the state of Minnesota," she said. "I've discovered, though, that this is about as far as I can go without alarming the authorities. McKenzie, I love this place so much. When my husband abandoned me I was—lost. I had no idea what to do with myself. I was thirty-eight years old and convinced that no one loved me; convinced that my co-workers were talking behind my back, my neighbors, asking themselves what I did to cause him to leave the way he did; wondering the same thing myself. I was a mess, to put it plainly. Working on this place, helping to build the gazebo is what kept me going."

"Then Charles Sainsbury threatened to take it away from you," I said.

"Motive for murder."

"People have killed for less."

"I know this will sound absurd considering everything that I said to the man in front of witnesses, yet the thought hadn't actually occurred to me; killing Charles, I mean."

"The prosecution will probably call it a crime of passion."

"Passion?" Carrell asked.

"For a moment or two your emotions ran so high and so hot that you snapped."

"Is that what you think happened?"

"I don't know what happened," I said. "Why don't you tell me?"

"I can't. I wasn't there."

"Where were you?"

"In my house."

"Not according to your neighbor."

"Kate was either mistaken or lying," Carrell said.

"Why would she lie?"

"We don't get along very well."

"She said that you did."

"That's what I mean," Carrell said. "You know what? Maybe the state of Minnesota should be looking at her instead of me."

Maybe it should.

"Katherine Hixson said she saw you carrying a shovel down the hill from the Circle; that was at about eleven P.M. The actual murder took place at about eleven A.M., though, the theory being that the killer bludgeoned Sainsbury with a blunt object, left the scene, and returned later to bury the body. Where were you at eleven A.M.?"

"Home."

"You don't work?" I asked.

"I took a buyout from my company when COVID first hit a year and a half ago."

"You retired early?"

"Not too early. Besides, I already told you that I was good with money. My house is paid for; my needs are few. I've earned a respectable income for the past thirty years, too, with no one to spend it on except me. It was easy to save and invest."

"You were alone at both eleven A.M. and P.M.?"

"I'm nearly always alone," Carrell said. "I prefer it that way."

"When I visited your house earlier, I found the toilet seat was up."

Carrell hesitated before she replied.

"What did that tell you, McKenzie?" she asked.

"I know what it tells my wife."

"I can't remember when I last used the downstairs bathroom,

possibly not since I cleaned it. One week ago? Two? I can't say why the toilet seat was up or if I'm the one who left it up."

Carrell didn't invent a story to explain the discrepancy and deliver it in a loud voice, which is what liars usually do, my inner voice told me, *or so you were taught at the academy.*

"Okay," I said aloud.

"I've come to a conclusion, McKenzie. Should I tell you?"

"Please do."

"I decided that I like you."

"I can't imagine why."

"You didn't call me a liar. Most people would have. It suggests that you have an open mind."

"The day's still young," I said.

Carrell thought that was funny enough to laugh. While she laughed, movement off to my right caused my head to turn. A man was approaching; I placed him at no younger than eighty. He was dressed in a suit with black dress shoes and a white dress shirt unbuttoned at the collar. He labored up the hill like it was the hardest thing he had done in some time. He was smiling broadly and brightly.

"There's my girl," he said.

Carrell came off the gazebo steps in a hurry.

"Carson," she said.

He held his arms wide as if he was expecting a hug.

"C'mon, Jacey," he said. "You know you want to."

Carrell hurried into his arms.

They embraced for what seemed longer to me than two good friends might; embraced until Carson nudged the woman away.

"Stop it now," he said. "You know how excited I get."

Carrell continued to hold the old man's hand even as she stepped back.

"What are you doing here?" she asked.

"Where else would I be?"

"I mean, where's Sara?"

"Sara? She better be in school if she knows what's good for her. Tell me, who's this strapping young man? Another one of your boyfriends?"

I stepped forward and offered my hand. He shook it; his grip was feeble and I made sure mine wasn't much stronger.

"This is McKenzie," Carrell said. "McKenzie, this is my dearest friend Carson Vaneps."

"A pleasure, sir," I said.

"Sir?" Carson repeated. "Polite. I like that. Only listen here. I've been friends with this young lady for ten years now . . ."

Ten years?

"If you don't treat her right, we'll have words."

"I'll remember that," I said.

"See that you do. Jacey"—Carson gestured with his hand at more or less the entire park—"look at this place."

"What about it?" Carrell asked.

"It looks great. The grass is cut, the clippings raked up. Don't tell me the neighbors are actually starting to lend a hand."

"The Westermeyers have taken over lawn mowing duties."

Carson's face suddenly went blank, although his lips moved as if he was attempting to pronounce a word that he was unsure of. Carrell pointed at a red tile roof.

"They live over there," she said.

Carson followed her hand, yet he might as well have been looking into the sun.

"Their daughter was married in the gazebo," Carrell added.

"Oh, oh, oh, that's right. Rebecca. Or was it Rachel?" Carson leaned his head close to Carrell's and spoke in a low voice. "My memory, Jacey. I've been having trouble with my memory, lately. I don't know what it is. I pour a cup of coffee and then another one and then another and all of a sudden I have a half dozen cups of coffee growing cold around me. Do you think I should see someone?"

"I think you'll be fine, Carson. None of us are getting any younger and I know how much you like your coffee."

"True." Carson straightened up and smiled some more. "Except for you. The rest of us are getting old, only I swear, Jacey, you become lovelier every time I see you. You have a painting in your attic, don't you? Wouldn't you agree—what's your name again?"

"McKenzie," I said.

"I'm lousy with names. It's a wonder I even remember my own. Do you know what I mean by a painting in her attic?"

"*The Picture of Dorian Gray*," I said.

"Good for you." Carson turned toward Carrell. "This one's smarter than the last guy. The last guy was dumber than a corn chip." Back to me, again. "Did Jacey tell you how we came to build this place, her and me?"

"I know the story," I said.

"It was after that asshole husband—"

"He knows the story, Carson," Carrell said.

"The whole story?"

"Yes."

"Well then, he's a better man than I am, Gunga Din. Remember that movie?"

"I remember it," I said.

"Cary Grant, Douglas Fairbanks, Jr.—what was the name of that guy they covered in shoe polish to make him look like he was from India?"

"Sam Jaffe."

"Can't do that anymore; cover a guy with shoe polish. I should take a look at the fire ring."

Carson began to move off in that direction, but Carrell tightened her grip on his hand.

"The fire ring is fine," she said.

"They delivered the paver stone? Already?"

"It's all been taken care of."

"Let's take a look."

"No, Carson, why don't you stay here and talk to us?"

"No, no, no, come between you and your boyfriend? No, no. Besides, don't you want to dance alone in the gazebo? I remember when you used to do that, you and . . . and . . . I forget his name."

"You danced with me, Carson. We used to dance together, remember?"

"After your husband was gone."

"Yes."

"I'm not much of a dancer."

"Let's see."

Carrell led Carson to the steps of the gazebo. I fumbled with my cell phone, looking for a likely song to play. It didn't happen, though. Sara Vaneps crested the hill. She was breathing hard and I wondered if she had run.

"Grandfather," she said.

"Who are you?" Carson asked.

"Five minutes. I turned around for five minutes."

Carrell waved her hand in a way that made it seem as if she didn't require an explanation and that Sara would be forgiven, anyway.

"Here's your granddaughter, Sara," Carrell said.

"Sara?"

Carson's brow furrowed and his eyes half closed as if he was attempted to grasp something that was just beyond his reach.

Carrell turned to the younger woman.

"We were just spending some quality time, together, Carson and I," she said. "Weren't we?"

"Like the old days," Carson said.

"Only now it's time to go home."

"Already?"

"Yes."

"All right, Jacey. Whatever you say."

The old man opened his arms again. Jeanette stepped into them again and they embraced.

"Gotta go, gotta go," Carson repeated.

Sara took the old man's arm the way a woman might take possession of her boyfriend and eased him away from the gazebo.

"Say good-bye to Jeanette," she said.

"There are no good-byes between me and her, are there, Jacey?"

"None," Jeanette said.

Sara and the old man began to descend the hill toward the Vaneps' house. They moved slowly. Carson looked at his granddaughter. His face was blank again.

"I don't remember your name," he said. "But I remember that I love you."

Carrell stood silently next to the gazebo until they were both out of sight. Her eyes were clouded with tears and I wondered what it would take for her to let them fall.

"*A quien los dioses quieren destruir, primero lo vuelven loco*," she said.

"Whom the Gods would destroy, they first make mad."

"You speak Spanish."

"Enough for that," I said.

"Buy you a drink, McKenzie?"

"Sure."

We entered Carrell's home through the back door.

"What will you have?" she asked.

"What are you drinking?"

"Jameson Irish Whiskey on the rocks. Not very ladylike, I'm afraid."

"Depends on the lady. I'll have the same."

"Go wander through my house. See if you can find a smoking gun or a knife dripping with blood. No, wait. A shovel. The shovel the deputies took was returned to me. Apparently it was bereft of brain matter. They actually asked if I had another."

"Do you?"

"Under the bed."

I moved through the house. It was shockingly clean. At least it was shockingly clean compared to the condominium that Nina and I shared. Possibly because Nina was too busy running Rickie's, her jazz club on Cathedral Hill that she had named after her daughter Erica, to devote much time to cleaning, and several decades of living the bachelor life had made me mostly indifferent to any untidiness that wasn't inconvenient or likely to cause illness or injury. I didn't get far into Carrell's house, though, before I encountered a wall covered with photographs in the corridor between the living room and the second-floor staircase.

Only a third of them portrayed Jeanette and all of those also contained someone else that she was hugging or laughing with. The other two-thirds were of people I didn't recognize except for Carson Vaneps and Sara. In one, Carrell was surrounded by a dozen young girls, including Sara. They all seemed happy.

There was not a single photograph of her alone or with a man who could have been her husband; there was not a single photograph that seemed to have been taken before she moved to the Circle.

Directly across from the photographs hung a black frame. Inside the frame was a diploma that proclaimed:

*The Board of Regents of the University of Wisconsin System
on the nomination of the faculty has conferred upon Jeanette*

Lee Fitch the Degree of Bachelor of Business Administration together with all honors, rights, and privileges belonging to that degree. In witness thereof, this diploma is granted. Given at Madison in the State of Wisconsin this sixteenth day of June in the year nineteen hundred and seventy-eight and of the University the one hundredth and twenty-nine.

Carrell came up from behind me.

"You're a Badger," I said.

She handed me a squat glass filled with more whiskey than I would have poured.

"I also look good in red. How aboat you?"

Aboat, again.

"I'm a Golden Gopher," I said.

"You poor thing."

I saluted her with my glass. She saluted back and took a sip.

"Fitch is your maiden name?" I asked.

"After my husband left me—his name was David Carrell, by the way. After he left me—three years after we were married he left me. I didn't know what to do. He wasn't dead, we didn't divorce, he just—I kept living as though he was going to walk through the front door at any moment; kept signing my name Mrs. Carrell when I paid the bills. My Comcast bill—it's still in his name."

"Aboat," I said.

"What?"

"You said aboat instead of about. You're Canadian."

She snorted into her glass.

"No," she said. "I'm a Minnesota girl from Faribault."

"Home to Shattuck-St. Mary's."

"I didn't go to an exclusive boarding school. I went to Faribault High. Before I became a Badger, I was a Falcon."

"Okay."

"My grandmother was a Canadian, though, from a place called Sault Ste. Marie near where Lake Superior, Michigan, and Huron join together. She practically raised me while my parents were both at work and some of her accent, if you want to call it that, leaked into my speech patterns. They're all gone now. My family. I've been an orphan for over thirty years."

When she said that, I noticed for the first time that the wall didn't contain any photographs of her as a child, either, or of anyone who could be her parents or grandmother.

"I'm an orphan, too," I said.

"Are you?"

"My mother died of cancer when I was in the sixth grade. I lost my dad about ten years ago."

"Do you have an extended family; aunts, uncles, cousins?"

"No."

"Neither do I," Carrell said.

"I have friends, though."

Carrell nodded her head as if that made all the difference in the world.

"Friends," she said. "I have a circle of friends. All these photographs. This one here with me and my girls; this was taken over twenty years ago. The young lady wearing the rabbit ears? She's at MIT now."

"Really?" I said. "What is she studying?"

"She's teaching. Biological engineering. This girl. Ryan. She works for NASA; a real live rocket scientist. I am so very proud of my girls."

"Sara said you looked out for them."

"I didn't want them to make the same mistakes I did."

"What mistakes were those?"

Carrell hesitated before she answered.

"Start with sacrificing their dreams for some guy. Why not

let the guy make the sacrifice if he claims he loves them so? If he doesn't . . . anyway."

"Carson Vaneps," I said.

I gestured at a more recent photograph of Carrell in the arms of her neighbor. There was love in that photograph. Not romantic love. Something else. A love between friends that transcended friendship. It was a love that I understood well. It caused me to flash on Bobby Dunston and his family, who had practically adopted me after my mother passed and on Shelby, who came later.

"An aberration," Carrell said. "Or at least a rarity in my experience. A genuinely kind and gracious man. Am I being too hard on your sex, McKenzie? I've been pretty since I was fourteen years old. At least men have told me so . . ."

"For what it's worth, the arresting officer says you're a babe."

"Of course he does. They all do. Each time they say it they expect to be rewarded, too, as if a compliment were an invoice, as if they should receive recompense; payment for services rendered. Except Carson. We met the day David and I moved to the Circle. 'Course, it wasn't the Circle then, just an underpopulated neighborhood. Carson welcomed us. He actually brought a casserole. A hot dish."

Carrell laughed at the memory.

"It was terrible," she added. "It had tater tots and green beans. But that man—not once did he look at me like he wished David wasn't there. And when David wasn't there . . . Friends, McKenzie. Unlike family, we get to choose our friends. Carson chose me and I chose him. He's twenty years older than I am, but it's like—it's like we went to high school together. Like we were both Falcons. Now, watching his mind disintegrate like that . . ."

Carrell stared at the photograph some more, her expression

suggesting that she wished she and Carson could go back in time. Or was she wishing he could go forward in time just as quickly as possible?

"Some people, neighbors, thought we were lovers," Carrell said. "His wife had passed a few years before I moved in and when David left me . . . It never mattered how many times I said it wasn't true. The more I said it was a lie, the more people believed it. People."

"From what Carson said, I gathered that you have not been without male companionship."

"After I reconciled myself to the truth that David wasn't coming back, I looked around to see if I could do better. I dated a few men from work; a few more that I came across here and there. I even attempted online dating; Sara was very insistent on the idea. I discovered, though, that it treats people as commodities instead of individuals. We're told to shop around, explore the marketplace until the laws of supply and demand determine the best consumer-to-goods match. In any case, while I found I could do much better than David, I quickly discovered that I couldn't do better than Carson. His company, as chaste as it has been, was far more preferable to me."

"Carson sold the Circle," I said.

"We're still trying to learn how that happened. Carson denies that he signed a contract, but you saw him. He thinks it's twenty years ago. Sara told me he gets up in the morning and dresses as if he were going to the office, going to General Mills."

I played the card I had kept up my sleeve since I had first learned what had happened on the Circle.

"Did Carson kill Charles Sainsbury?" I asked.

"What?"

"You're not allowing the accusations against you to stand in order to protect him, are you?"

"You saw Carson. How could that old man kill anyone?"

"I saw him today, not six months ago."

Carrell sipped some more whiskey before she replied.

"I didn't kill Charles and neither did he," she said.

"How do you know? You said you weren't there."

"That great and gentle man—no, McKenzie. No. Please."

I took a sip of the Jameson and waited. Sometimes if you wait long enough, people will tell you the most amazing things. Carrell didn't speak a word.

"I've come to a conclusion, Ms. Carrell," I said. "Would you care to hear it?"

"Please."

"I've decided that I like you, too."

"Even though I've been accused of bludgeoning old man Sainsbury to death?"

"Even though."

"In that case, you may call me Jeanette."

"Not J. C.?"

"Give it time, McKenzie. Give it time."

The sign on the front entrance read EFFECTIVE IMMEDIATELY ALL GUESTS ENTERING THE RICKIE'S BUILDING WILL BE ASKED TO WEAR A MASK AT ALL TIMES, EXCEPT WHEN SEATED AT THEIR TABLES. So, I put on a mask. I didn't like it, but who did?

All of Rickie's staff were wearing masks, as well, including the boss. She was standing at the bottom of a spiraling red-carpeted staircase. The mask was black. Nina Truhler was wearing blue.

Rickie's was divided into two sections, a casual bar on the ground floor with a small stage for happy hour entertainment and a full restaurant and performance hall upstairs. When

COVID hit, Nina had also built a stage under an enormous canopy in her parking lot that she surrounded with socially distanced tables for parties of two and four and a custom heating system. She was debating whether or not to retain the "outdoor performance hall" as she called it for the upcoming winter. Probably she would, she told me that morning. There were still many people who were hesitant to go indoors despite vaccinations and mask mandates and given the rapid spread of yet another coronavirus variant, who could blame them?

"Hey, you," she said when I approached. We hugged yet did not kiss, another reason I hated masks. "How's Evangeline?"

"Fine."

"What did she want?"

"She wanted me to help a friend who has a friend who's been accused of murdering her neighbor and burying the body in the woods behind her house."

"That's what you've been doing all day?"

"Pretty much," I said.

"So, did she do it, this woman who's been accused of murdering her neighbor and burying the body in the woods behind her house?"

"I honestly don't know yet. I hope not. I like her."

"But you'll help nail her to a cross if she's guilty," Nina said.

"Once a cop always a cop."

The bar was crowded for an early evening and the customers seemed to be in a festive mood.

"Business is good," I said.

"Business hasn't been good since the coronavirus hit, but it's much better. Come with me."

Nina led me to her office behind the downstairs bar. Once inside, she closed the door and removed her mask. This time we did kiss.

"I miss you when you're not around," she said.

"You have no idea how much I appreciate hearing that."

"Show, don't tell."

We kissed some more.

"Why is it that no one ever asks you to give them a ride to the airport or if you'll help them move?" Nina asked.

"Excuse me?"

"It's always murder or an art theft or a missing boyfriend who turns out to be a fraud or something like that."

"I'm sorry," I said. "My mind was elsewhere. What are you asking?"

"I was thinking about the favor you're doing for Evan."

"While you were kissing me?"

"Oh, guess what? Bobby and Shelby are upstairs right now having a romantic dinner for two."

"No kidding? I should go up and say hi."

"What part of 'romantic dinner for two' did you not get?"

"All right, all right," I said. "I'll keep my distance. What's the occasion, did they tell you?"

"No, but Victoria has been sending out applications for various colleges and universities and I think they're feeling a little old."

"Meanwhile, your own daughter, my stepdaughter—I like saying that, by the way—your own daughter will be graduating from Tulane this year."

"Yet I don't feel old at all."

"Nor do you look old," I said.

"As long as you keep thinking that. You know, my new manager has proven to be extremely competent. I could take the night off."

"Do you have anything in mind?"

"I was thinking a romantic dinner for two."

"Where? Here?"

"Home," Nina said. "I do my best romancing at home."

I certainly liked the sound of that. Before I could answer though, my cell phone began playing the opening notes to Louis Armstrong's legendary cover of *West End Blues*. I checked the caller ID.

"I sent Evan a text before I came here; this is her calling me back." I turned my back on Nina and stepped away. "Evan."

"So, what's going on?" she asked. "Have you figured it out yet?"

"Not yet. Listen, I need a favor."

"God knows I owe you a few," Evan admitted.

"I have the names and addresses of all the people who live on the Circle; they were in the notes taken by Jeanette's attorney. What I would like for you to do is call them, at least those people you know well enough to call, and tell them that I'll be by to ask questions on Jeanette's behalf; tell them that I'm working with her attorney. If you could convince them to chat openly, that would be good, too."

"I can do that. Also, the book club—we have a book club; it's meeting around the fire circle tomorrow night. I'll be happy to introduce you. You can hear the latest gossip, for whatever that's worth."

"Thank you. I appreciate that."

"We call ourselves the Plot Whores," Evan said.

"The what?"

"We're whores for a good plot."

"You couldn't come up with a better name?"

"What's wrong with the name?"

"If I called you that, you'd burn me at the stake."

"You would deserve it, too."

"Is Jeanette Carrell a member?"

"Emeritus. She's not a member any longer but she's always welcome."

"Will she be there tomorrow?"

"I doubt it. We haven't seen much of her since they attached that GPS tracker to her ankle."

I thanked her, we said our good-byes, and ended the conversation. Nina was watching me.

"Anything I should know?" she asked.

"I was just thinking how hungry I am."

FOUR

Jennifer Carlson greeted me at her front door the next morning wearing a dark blue skirt and matching jacket, white shirt, black pumps, and a gold necklace adorned with stars and half-moons and my first thought was to apologize to her.

"I hope I'm not keeping you from your job," I said.

"Oh, no," she said. "I've been working from home since COVID; we have a guest room that I use for an office. I like to dress like I'm going into the office, though, because it makes me feel more professional. I know that's silly; people say I'm being silly and if you see how people dress when we Zoom, when we have online meetings . . . except for my boss. She always dresses like she's in the boardroom, so I do, too. Would you like coffee? Since COVID, I have become a connoisseur of coffee."

"I'd love some."

"I'm Jenny, by the way, except at work." Jenny led me through her living room and dining room into her kitchen. "At work I'm either Jennifer or Ms. Carlson. We tended to be very formal in the office when we all still worked in the office and my boss still is, formal, I mean. She doesn't work in the office, either, although I know she wants to and, yes, I'm being obsequious. There are spots opening up above me and I intend to move into one of them; get a nice office instead of a cubicle when we actually do move back to the building, assuming that we do. It keeps getting postponed."

The kitchen was large, spacious, and immaculate. If you had told me it was a display room used by a home builder or remodeling firm to entice potential customers instead of a place where someone actually cooked and consumed meals, I would have believed you. We halted at a counter where a machine sat sporting enough doohickeys and thingamajigs that I was sure that along with brewing coffee, it could guide ships at sea.

"I have all the ingredients because my husband won't drink a black cup of coffee to save his life," Jenny said. "I wonder if that's a millennial thing; people who grew up with a Starbucks on every corner. Anyway, I want you to try this coffee black, first. Tell me what you think. Here."

Jenny filled a mug and I tasted it.

"Wow," I said.

"New Orleans Café Noir, or just plain New Orleans hot coffee if you don't want to sound pretentious. It's made with chicory."

"This is excellent."

"I can offer you French Crème . . ."

"No, no this is fine."

"You're not just being nice . . ."

"Not at all."

"Evan said you were the nicest guy," Jenny told me.

"Hardly."

"She said you were trying to help Jeanette Carrell. I hope you do. I feel so bad about all of this. My husband says I'm being silly. He's not here, by the way. He works at home, too, only he went out jogging just a little while ago. I told him he should wait until we talk to you but he runs when the mood hits him; sometimes at night. He runs a lot more now than he did before COVID. I read somewhere that exercising is up like eighty-eight percent. I don't know about that. I read somewhere else that forty percent of the population has gained weight. I know I've gained ten pounds in the last year. Do you think I look fat?"

"No."

"My husband does. You don't want to hear that, though. You want to talk about Jeanette. I don't know what to tell you."

I had decided to call on Jenny Carlson first among all the other potential witnesses who lived on the Circle because, according to the criminal complaint, she was the one who had first discovered Charles Sainsbury's body.

"Start with that," I told her.

"I didn't actually find the body. It was the dogs. Cadaver dogs; I didn't even know there was such a thing. All I did was call—I almost called Jeanette first. 'What's that smell near the fire ring?' I was going to ask. Instead, I called the deputy. He talked to everyone living on the Circle when Sainsbury disappeared, asked us questions; gave us his card and told us to contact him if we remembered anything that we might have forgotten, that we didn't say when he was interviewing us. So, I called his number. My husband said I shouldn't have. I should have minded my own business, he said. I don't know. McKenzie, what would you have done?"

"I would have made the call."

"Now Jeanette is in trouble. I like Jeanette. She's my friend. At least she was. I don't know what she is now. We haven't spoken."

"I would have made the call," I repeated.

"The smell, McKenzie. I'll never forget the smell. Sometimes I still smell it. Probably it's a psychological thing. My husband—at first it wasn't so bad, the smell. We were sitting around the fire ring just watching the fire when I first noticed it. 'What is that?' I asked. My husband said he didn't smell anything. The next time I went up there, it was a couple of days later—I can't believe no one else smelled it. Or maybe they were all like my husband; they didn't think it was a big deal. Only it was a big deal, wasn't it?"

"Yes."

"Now Jeanette is accused of murder. What did I do?"

"You did what you're supposed to do."

"I don't think my neighbors agree. Derek doesn't agree. Derek is my husband. We've been married—McKenzie, have you ever heard the phrase 'Absence makes the heart grow fonder'? It's true. The opposite of that is also true. Derek and I have been cooped up together in this house for a year and a half and we, and we—we gotta get out of this place."

"Where were you on April nineteenth?" I asked. "Do you remember?"

"At around eleven o'clock when Sainbury was killed? I was working in my office, well, the guest bedroom. I was in a Zoom meeting with my boss and some others—"

Jenny was interrupted when her front door was opened and a man stepped inside her house. He was in his early thirties, like her, and was wearing jogging shorts and a black T-shirt with a Nike swoosh above his left breast. His hair was mussed and his skin was pale, yet his breathing seemed normal.

Jenny moved toward him.

"How was your run, dear?" she asked.

Derek was six inches taller than his wife. He looked over the top of her head at me and, instead of answering her question, took hold of her shoulders and moved her to the side.

"Are you McKenzie?" he asked.

"Yes."

"I was told that you might drop by. You're here to get some dirt that might help J. C."

J. C.? my inner voice asked. *He gets to call her J. C.?*

"In a manner of speaking," I told him. "How was your run?"

"Fine. I try to get in 10-K a day."

"How much did you run today?" I asked.

He seemed surprised by the question.

"10-K," he repeated.

Then why is your T-shirt mostly sweat-free?

"That's what?" I asked aloud. "An hour?"

"I can run it in under fifty minutes, depending on the conditions." Derek glanced at his wife. "Took me a bit longer, today." And back at me. "Do you run?"

"Yes, but I only get in about three miles every other day."

"5-K then."

Half the distance yet three times the sweat.

"There are a lot of 5-K and 10-K races you can enter," Derek told me. "I'm running in the Autumn Woods Classic in Maple Grove next week and on Thanksgiving Day I'm doing the Turkey Trot in St. Paul." He glanced at Jenny again and smiled; she did not smile back. "I've been trying to convince Jennifer to run, only she can't be bothered."

She said, "Maybe if we ran together," but Derek wasn't listening.

"It shouldn't be much longer before J. C.'s trial begins, should it?" he asked.

"No," I said.

"It would be so much better if the prosecutor would just drop the charges."

"I'm sure Ms. Carrell would agree."

"What would it take for that to happen?"

"If there was evidence to prove that Ms. Carrell didn't commit the crime or at least enough to convince the ACA that he probably wouldn't win the case."

"Evidence like that, would it need to be made public?"

"I guess that would depend on the ACA. Why do you ask?"

"Just thinking out loud."

"That's really a thing, isn't it," Jenny said. "It doesn't matter if someone is guilty or innocent. What matters is what the prosecutor can prove in court."

"That's what matters," I agreed.

"You're starting to get worked up again," Derek said.

"I don't want Jeanette to go to prison," Jenny answered.

"Then you shouldn't have called the deputies, am I right?"

I really didn't want to get in the middle of a family dispute, so I interrupted.

"Mr. Carlson," I said.

He turned to look at me.

"Where were you when Charles Sainsbury was killed— approximately eleven A.M. on April nineteenth," I added.

"I was here. Working out of the house because of the virus. I'm a marketing consultant for a tech firm based in Golden Valley."

"No," Jenny said. "You weren't."

Derek turned on his wife, his expression suggesting that he was outraged that she would contradict him.

"What?" he said.

"You were running," Jenny said, quickly adding, "That's what you told the deputy when he came to interview us."

Derek hesitated before responding.

"That's right," he said. "I forgot. Thanks for reminding me. McKenzie, I was running."

"Do you run on the Circle?" I asked.

"Not really. Mostly I run around it and up and down the streets all through Shoreview. I have a 10-K route all mapped out that I follow. I'm careful with hills."

"Did you see anyone else around the Circle?"

"No; what I told the deputy."

"Did you know Sainsbury well?" I asked.

"He was an asshole."

"He was not," Jenny said.

Again Derek spun toward his wife, a look of disgust on his face.

"He was an asshole," he repeated.

Jenny angled her head around her husband to look at me.

"The five years we lived on the Circle, Charles seemed like a nice man. I spoke to him many times and he was always very pleasant. I was surprised as anyone when we learned what he was going to do."

"That's what made him an asshole," Derek said.

And what made you an asshole? my inner voice wondered. *Don't tell me it was COVID.*

"Did anyone else feel the same way as you do?" I asked.

"Just about everyone on the Circle wanted to—" Derek stopped speaking midsentence. I knew why, too. He was afraid he was talking himself into a hole. After a few moments to collect himself, Derek said, "A lot of people were upset with old man Sainsbury. Not just me. Not just J. C."

"You told the investigators that you were out running when Sainsbury was killed . . ."

"That's right, the 10-K."

"You don't remember seeing anyone."

"That's right."

"Did anyone see you?"

Derek knew exactly what I was asking. He glared at me just like he had at his wife. I almost didn't hear his answer because of the way his teeth were clenched.

"I don't know," he said.

"Yeah, I've seen him running." Rebecca Westermeyer Sauer was leaning against a counter in her kitchen and sipping coffee from a mug adorned with flowers. "Derek's one of those guys who likes to take his shirt off when he runs, you know what I mean?"

Rachel Westermeyer Wright laughed at the image.

"I know exactly what you mean." She spoke from her chair at the kitchen table. "Look at me, look at me; I have perfect pectorals."

"On the other hand," Rebecca said, "I like me a man who's pectorally perfect."

"Is pectorally even a word?" Rachel asked.

"I'm sending it to Merriam-Webster right after I finish my coffee."

As entertaining as I found the two sisters, I was compelled to keep them on track.

"I wonder if anyone else on the Circle finds Derek to be pectorally perfect," I said.

"You mean besides Jenny?" Rebecca said.

"I think her interest is beginning to wane with the way he treats her," Rachel said.

"I suppose there are some people. I don't know. Do you know?"

"I don't know anything, but . . . maybe Linda? I'm just guessing."

"Linda doesn't like him."

"She doesn't like Derek in public. We have no idea what she thinks of him in private. Although, I admit, he's tall and rectangular and she's short and round. It'd be like putting a square peg in a round hole."

"That is so cheap, Rach."

"I've been cheaper."

"True, very true. On the other hand, if Linda was going to screw someone off the books, it would be Sainsbury."

"That's true, too."

"Wait," I said. "Charles Sainsbury?"

"No, no, no," Rebecca said. "William Sainsbury."

"He's the one who's responsible for all of this," Rachel said. "Tearing down the Circle, I mean. He's the one who talked Vaneps into signing the contract. It was never his father."

"You don't know that," Rebecca said.

"That's what Ruth said. The wrong Sainsbury was killed, that's what Ruth told me."

"How does she know?"

"She lives next door to them."

"Ruth is Ruth Krider?" I asked.

"Yes."

"And Linda?"

"Linda Welch," Rebecca said. "She lives two houses down from me. She's been divorced—how many years has she been divorced now?"

Rachel held up three fingers.

"What do you mean by 'screw someone off the books'?" I asked.

"Linda's not married, but William Sainsbury is," Rebecca said.

"I've never heard adultery described that way."

"I'm going to send that phrase to Merriam-Webster, too. You know 'dad bod,' for men who are a little overweight and not particularly muscular? That was me."

"God, Becca," Rachel said. "It was not."

"She's just upset because I first used it to describe her husband."

"Not everyone can be pectorally perfect."

"Linda Welch," I said. "Do you believe she's having an affair with William Sainsbury?"

Rebecca paused long enough to drain half of her coffee before she answered.

"It's just a feeling I have," she said. "I mean, I can't prove anything. I've never seen them together except on the Circle and other people were always there. She was the only one who defended both Charles and William when we found out about their development plans, though. They're going to build mini-mansions on the hill that will look right down into the bed-rooms of every house in the Circle."

"Your husband might like that," Rachel said. "Open the shades . . ."

"It's not funny, Rach."

"Does everyone feel the way you do?" I asked.

"Everyone."

"Except for Linda," Rachel said.

"Yes, Linda."

"Were you there when Jeanette Carrell threatened Charles Sainsbury?" I asked.

"I was," Rebecca said. "All the years I've known her, I've never seen her step out of character like that. It was like—it was like for a minute she became a completely different person and I've known her since—can it be twenty-five years now? When Rach was married . . ."

"I was married in the gazebo," Rachel said. "Very intimate."

"I had a huge wedding," Rebecca said. "Turned into a catas-trophe. Everything went wrong."

Although, the way both Rebecca and Rachel laughed, I wasn't sure of that.

"The zipper on my dress broke," Rebecca said. "Mom had to sew me into my dress."

"You never did tell me how you got out of it on your wedding night."

"How do you think?"

"Then the water pipe . . ." Rachel said.

"A water pipe burst like an hour before the reception, not in the hall, but just outside," Rebecca said. "The entire street was flooded. Then the hall flooded. And the caterer couldn't work under those conditions."

"When my turn came, we went very small," Rachel said. "There were a lot fewer moving parts. Jeanette—she helped to decorate the place and set up a sound system . . ."

"She was J. C. taking care of her girls," Rebecca said. "The woman who threatened to gut Charles Sainsbury like a fish—I have no idea who that was."

"I heard that other people said similar things," Rachel told me.

"You heard?" I asked.

"I don't actually live on the Circle anymore. I live a couple of miles away. I just orbit the Circle like a satellite now."

"A circlelite," Rebecca said. "Hey, I just invented another word."

"You did not."

Rachel pulled her cell phone off the kitchen table and began to access it.

"We grew up here," Rebecca said. "Mostly grew up here. I was ten and Rachel was eight when Mom and Dad bought the house about twenty-five years ago. They decided to downsize after Dad retired and moved to an apartment; my husband and I bought the house from them. They gave us a great deal."

"Which I expect to see reflected when we receive our inheritance," Rachel said.

"Rach wasn't on the Circle when Jeanette had her meltdown."

"Who was?" I asked.

Rebecca recited a list of names that were already in my notebook.

"Derek Carlson said 'I could fucking kill him,'" she added. "That's a direct quote, by the way."

Which isn't in your notebook, my inner voice reminded me.

"Kate Hixson said 'I'd like to bury him myself,' also a direct quote."

Which also isn't in your notebook.

"Did anyone take them seriously?" I asked.

"I don't think so."

"But Jeanette Carrell . . ."

"It was so unexpected coming from her that yeah, everyone took it seriously."

"The day that Sainsbury was killed—" I began.

"We weren't here." Rebecca pointed a finger at her sister and then herself and waved it back and forth in case I didn't know who she meant by "we." "Rach and I were at the Rosedale Center. The kids were out of school so we took them to SeaQuest, the petting zoo and aquarium they have there."

"I petted a Burmese python," Rachel said. "Sometimes you need to be brave for your children, McKenzie."

"Now her daughter wants one," Rebecca said.

"Hey." Rachel was still looking at her smartphone. "If you spell 'circlelite' with two *l*s, I think you did invent a new word."

FIVE

Because of the trees, you couldn't see much of the Circle and none of the gazebo from Linda Welch's backyard, yet I assumed that's what she was talking about when she waved her coffee mug and asked, "Is that worth murdering someone over?"

I nearly answered, telling her that my experiences as a police officer and what I do now had taught me that people kill for astonishingly small and petty reasons. Like the guy who knifed a woman over a parking space. Only I didn't think she'd appreciate the lecture. No one ever does. Instead, I said, "People are accusing Jeanette Carrell of killing Charles Sainsbury for just that."

We were outside—apparently Linda couldn't think of a reason to invite me inside—and sitting on heavy lawn chairs at a heavy metal table with a round hole in the center for an umbrella that wasn't there. That was fine with me. The weather, although colder than the day before, was still warmer than the October average by ten degrees. Linda hadn't offered me coffee when I arrived, which was a direct violation of the Code of Minnesota Nice, yet that was fine, too. By then I was all coffeed out.

"People talk about Carrell like her shit doesn't stink," Linda said. "Trust me, it does."

"Why do you say that?"

"Let me guess, you're on Team Carrell, too."

"Not necessarily. I just want to know what you're thinking."

"I'm thinking that Carrell is all sunshine and lollipops with her friends but if you're not her friend she'll—you know what? If you're not her friend she'll hit you over the head with a shovel and bury you in a shallow grave."

From her laughter, I guessed that Linda thought that was funny.

"I take it you two are not friends," I said.

"We got along just fine until the Sainsburys decided to develop the hill. Vaneps sold it to them; why shouldn't they develop it? But everybody, they're all, like, not in *my* backyard. If they were putting up a housing development two blocks away no one over here would give a shit."

"I heard that the Sainsburys were divided on the project; that William wanted to develop it but his father was against it."

"That's true. Charles kept saying they needed to think about the people who live here and William kept asking him, what about the people who want to live here and who would buy our houses if we built them? Let's think about them, he said."

How does she know this? my inner voice asked.

"How do you know this?" I asked aloud.

"William told me. Everyone else might be angry at him, but I'm not. William is a nice guy. He talks to you like an adult. Carrell talks to you like you're an elementary school student and she's the teacher. You know what? I'm surprised she doesn't carry a ruler wherever she goes. Whack, whack, whack."

"The day Charles Sainsbury was killed . . ."

"You want to know if I have an alibi," Linda said. "The cop, the one I spoke to after Charles disappeared and later when they discovered his body, what's his name?"

"Deputy Sergeant Michael Swenson."

"Yeah, yeah, yeah. He asked the same thing. Where was I

at eleven A.M. on—I forget the day. The thing is, I don't have an alibi. I mean, I was here, but there's no one to vouch for me."

"You live alone," I said.

"After my husband and I divorced—there's so much sleaze out there, McKenzie, so much sludge. Try to find a decent man, someone my age. I'm forty-four. The two years I've been looking, the only decent men I've met were already married."

I flashed on what the Westermeyer sisters told me earlier.

"Does that matter to you?" I asked.

Linda stared while I waited for her to throw me out. She didn't. After a few moments, she said, "You heard the gossip, I take it."

"Gossip?"

"Some people on the Circle think I've been sleeping with William Sainsbury because I keep saying nice things about him when nobody else does."

"Are you?"

"Did you ask your friend Carrell that question? Because people say she's been fucking Carson Vaneps for the past thirty years."

"Yes, I did," I told her.

"You did?"

"She denies it, by the way."

"Oh, well then, okay, to be fair—I haven't been sleeping with William. We're just friends. Is that so hard for people to believe?"

I thought it was a good idea to change the subject, so I did.

"If William was responsible for trying to develop the Circle, why was everyone so angry at Charles?" I asked.

"Because they didn't know," Linda said. "That time at the gazebo when Carrell went batshit crazy? No one knew it was William who arranged everything. I didn't know. That came out later when the Vaneps filed the lawsuit. You know what? Carson is suffering from Alzheimer's now, but at the time, we're talking six months ago, he seemed fine to me. I don't know how they can say he wasn't."

"Why did William do it? Did he tell you why he went against his father?"

"It was his business; he was running it even back then. His father was just the figurehead and William wanted to make a splash, let everyone know that Sainsbury Construction under him was everything it was supposed to be. Besides, he needs the money."

He needs the money? Walk softly here, McKenzie.

"Is that what he told you?" I asked.

"You know what?" Linda said. "There's no way I should be talking to you about William. I've already said too much. If you want to know anything more about him and his business, you should talk to him."

Dammit!

"I mean, really," she added.

"Let's say just for argument's sake that Jeanette Carrell is innocent," I said. "Just out of curiosity, who do you think would have reason to kill Charles?"

"Seriously?"

"Yes."

"Because as much as I dislike her, I never thought Carrell did it. My guess—you know what? I think you should talk to Ruth Krider."

"Why?"

"Because the road and sewer pipes and all that shit people need so they can live in the new development, it'll run right alongside her property line."

Ruth Krider carefully positioned herself along the edge of her yard.

"See the little tree near the boulevard?" she asked. "Now where I'm standing? And those trees closer to the hill? Draw a line and that's where my property ends."

"Okay," I said.

"You see the problem, don't you?"

Her house was only about ten yards away from where we stood.

"Yes," I said.

"I could spit out of my kitchen window and hit passing cars because you know this is exactly where Sainsbury is going to build his damn road, as far away from his own house as you can get. Look. Look at how far away it is. Thirty yards? Forty? Closer to forty. I don't know. My house was built long before his, in the sixties. His was built in the mid-eighties and you can see that the builder put it as far away from me as he could get. Well, not me. My husband and I bought our house in the early eighties. He passed a few years ago and my kids and grandkids are all scattered hither and yon, so it's just me now. My point—you just know that once the road is built and the Circle is developed, Sainsbury's gonna sell it. Why not? It was his father's house, not his. He doesn't live here anymore."

"Who does?"

"His niece has been house-sitting since Charles was killed," Krider said. "She goes to the U. She's very nice. Like her mother. Her uncle—I've lived on the Circle even longer than J. C. has so I was able to watch William grow up. He's always been a selfish bully. One of those kids who was born on third base and figured he hit a triple, you know what I mean? His sister, though, Bethany—almost the exact opposite."

"Was she one of Jeanette's girls, too?" I asked.

"Sure, she was. They all were. Back in those days, J. C. was like everyone's favorite aunt who drove a convertible. They gravitated to her, listened to her stories; listened to her advice about being their own women. Bethany was older than most of them, Sara Vaneps, the Westermeyer sisters, which is why I think she took what J. C. had to say more seriously. Bethany is a partner in Sainsbury Construction, by the way, but only a junior partner. That's the way Charles wanted it. He wanted his daughter to benefit from his business, his hard work, yet to be an equal partner, actually help run things? Oh, no, no, no. That's a job for the men in the family."

"Meaning his son."

"Meaning his son," Krider said.

"I'm sure that made Bethany happy," I said.

"Let's just say she wasn't surprised and let it go at that."

"The people I've spoken to seem evenly divided. Half blames Charles for trying to develop the Circle and the other half blames William."

"It was both of them," Krider told me. "Charles had always wanted to turn it into a development for mini-mansions, only he could never convince Carson Vaneps to sell and after a while he just gave up and decided to enjoy the Circle like everyone else. It didn't hurt his business any, that's for sure. He's had developments of one sort or another in half the suburbs surrounding the Twin Cities. Only then the housing shortage hit. I read somewhere that it's worse here in the Cities than anywhere else in the country, so it became a thing again, the Circle.

"Somehow William managed to convince Carson to sell," Krider added. "Personally, I think Carson realized six months ago that he was headed for a bad end and made the move to guarantee his children, his grandchildren, a nice inheritance. Not that it really matters, except maybe for tax purposes. If Carson passed tomorrow, his family would absolutely sell the Circle. They'd do it in a second. Why not? They don't live here, either. If you ask me, I'd say the only reason they filed the lawsuit to stop the sale is because they don't know what it would do to Carson. From what I've seen, the Circle is the only thing that's keeping him anchored to reality. Besides, it's not like the property will suddenly lose its value. They can afford to wait. Heck, McKenzie, maybe I should sell, too. My kids are always harping at me to downsize. They think the house is too big for me to take care of, except it's my home, you know, and I've been taking care of it since before they were born."

"What does Bethany think about it all?" I asked.

"The last time I spoke to her, she seemed ambivalent. On the one hand, she'd hate to see the Circle go away. She grew up here, after all. On the other hand, she lives in Mounds View now. She moved there after she married Steve Gilman. I'll tell you one thing, though; what she told me the last time we spoke maybe a month ago—she doesn't believe that Jeanette Carrell killed her father."

"Who does she suspect?" I asked.

Krider hesitated before answering.

"You should ask her," she said.

Yes, you should, my inner voice agreed.

I thanked Krider for her time and asked if I could call on her if I had more questions. She told me that she would welcome my company.

"I don't get out as much as I used to," Krider said. "Given my age and COVID, going to the grocery store has become a major social event."

I waved at her property line.

"I hope this works out for you," I said.

"Who knows, maybe I can convince the homeowner's association to let me build a big wall like Katie Hixson did."

Wait. What?

"Homeowner's association," I repeated. "There's a homeowner's association?"

"Chippewa Woods HOA. McKenzie, this whole neighborhood

is part of what they call a housing estate. It was established in 1986 when they developed the area and the houses that were already here like mine and J. C.'s and Carson's were incorporated into it. Didn't you see the signs?"

"No."

"Well, there are signs. One of the HOA's rules—no fences of any kind, only Kate somehow convinced them to let her build a wall, so maybe I can, too."

"The five-foot-high wall between her backyard and Jeanette Carrell's backyard," I said just to keep things clear in my head.

"Yes."

"Why did she want a wall?"

Krider stared at me as if she was surprised by the question.

"You don't know?" she asked. "You said you've been speaking to people who live along the Circle. I'd of thought someone would have told you."

I shook my head.

"Kate Hixson has two kids, young boys, and they were always wandering into J. C.'s backyard, chasing balls, whatever," Krider said. "J. C. kept telling them to stay out; that she didn't want them messing with her gardens. They never listened. One day she shot them with a hose."

"What?"

"She sprayed them with her garden hose. From what I heard, the kids thought that was hysterical. Their mother, not so much. Kate called the police, but I don't think anything ever came of that. Then she went to the homeowner's association. I wasn't at the meeting so I don't know what happened exactly. But they let her build a wall, so . . ."

Patrick Hegarty was a retired mail carrier in his late sixties who lived three blocks over from the Circle. Unlike Linda Welch, he offered me a beverage thirty seconds after I knocked on his front door. I told him I would have what he was having, so we ended up sipping hot chocolate laced with rum and topped with mini-marshmallows at his kitchen table, "To take the chill from our bones," he told me.

"Funny how it works," Hegarty said. "Sixty-six degrees in October and people 'round here think it's cold; I think it's cold. I'm this far away"—he held his thumb and index finger a half-inch apart—"from turning on the heat. Sixty-six degrees in March, though, or April, people will be running around in shorts and flip-flops."

I agreed with him. At the same time . . .

"Do you know Jeanette Carrell?" I asked.

"Is that what this is about? You want to talk about Jeanette Carrell? I know who she is because of the murder thing, only I've never met her. I talked to her once on the phone, but that wasn't more than a three-minute conversation."

"What did you talk about?"

"The wall her neighbor wanted to build," Hegarty said.

"Could you tell me about that, Pat?" I used his first name because we were friends now and I wanted him to speak freely.

"That was what?" he asked. "August of last year? This woman—what was her name? Karen?"

"Katherine."

"Katherine Hixson. There you go. We meet once a month, the Chippewa Woods Homeowners Association. Usually, there's not much to talk about, although, this one time, this was a couple years after I was first elected—I was elected president of the HOA ten years ago and keep getting reelected every two years because nobody else wants the job. If somebody, anybody, put their hat in the ring, I'd be voting for them. Otherwise, unless I screw up, it looks like I have the job for life. What did you ask me again?"

"Katherine Hixson."

"Oh yeah," Hegarty said. "So, we're having our monthly meeting and this woman comes in screaming that her kids were being abused by her next-door neighbor and we better do something about it or she was going to sue us. You mentioned Jeanette Carrell. Turned out, she sprayed Katherine's kids with a water hose cuz they wouldn't stay out of her gardens, the gardens she had in her backyard. Hixson wanted her arrested, but we don't have the authority to do that. Then she wanted Carrell evicted, but we can't do that, either. Then she wanted her fined and we were thinking, what? Way we saw it, it was them kids of hers that were in the wrong, messing in other people's backyards. They're the ones who should be arrested or fined or whatever. Finally, Hixson said she wanted to build a fence.

"Now I'm a big believer that good fences make good neighbors, what Robert Frost said. If Hixson had a fence, none of this would have happened. But the association has a rule. No fences. None. Zero. Zip. Nada. Had the rule since, what? Nineteen eighty-six? That's what I was going to tell you before. Couple years after I was first elected, some guy built a fence around his yard without getting permission from the association and people complained. If he can have a fence, why can't we, they said. So we had to make him take it down. Almost we didn't; almost we changed the rules because it turned out that the man was a nudist; his wife, too. Only if you looked at them, you'd say, hell yes, let them build a fence; no one wants to see that. Only the vote was five to two against. Instead, we let them put up a hedge.

"Then Katherine Hixson came to us and she wanted a fence, too, so we compromised again," Hegarty added. "We ruled that she could build a five-foot-high wooden wall, gotta be tasteful, that only runs the length of the backyard between the two properties, that couldn't be easily seen from the street.

"Before we gave her permission, though, we put in a call to her neighbor, to Jeanette Carrell, to hear what she had to say. She wasn't at the meeting, you see. Didn't know anything about what was going on. So I called Carrell, put her on speakerphone so the other members could hear. Told her about Hixson and her request and she laughed. I remember that. Carrell laughed, which made me laugh, and she said, 'If that's what it takes to keep those young ruffians out of my chrysanthemums, that's fine with me.' So we let Hixson build her wall. Sent a board member, I can't remember who, it wasn't me. We sent a member to make sure the wall was tasteful."

"This was August of last year?" I asked.

"Could've been July. I can find the exact date if you need it. We do keep records, after all."

"Tape recordings? Transcripts?"

"Uh-huh, both," Hegarty said. "Video, too. We elect a secretary who takes care of all that in case there's a problem down the road, you know, legally."

"The way you told the story, I take it that Hixson was quite upset when she came before the HOA."

"Now there's an understatement," Hegarty said. "The woman was—we're talking gnashing-your-teeth, foaming-at-the-mouth mad. I mean, she called Carrell names, if I said them I'd be lynched."

"Pat, will her exact words be in the records?"

"Well, yeah, that's why we keep them."

"Do you think the secretary could send me copies?"

"I'll give him a call."

I left Patrick Hegarty's house feeling pretty good about myself.

Eyewitness testimony was notoriously unreliable, a fact that Jeanette Carrell's attorney would no doubt impress on the jury when cross-examining Katherine Hixson. He'd explain, probably in painstaking detail, that numerous studies have proved that over fifty percent of wrongful convictions of innocent people were the direct result of mistaken eyewitness identification. And the jury would listen intently. And nod their heads. And then ignore him. That's because studies also prove that juries *love* eyewitness testimony. For one thing, eyewitnesses nearly always provide the most dramatic and theatrical moments in a trial. They're not law enforcement officers or evidence technicians explaining, usually in a monotone voice, the specific details of a crime. They're *real* people pointing at the defendant and saying, "It was her. There's no doubt in my mind." Why wouldn't they believe the witness?

Only now Alexander Brandt would have the means to explain why Hixson made a grievous mistake in identifying Jeanette Carrell as the person who was carrying a shovel down a hill in the dark. He'd say that her memory was contaminated. He'd say it was because Hixson expected it to be Jeanette Carrell. That she wanted it to be Jeanette Carrell. Because she hated Jeanette Carrell, despite her recorded remarks that they were "neighborly," that "we get along just fine."

That would go a long way toward impeaching Hixson's testimony, I told myself.

Only will it be enough to get Carrell off? my inner voice asked.

Good question. After all, most criminals are convicted based solely on circumstantial evidence, not direct evidence, for the simple reason that most people don't commit their crimes in front of witnesses. Even without Hixson's testimony, that left the death threats, the diamond-crusted pendant, and the fact that Charles Sainsbury was buried, after all, in Carrell's backyard.

So, what next?

The answer was announced by Louis Armstrong's trumpet and my smartphone's caller ID that read "Sergeant Mike Swenson."

"Michael," I said.

"McKenzie. I thought I'd give you a call and tell you that I finally remembered what it was about the Carrell homicide that I forgot yesterday, and no, I didn't put it in my sups."

"What?"

"The day we arrested Carrell, actually the day that the St. Paul *Pioneer Press* reported that we arrested Carrell, I received a phone call from Dominic Belden. You know Belden?"

"No."

"He did thirty years with the county," Swenson said. "He retired, I want to say ten, fifteen years ago, something like that."

"Okay."

"Anyway, he called me. My name was in the paper as arresting officer. He called and said that he was glad that 'Someone finally got the bitch.' That's a direct quote, by the way."

"'Someone finally got the bitch'?" I repeated.

"Yeah."

"He was referring to Jeanette Carrell?"

"Turns out he was secondary on the case when Carrell's husband disappeared. I looked it up. Twenty-seven years ago, David Carrell disappeared and no one has seen or heard from him since. Belden told me that he was convinced at the time that Jeanette Carrell made him disappear."

I hesitated before asking, "Was he?"

"You're going to ask me questions, McKenzie. I don't have any answers, though. At the time he called, well, I'll tell you about that later. Interested?"

"Very much."

"Want to talk to the man?"

"Yes."

"What if he tells us something that can be used against your friend?"

"Depends on what the something is."

"Fair enough."

"When can we meet?"

"Right now."

SIX

Lauderdale was one of those cities that didn't have a reason to exist accept that about five hundred and thirty families lived there. It was a four-tenths-of-a-square-mile sliver tucked among St. Paul, Roseville, Falcon Heights, and Minneapolis and you would not have known that it was there unless your GPS app told you so.

Sergeant Swenson and I arrived at Belden's house in Lauderdale at pretty much the same time. The house was small and looked run-down. Directly behind it loomed a much taller wooden noise wall badly in need of paint that had been built to block the sounds of the heavy traffic coming from Highway 280 on the other side. The wall didn't do a very good job.

We found Belden sitting on a lawn chair in his front yard and drinking beer from a bottle. He looked to be in his seventies and was bundled as if it was ten degrees below zero instead of sixty-six degrees above. I was wearing my uniform—polo shirt under a black sports jacket, jeans, and Nikes. I didn't think it was cold until I looked at him.

Belden waved a beer at us.

"C'mon in," he said.

There was a low cyclone fence enclosing the front yard and a pair of black Labrador retrievers roaming freely inside the fence. We found a gate, opened the latch, and stepped inside. Immediately, the dogs were on us, jumping and barking and wagging their tails as if we were the best friends they had in the world. Belden did not make a move or say a word to restrain them. Instead, he asked, "Want a beer?"

"I'm on duty," Swenson said.

Belden laughed at him.

"Never stopped me," he said. "You must be McKenzie. You want a beer?"

"Sure," I said, just to be polite.

He bent down and removed a bottle of Busch Light from a cooler at the foot of his chair. While he opened it, Swenson spied a couple of lawn chairs leaning against Belden's house and went to retrieve them. The dogs followed him there and back. I took a sip of the cheap beer, wishing I had kept my mouth shut, while Swenson set up the chairs and we sat. The dogs circled us until they became bored and wandered off.

"I know you, McKenzie," Belden said.

"Have we met?" I asked.

"I know you from when you won the lottery. Yeah, yeah, yeah, what was it? Ten years ago? You were with St. Paul PD. Then you won the fuckin' lottery; sold your badge to take the reward on an embezzler you collared."

"Is that what I did?" I asked.

"That's what it looked like," Belden replied. "How much did the insurance company pay you to quit the cops?"

"A little over three million before the government took its cut."

"Can't say I wouldn't a done the same thing. Lotta us was saying we'd a done the same thing."

"For what it's worth, I was hoping to give my father a comfortable retirement, only he passed six months later."

Belden tilted his beer at me.

"Life is a bitch, ain't it?" he said.

"She has her moments."

"Now you're workin' private is what my friend Swenson tells me."

"Yeah."

Belden pulled on his beer until he drained the bottle, dropped it on the ground next to three other empties, and reached inside his cooler for another. The dogs trotted over as if they thought he might be fetching a treat for them and went back to wandering around the yard when they discovered he wasn't.

"Jeanette fuckin' Carrell." Belden opened his beer and threw the cap on the ground. "You here to help her?"

"Help her if she's innocent," I said. "Get out of the way if she's not."

"I don't know nothin' about the guy on the hill, but I know she did her husband." Belden pointed a finger at Swenson. "Why didn't you call me back? It's been six months!"

"The ACA," Swenson said. "He didn't want to complicate his case by bringing in a second body, especially one that was twenty-seven years old. Keep it simple, he said."

"Fuck." Belden shook his head in disgust and drank more beer. "They're all the same."

"If you knew Carrell killed her husband, why didn't you take her down?" I asked.

"Because they're all the same, every one of those fuckin' politicians tellin' voters they're tough on crime so they can run for higher office. You want to know what happened? The county attorney called me. Not the assistant county attorney. Nah, nah. The actual county attorney. When was the last time that happened, I wonder? Never happened to me except for that one time, the county attorney calling an investigator workin' a case. Empson it was, back then. Little Jerry Empson. He called me and said to drop the case. Said it was a domestic matter between Carrell and his wife. Domestic matter, my ass. Jeanette

(87)

Carrell killed her husband David Carrell. See, I even remember his name after all this time. She killed him and somehow disposed of the body. Hell, maybe she buried him on the hill behind her house same as the other guy."

"How do you know this?" I asked.

"I just know. You work the job as long as I did, you know. The way she acted. Calm. Not a tear in her eye or a tremor in her voice . . ."

That sounds like her, my inner voice said.

"She answered all of our questions like she had practiced the answers before we got there," Belden added. "Not once did she deviate from those answers. Not once did she seem confused and we tried to confuse her a lot, you know how it works."

"Dominic . . ." Swenson said.

"No, listen, okay? The man, David Carrell, he didn't make any withdrawals from his checking or savings accounts, didn't cash in any of his investments, not a nickel's worth. He didn't write a check. He didn't use his credit cards. Something else—he didn't pack a bag, either; didn't pack his electric shaver. He just disappeared. Couple days later, we found his car at the airport, the Minneapolis-St. Paul International Airport.

"Now this was years before nine-eleven," Belden added. "Long before the attack on the World Trade Center. They didn't have anything close to the airport security in those days like they do now; cameras everywhere, eyeballs on everything. People used to go to the airport for fun in those days; kids running around the terminal watching the planes landing and taking off. Remember that? So, we had nothing but the car. Only here's the thing. The car was wiped clean. No fingerprints at all on the steering wheel, the dashboard, the leather seat, the mirrors. What does that tell you, huh? Would David have done that if he was just flying off to parts unknown to start a new life? Even if he was, why didn't he take what was his, his money, his clothes? Why not just divorce his wife, say 'See ya, bitch,' and fly off to California or some such?"

Those are all very good questions.

I didn't have any answers, yet I did have another question.

"What did David Carrell do for a living?" I asked.

Belden waved his finger at me.

"Now you're thinking like a cop." He pointed his finger at Swenson. "Why didn't you ask that?"

"Because I know the answer," Swenson said. "He worked for a finance company that specialized in bankrolling real estate projects. North Country Properties. It doesn't exist anymore."

"You read the case file."

"Of course, I did. Right after you called me. There wasn't much there."

"That's because of little Jerry Empson. He was working for them; he was one of their stooges."

"Who is 'them'?"

"You don't think that Jeanette Carrell made her husband disappear all by her little self, do you? She had help."

"Who helped her?" I asked, expecting to hear Carson Vaneps's name.

"The mob," Belden answered instead.

"What mob?" Swenson asked.

"What do you mean 'what mob'? The mob, the mob, the mob running the Twin Cities."

"There's no organized crime presence in Minnesota," I said. "Not since they sent Isadore Blumenfeld to federal prison for white slavery and jury tampering in the early sixties."

Belden thought that was awfully funny.

"You kids." He called me and Swenson kids. "Don't you see? The greatest trick the mob ever pulled in Minnesota was convincing people that it didn't exist. You don't believe me? Two words—Omer Berenson."

"I don't know who that is," Swenson said.

"See?"

"I don't know who that is, either," I said.

"He's a gangster."

"Why would a gangster help Jeanette Carrell murder her husband?"

Belden emptied his beer bottle and dropped it next to the others.

That didn't take long.

"You want another?" he asked me.

I raised my bottle.

"I'm good," I said.

Belden reached into his cooler for his sixth beer, by my count, and opened it.

"Dominic," Swenson said. "Why would this Omer Berenson help Jeanette Carrell?"

"I don't know. Little Jerry Empson pulled us off the case before I could find out."

"Then why do you think . . . ?"

"Him and David Carrell knew each other. David worked for him over at North Country Properties."

"David Carrell was involved with organized crime?" I asked.

"Yeah, yeah, yeah. My guess, Berenson also knew Jeanette. I don't know what she looks like now, but in those days, fuck. I'd say Berenson helped Jeanette kill David in exchange for some pussy, only I didn't get a chance to prove it."

It went on like that for a few more minutes, Swenson and I asking questions and getting answers that seemed even more outlandish until Belden became nearly incoherent. We let him finish another beer before we thanked him for his insight, said we'd look into it, and left him on his lawn chair surrounded by his fence and dogs. As we walked to our cars, Swenson told me that on the way to Belden's house he passed a church.

"Meet me there," he said.

The parking lot for the Peace Lutheran Church turned out to be half a dozen diagonal spaces hard against the wooden noise wall. I pulled into one. Swenson pulled into another and joined me in my Mustang.

"Nice car," he said. "Did you buy it with the reward money?"

"My wife gave it to me for my birthday."

"It's good to be you."

"Opinions differ. What do you think about Belden?"

"When he called me six months ago, he was even drunker than he was today. That's one of the reasons I didn't include the conversation in my sup. Another reason, nothing he said made any sense much less could be proved in court. There was nothing in the case file that even hinted at what he told me on the phone and now in his front yard; a case that's nearly three decades old."

"You never mentioned it to the ACA?" I asked.

"No. I made that up for Belden's benefit."

"When Jeanette Carrell told me that her husband had deserted her twenty-seven years ago and Ramsey County concluded it was a domestic matter, my very first thought—David had walked out on her, probably with another woman, maybe a guy. It never occurred to me that he was ghosting. I mean, it could be done. Sara Jane Olson, remember her? Robbed a bank and rolled pipe bombs beneath LAPD patrol cars. She was ghosting for over twenty-three years before the cops finally caught up with her in St. Paul, and the cops were actively looking for her. No one is looking for David. Although, the fact that David Carrell's car was wiped down . . ."

"I know, and if it wasn't twenty-seven years ago, I'd be all over it," Swenson said. "But gangsters?"

"Could be that's why he's hiding."

"Unless David *is* buried on the hill behind Jeanette Carrell's house like Belden suggested."

My Mustang had all the latest electronics, so I made a hands-free call. Both Swenson and I were able to hear a phone ringing on my speaker and a man answering.

"Special Agent Brian Wilson, Federal Bureau of Investigation," he said.

"Harry," I said.

"McKenzie, how many times have I told you not to call me that?"

"Who keeps count? Harry, is there an organized crime presence in Minnesota?"

He paused before replying.

"Who wants to know?" Harry asked.

"Besides me?" I gestured toward Swenson. "Tell him who you are."

"Special Agent Wilson, my name is Sergeant Michael Swenson. I'm with the Ramsey County Sheriff's Department's Criminal Investigations Unit. I don't know what you're relationship with McKenzie is, but I'm working an active case and if you could answer a couple of questions?"

"Such as?"

"Is there an organized crime presence in Minnesota?"

Harry agreed to meet Swenson and me at Rickie's during happy hour. The three of us sat at a table near the small stage where Joel Shapira played jazz guitar, which I found distracting because Shapira was very, very good at it. Nina gave Harry a hug, COVID be damned, and called him "Brian." I don't know which he appreciated more, the hug or hearing his given name. I called him Harry because of his uncanny resemblance to Harry Dean Stanton, the award-winning character actor, but nobody else did.

After we were served our drinks, for which we would receive no check but I would leave a massive tip, we all leaned forward.

"Is there organized crime in Minnesota?" Harry asked. "You tell me. For decades, a city in northern Minnesota refused to change zoning laws or issue permits that would allow for the construction of a shopping mall at the intersection of two main highways because it didn't want to take business away from its downtown until three of the five council members met privately with a developer and changed their votes. The shopping center was built and the three council members later retired to their brand-new condominiums in Florida. Organized crime or a persuasive businessman?

"A developer personally financed a special interest group that lobbied state legislators during the height of COVID to pass a tax law that would help homeowners avoid foreclosure if they fell on hard times and couldn't pay their bills, then he used that same law to avoid paying over four million dollars in property taxes while he developed his properties. Is that organized crime or just a savvy entrepreneur taking advantage of the system?

"A government organization that helps fund infrastructure projects that are supposed to broaden economic development and create jobs around the state, awarded grants totaling over two million dollars to the same firm. Is that organized crime or a guy who has friends in high places?

"A loosely affiliated group of developers got together and decided to slow construction projects throughout the greater Twin Cities area until the housing shortage became so acute that they are now actually being encouraged to build homes pretty much wherever they want and sell them for twice as much as they were worth just a few years ago. Is that organized crime or wily wheeler-dealers reaping the benefits of the law of supply and demand?"

"You keep mentioning developers," I said.

"You both know who Isadore Blumenfeld was?"

Swenson and I nodded our heads.

"Do you know what happened to him?" Harry asked.

"He was convicted of violating the Mann Act and jury tampering and ended up in Leavenworth," Swenson said.

"I mean after that," Harry said.

"No."

"Kid Cann, as he was called, did four years in federal prison and then moved to Miami, where he became involved in the real estate business with Meyer Lansky."

Swenson and I responded almost simultaneously.

"Real estate," he said.

"Meyer Lansky," I said.

Harry smiled at us.

"Meyer Lansky who helped found the American mafia with Lucky Luciano, that Meyer Lansky?" I asked.

"That's the one," Harry said.

"He and Blumenfeld were pals?" Swenson asked.

"Lansky once said 'I wouldn't trust that bastard with my pocket comb,' so no, not pals. Merely business associates. The Miami newspapers once reported that together, Blumenfeld and Lansky had financial stakes in ten of the city's biggest and best hotels."

"In Miami."

"Yes."

"What about Minnesota?"

Harry wagged a finger at Swenson.

"No," he said. "But, do you know who Omer Berenson was?"

Swenson and I ended up staring at each other.

"I take it you do," Harry said.

"I never heard the name until about three hours ago," I said.

"Me, neither," Swenson said.

"Berenson was one of Kid Cann's younger lieutenants," Harry said. "Very smart man if you want to use that adjective to describe a gangster. He kept a very low profile. Most of the old-time gangsters, it wasn't enough that they were crooks; they wanted to be famous crooks. Kid Cann, his favorite outfit was a maroon suit, maroon suede shoes, a canary yellow shirt, and matching socks. Who dresses like that? I mean, besides the University of Minnesota mascot? Berenson was the opposite, though. He didn't want anyone to know his name. He also realized that the days of the tommy gun were over long before Kid Cann did. He got out of the liquor business; he got out of the protection rackets, loan-sharking, gambling, prostitution; never touched drugs."

"What did he do?"

"He went into real estate. I think that's where Kid Cann got the idea."

"Ah, that's what you meant," I said. "The examples you gave."

"Ever hear of the Polachek Companies?"

"They're everywhere."

"Berenson owned it. Berenson was Jewish, by the way. His people emigrated here from Poland around 1910. Polachek translates to a 'Pole from Poland.' Blumenfeld was Jewish, too. He came from Romania. And people think only Swedes, Danes, Norwegians, and Lutherans live in Minnesota."

"So, Omer Berenson went straight and became a real estate developer," Swenson said.

"I didn't say he went straight," Harry said. "He just evolved into a different kind of criminal. He didn't murder journalists like Kid Cann did; he didn't shoot people down in the street. Money was his chief weapon of coercion, followed closely by blackmail, not guns. If a business owner or a politician couldn't be bought or bullied, which would make him a very rare individual indeed, Berenson simply moved on to the next project. There were always opportunities for the enterprising young man was the way he looked at it."

"You never busted him, the bureau, I mean."

"Yes, we did. He was indicted for tax evasion, mail and wire fraud in 1991. Unfortunately, he died, in bed, shortly before his trial was set to begin. His company paid a 2.7 million special assessment and that was that."

"Wait," I said. "Nineteen ninety-one?" I turned to Swenson. "David Carrell disappeared in July 1995."

"Berenson couldn't have been involved despite what Belden had to say."

"You guys want to tell me what's going on?" Harry said.

We did.

"So, you're thinking of opening a twenty-seven-year-old cold case based on the suspicions of a retired deputy that, by your own admission, isn't all there," Harry said. "Good luck with that."

We all leaned back in our chairs, sipped our beverages, and listened as Joel Shapira's nimble fingers danced over the strings of his vintage guitar. We were three songs in when Harry leaned forward again.

"In case you didn't know, Omer had a son," he said. "Adam Berenson."

"What?" I asked.

Swenson and I huddled with Harry once again.

"A son?" Swenson asked.

"Adam took over the Polachek Companies when his old man passed. He was thirty-five at the time. He's the one who paid the tax bill, although he claimed that he did not believe his father committed the offenses he had been accused of. He said he paid the assessment because he didn't want his father's name to be tarnished after his death. Oh, and the examples I listed earlier—is this organized crime or smart businessmen? They're all recent."

"Is the FBI currently investigating Adam Berenson and the Polachek Companies?"

"Gentlemen, you know that the bureau never discloses details of an investigation in order to both preserve the integrity of the investigation and to protect the rights of individuals not yet charged with a crime. Besides, it's against the law."

"Then why are you telling us this?" Swenson asked.

"I haven't told you anything," Harry said. "I'm just having a drink with an old friend and his new BFF. Isn't that right, McKenzie?"

"Nina was saying just the other day that we don't see enough of you and your wife," I said.

In reply, Harry saluted me with his drink.

Joel Shapira finished his set and Harry finished his drink. He said that his wife was waiting dinner for him and left Swenson and me sitting alone at the table.

"Did he just do what I think he just did?" Swenson said.

"What did he do?"

"Your friend all but told us to go ahead and investigate Adam Berenson."

"For a twenty-seven-year-old murder while he sits back and watches? Question is—do we want to do that?"

"Hell no. McKenzie, whether Jeanette Carrell killed her husband, or Berenson did it, or they did it together—that crime has nothing to do with Charles Sainsbury's murder."

"You're probably right," I said.

"I do not want to have to go to the ACA and explain all of this to him. He'll think I'm an idiot."

"Then don't."

"Except, you're going to tell your guy, aren't you, Carrell's attorney."

"Yeah, I thought I might."

"For God's sake, why?" Swenson asked.

"Sainsbury worked in real estate."

"I can't believe this is happening. McKenzie, remember yesterday afternoon in the cafeteria at the LEC when I said I was happy to see you? I changed my mind."

SEVEN

The fire was roaring away nicely by the time Evangeline and I reached the top of the Circle. It looked as if it had been set by someone who knew what she was doing and I wondered which one of the dozen members of the Plot Whores Book Club that had gathered around the fire ring had been a Girl Scout. In Minnesota in early October, the sun set at about six fifteen P.M., with twilight descending a half hour later. The fire was the only light above the tree line and it flickered across their faces. Everyone was sitting on lawn chairs that they had carried up the hill. Jenny Carlson was there and so were the Westermeyer sisters. I was surprised to see Linda Welch. She didn't strike me as being either a reader or particularly sociable. I hadn't met the others.

Evan set two bottles of wine on a card table near the fire ring that had already been filled with several other opened bottles, plastic cups, and treats.

"Everybody." Evan pointed at me. "This is my friend McKenzie. I told you he was coming."

"The detective," Jenny said.

"Detective?" one of the Plot Whores asked. "Like Sam Spade, Philip Marlowe, Lew Archer . . . ?"

"C. Auguste Dupin," someone else said.

"Apparently, McKenzie has only one name, like Spenser and Rockford."

"Rockford had a first name," someone added. "It's Jim."

"I know. Inspector Japp."

"Who?"

"McKenzie always reminded me of Encyclopedia Brown," Evan said.

"When he was at the house this morning, I kept thinking Veronica Mars," Rebecca said.

I couldn't help but notice that Rachel thought that was awfully funny.

"Actually," I said, "I always thought of myself more of a Nancy Drew type."

"Hey, Evan," a woman said. "Does that make you George?"

"He's here to find out who killed Charles Sainsbury," Linda Welch said. Unlike the others, her tone of voice was dead serious.

"I thought it was J. C.," one of the unidentified women said. "Wasn't it?"

"That's the consensus," I said.

"Only you don't believe it."

"I was hoping you'd tell me what you believe."

"Motive, means, and opportunity," another woman said. "The holy trinity."

"What about it?" someone asked.

"You start with motive, don't you? That's how it works, right, McKenzie?"

"Sometimes," I said.

"Well, then, everyone who lives on the Circle had a motive."

"Not everyone," Linda said.

"You know, it might not have had anything to do with the Circle," Jenny said. "Charles could have been killed for a completely different reason."

"What reason?" a voice asked.

"You tell me," I replied.

I was impressed by how freely the women spoke to me and to one another. I wondered if the wine they had consumed and kept consuming had something to do with it. Or the fact that, except for the fire, they were all wrapped in darkness. Or perhaps it was familiarity. They seemed to know one another very well.

"He was killed for what he knew," one of the Plot Whores said.

"What did he know?" another asked.

"He was killed before he could tell us."

"It had to be a deep, dark, dangerous secret," Rachel said. "Becca?"

"Stop it," her sister replied.

"This is certainly more exciting than talking about Wendy Webb's new book," another woman said.

"I could feel the icy wind coming off of Lake Superior while I was reading it," said someone else.

"I'm feeling it now."

"This should be a book. *Murder on the Hill*."

"*The Case of the Gazebo*—what goes good with gazebo?"

"*The Case of the Gazebo Rub Out*."

"Nah."

"*The Circle of Death*."

"No, no, no. Call it *The Seventh Circle*."

"That's awfully specific."

"In the *Inferno*, the first part of Dante's *Divine Comedy,* the Roman poet Virgil gives Dante a tour of the nine circles of hell. The first ring of the seventh circle of hell, a river of boiling blood and fire, is where murderers and bandits are punished."

"I never read it."

"If you had attended a real college instead of St. Catherine's . . ."

"Oh, we're going there again."

"We have the violence," a member of the reading group pointed out. "But where's the sex?"

"You don't think J. C. has had more than her share?" Rebecca said. "I mean, look at her. Given half a chance, you would do her."

"I don't know," Rachel said. "She's a little tall for me."

"She's a love-'em-and-leave-'em gal," someone else said. "Have you ever known J. C. to date someone more than a month? She screws 'em and kicks them to the curb."

"Sounds like half the men I knew in college. Yes, I knew men when I went to St. Kate's."

"A private all-women's university, I bet you knew a lot of girls, too."

"Oh, you are asking for it tonight."

"Who's the hero of *The Seventh Circle*?"

"McKenzie. He's a little old for the part . . ."

Hey, now! my inner voice cried.

"What did we decide during our meeting last month? There are only two kinds of stories. Someone goes on a journey or a stranger comes to town. He's new in town. Sorta."

"Yes, but then who's the villain?"

"Ruth Krider," Linda Welch said.

"What do you have against Ruth, anyway?" Jenny Carlson asked. "She's always been nice."

"Nice to you, maybe," Linda said. "Listen, I have nothing against Ruth. But if you want a villain, why not her? Her house, her property will probably lose a lot of value if they build a road next to it and living so close to Charles Sainsbury for all those years, I bet she has a lot of reasons to club him over the head."

"Ruth is in her seventies."

"Charles was in his eighties."

"William Sainsbury," Evan said.

"What?"

"There's an idea," Rachel said. "If you want a motive, how 'bout William kills his father to inherit the business."

"The king is dead, long live the king," Rebecca said.

"Wasn't William already running the business when Charles was killed?" Jenny asked.

"He was running it, but did he own it?" Evan asked in return.

"That's bullshit," Linda said. "You're just saying that because you don't like him."

"You like him, though, right?" a woman asked.

"Yeah, Linda," one of the other Plot Whores said. "Maybe you killed Charles as a favor to William."

"Sex and violence," added another.

Linda Welch rose quickly from her chair. I expected her to articulate her outrage in no uncertain terms with a long string of earsplitting expletives. She didn't. Instead, she folded her chair and started carrying it silently across the hill. A voice I hadn't heard before called to her from beyond the fire ring.

"Linda," it said.

She paused.

"Don't go away mad," the voice added. "Just go away."

"Fuck you, Gilman," Linda said.

There you go.

While Linda retreated into the darkness, the woman who spoke stepped close enough to the fire that she was easily recognized.

"Bethany," one of the Plot Whores said, "we're so sorry. We didn't mean any disrespect to you or your family. We were—we were just wondering who might have killed your father."

"That's okay," Bethany said. "So have I."

"We didn't mean to be rude."

Bethany brushed the apology aside with the wave of her hand.

"Are you McKenzie?" she asked.

"Yes, ma'am."

"I was just talking to Ruth Krider. I met her when I drove over to see if my daughter had burned down my father's house yet. She said you might be up here chatting with the Whores."

Would you people please get a new nickname!

"I was wondering if they had any ideas concerning who might have killed your father," I said aloud.

"I have an idea. Just so you know; it isn't my brother or Linda or J. C."

It felt as if everyone around the fire ring was leaning toward her when I asked, "Who?"

Bethany Gilman's response was to move to the card table and casually examine the labels of several wine bottles before she chose one she liked and half filled a clear plastic cup with the contents.

"Who?" Rebecca repeated.

"Don't you gals have anything better to do than gossip around a campfire?" Bethany asked.

"Oh, c'mon," Rachel said.

"Seriously, I thought you came up here to talk about Wendy Webb's book, *Daughters of the Lake*."

"Ms. Gilman . . ." I said.

"I said I had an idea, not a suspect," Bethany said. "There's no one I would actually accuse."

"I'd still like to hear your idea."

"When you finish chatting with the Whores, come down to the house. We'll talk."

Bethany pivoted away from the table and headed in the

direction she had come. She didn't leave right away, though. There were several hugs to be had and parting words with her friends that lasted at least a quarter hour. We call it a Minnesota Good-bye.

I remained with the book club members for a half hour more, yet didn't learn anything particularly useful. Finally, the fire burned down and the Whores gathered their chairs and other belongings and began to wander back to their homes by the light of the moon. One of them was Evangeline, who grasped the necks of the two wine bottles she had brought to the gathering, both of them now empty.

"Stop in before you leave," she told me.

I said I would.

I dodged several trees as I made my way down the hill toward the lights shining through the windows of Charles Sainsbury's home. Instead of going to the back door, I circled to the front and tapped the doorbell. The front door was pulled open by a young woman wearing a ponytail and a gray sweatshirt with MINNESOTA printed across the front in maroon and gold.

"Hi," I said. "My name is McKenzie."

That's all she needed to hear. She held the door open for me as she spun toward the interior of the house.

"Mom!" she shouted. "Your boyfriend is here."

"Boyfriend?" I asked.

"Private joke," the young woman said. "Mom's always picking on me about my boyfriends, so . . . Mom!"

Bethany Gilman appeared behind her, a look of exasperation etched on her face.

"Stop shouting," she said. To me, she added, "This is my daughter, Maren. You'll have to excuse her, McKenzie. Apparently, her parents did a poor job of teaching her manners."

The young woman thought that was funny enough to chuckle at as she disappeared into the house. Bethany took charge of the door and closed it when I was inside. In the bright light of the house I placed her at early to mid-forties.

"I just opened a bottle of wine if you care to join me," she said.

"That's kind of you. Thank you."

I followed Bethany through an opulent living room to the dining room where her daughter sat taking notes from a textbook with a purple flower on the cover that I couldn't identify beneath the title *Campbell Biology*.

"Should I leave?" Maren asked.

Her mother smoothed her daughter's hair and said, "No, no, finish your homework," as she moved into the kitchen. I followed her there.

The wine bottle was resting on a counter next to a half-filled glass. Bethany opened a cupboard, found an exact duplicate of the glass, and filled it. She handed me the glass and took a sip from her own. She didn't sit at the table, so I didn't either, the two of us leaning against kitchen counters across from each other.

"Ruth told me that you're working for J. C.," Bethany said.

"I was asked to help her."

"Does she need help?"

"Yes."

"When my father was killed and they said J. C. killed him, I can't tell you how angry I was; how much I wanted to kill her. It was bad enough that my father had been murdered, but that this woman was responsible, a woman who had been a friend to me all of my life. The pain wasn't just emotional, it was physical. I could feel it. Sometimes I still do."

Bethany drank much of her wine and added more to the glass.

"Except, after time, the pain subsided like clouds vanishing from the sky, and when it did, I could see that it was impossible. I've had six months to think about it, McKenzie, and the more I've thought about it the more convinced I became that J. C. didn't do it; that she couldn't have done it. Yes, I know I might be deceiving myself. At the same time . . ."

"Did you tell the county deputies that; the assistant county attorney?"

"Not when it happened, but I would now."

"In court?"

"Yes."

Bethany drank more wine.

"You said you had an idea who killed your father," I reminded her.

"My father made a lot of enemies over the years, not so much for what he built, but for what he tore down in order to make room for what he built. Why not one of them?"

"Did anyone threaten him?"

"Yes."

"Just before he died?"

"You're asking me the same questions the sheriff's department asked. The answer is no, not just before he died. He wasn't that active in the business back then; hadn't been for a couple of years except to supervise William and make sure he didn't screw up which, of course, he did. That doesn't mean someone who was angry at Dad five years ago, ten, wasn't still angry, does it?"

"No," I said.

"Besides, Sainsbury Construction was my father and my father was Sainsbury Construction. Look up either on the internet and that's what you'll see. If you were upset at the company for something, that meant you were upset with him personally whether or not he had anything to do with what was making you angry."

"Okay."

"You don't believe me."

"I do believe you, Ms. Gilman."

"Bethany," she said. "Or Beth."

"The problem, Bethany, is that it's a very hard thing to prove."

"Proving that it was J. C. who killed him, though, that's easy?"

"Easier, anyway."

"Because people heard her threaten my father . . ."

"Yes."

"Because someone claims they saw her on the hill . . ."

"Yes."

"Her diamond pendant . . ."

"I'm afraid so."

"Only it's not true," Bethany said. "I just know it."

"You were one of Jeanette's girls, weren't you? I was told by several sources that she practically adopted the girls who grew up on the Circle."

"I don't know if she adopted us so much as we adopted her. J. C. was so beautiful, McKenzie. So smart, so willing; so un-encumbered. We were always welcomed in her house day or night. We went to her with our problems and she tried to help us solve them. She happily answered every question we asked about anything. No subject was off-limits. Sex. The 'talk' we got from her was so much more informative and honest than the one we got from our mothers. She was always encouraging us to do whatever the hell was in our heads at the time, too. Some-thing else, probably the most important lesson—she told us to never put ourselves second to anyone."

"Amen," Maren shouted from the dining room.

"It's impolite to eavesdrop, young lady," Bethany said.

"It is? My parents should have told me."

Bethany smiled.

"I taught Maren what J. C. taught me," she said. "Which was the exact opposite of what my father believed. He believed that the man should always be in charge. He claimed that the Bible said so and that the church agreed, although I don't think he had ever read the Bible or set foot inside a church in his entire life. You don't need to hear that, though."

"Yes, I do," I said.

"I worked for Sainsbury Construction; I worked there in one capacity or another since I was a junior in high school. I even worked a few construction sites. It was mostly just fetching and carrying, but I was there because Dad said it was important that I understand how things worked. Yet, when the time came, he put William in charge, even though I was older and had more experience.

"No, McKenzie—I can tell by the expression on your face what you're thinking. I wasn't angry at my father; certainly not angry enough to kill him. I knew from a very young age that my father didn't value girls nearly as highly as he valued boys. He didn't even value my mother until she passed and he was left with two teenagers to raise. Putting William in charge and leaving him controlling interest in the firm after he died, that didn't surprise me one little bit."

"Tell me about the Circle," I said.

"That was my father's dream project, building mansions on the high hill with a view of all the houses around them. I don't know why, but that was something he always wanted to do. He was absolutely delighted when William announced that he had convinced Carson Vaneps to sell."

"How did your brother manage that?"

"William simply went to Carson one day and told him that

he wasn't getting any younger and if he wanted a big payday for his family before he passed, now was the time. At least that's what he told me and Dad. He kept the deal a secret, too, while he gathered together all the building permits that he needed. Then, right before he was ready to send his bulldozers up the hill, some of the neighbors found out what was happening. Sara Vaneps found out. They went to Carson and asked him about it. Carson claimed he didn't know what everyone was talking about, that he didn't sell the Circle. That's when Dad stepped in and told William to hold off for a while; give our neighbors a chance to settle down and accept what was happening. William didn't want to hold off. He was ready to go. I remember him standing in the office and waving the permits and the contract with Carson's signature on it in the air above his head. Dad said, 'Do it for me, these are my neighbors.' So he agreed to give it a week, ten days max. Only that gave the Vaneps time to file a lawsuit to keep him off the hill and now he's sitting and waiting for the court to reach a decision."

"I was told that your brother needed money," I said.

"By who? Let me guess—Linda Welch."

"I really can't say."

"She's such a . . . Linda's not all that much to look at, but William said she's an animal in bed or anywhere else they screwed, for that matter."

"He told you that?"

"My brother likes to brag and he isn't always smart about who he brags to, one of the reasons his wife is divorcing him. One of the many reasons his wife is divorcing him. My father was livid about that, by the way. He disliked Linda immensely and he called William's affair with her 'a disappointment of character.'"

"Amen to that, too," Maren Gilman said from her perch at the dining-room table.

"Aren't you supposed to be studying?" Bethany asked.

"The book says that the human race is evolving. Makes me question its veracity."

Veracity, my inner voice repeated. *Ah, to be young and in college.*

"Money," I said aloud.

"You need to know how the real estate business works, Mc-Kenzie," Bethany said. "Developers, sometimes alone, sometimes with investors, will build a building, develop a property, and then sell it for a profit. Often they'll have an interested buyer when they begin the project, sometimes they don't. In either case, they rarely operate an apartment building, a shopping mall, on their own. Instead, they flip it. That's how the developer and his investors make their money. Only William has been sitting on this project for over six months now with money going in, such as legal fees, and nothing coming out so, yeah, he's feeling the pinch. Truth is, if it hadn't been for Dad, the project would have been completed and sold by now."

"How much debt is he carrying?"

"I have no idea. I don't work for Sainsbury Construction any longer."

"Why not?" I asked.

"Let's just say that management and I had a disagreement concerning the direction the firm was heading and we decided that it was best that we go our separate ways."

Bethany's daughter spoke up from the dining room again.

"Slapping my uncle was part of her severance package," she said.

"Young lady, we do not air our family's dirty laundry . . ."

"Mom, twenty people saw you do it."

Bethany closed her eyes and shook her head slowly, although the way she smiled suggested that she didn't regret the memory.

"I get thirty-three-and-a-third percent of the firm's profits whether I put up with my brother's verbal abuse or not," she told me. "But that has nothing to do with this."

"Up on the hill, you said that you had an idea who killed your father," I told her.

"My brother . . ."

"You just said that you didn't think it was him."

"McKenzie, no. I don't think it was him any more than I believe that J. C. did it. What I meant, Dad might have been killed because of my brother. Dad did very well with the business. When William took over, he wanted to do even better. He became involved in an apartment complex in St. Paul. He couldn't manage it alone, for various reasons, so he brought in a partner. This is not a big deal, McKenzie. This happens all the time. Except the deal went sour, again for a lot of different reasons, and his partner wanted his money back. The Circle project would have allowed William to pay off his debts. Except, when Dad put the project on hold and the lawsuit was filed . . ."

"You think that William's partner might have done it?"

"For six months, I've been thinking about this and I can't come up with a better explanation . . ."

In six months we could come up with a hundred outrageous theories, my inner voice told me.

"I know it wasn't William," Bethany said. "He was in the office when they say Dad was killed. I was with him."

"I don't know, Bethany," I said. "What would your brother's partner have gained by killing your father?"

"Revenge."

That's very, very thin.

"I don't know," I repeated.

"That's why they say J. C. murdered Dad, isn't it?"

Good point.

"Anyway, you can look into it, can't you?" Bethany said. "You were asked to help J. C. This might help her, wouldn't it?"

"I suppose it might."

"Well, then," Bethany said.

"Do you think your brother would agree to speak to me?"

"Yes, probably. He loves to talk about himself."

"A lot of people do."

I thanked Bethany for her time and we wandered from the kitchen into the dining room where her daughter was busy gathering up her schoolwork.

"Do you want me to stay for a while?" Bethany asked.

"No, Mom. I'm good."

"It worries me that you're always alone in the great big house."

"Mostly I just sleep here," Maren said. "Usually, I'm on campus, you know that. When I am here, I almost always have a bunch of my friends hanging around. They're not here now because we knew that you were coming over, so . . ."

"Friends plural or one friend in particular?"

"Plural, Mom."

"What do you do here, you and your friends? Party all night?"

"Mother, how can you ask that? We study hard all night just like you did when you were in school."

Maren said that with all seriousness, even though the way she winked at me in clear view of her mother suggested otherwise.

"Maren has been house-sitting for William ever since my father died," Bethany told me. "I worry."

"Would you worry less if I was still living in that expensive apartment off campus?" Maren asked.

"All right, all right."

"Give Dad a hug and a kiss for me."

"I will."

"A pleasure meeting you, McKenzie," Maren said. "I hope

you can help Jeanette. From what I know of her, she seems awfully special."

"I'll do my best."

Bethany and I left the house. She was parked in the driveway. My car was on the other side of the hill in Evan's driveway. We said good-bye just outside the front door.

"Should I contact my brother and tell him you'll be calling?" she asked.

"That might not be a bad idea," I said.

"First thing in the morning."

"Thank you. Oh, Bethany. You mentioned earlier your suspicions concerning your brother's partner. Who is the partner?"

"The Polachek Companies."

The Polachek Companies.

The name bounced around in my head as I slowly threaded my way through the trees behind Sainsbury's house and climbed the hill. Images from gangster movies appeared and disappeared alongside it, including the scene in *The Untouchables* where Billy Drago shot Sean Connery down with a tommy gun. As I was cresting the hill, though, another image caught my eye and stayed.

It was a figure of a man in jogging shorts and a dark T-shirt trotting steadily past the gazebo. The quarter moon and a few stars gave me light, yet not enough to identify him by.

I remained hidden in the shadows of the tree line and watched.

He ran away from the gazebo and toward the fire ring. Before he reached it, he altered course.

I moved along the tree line and put myself in a good position to watch him as he reduced speed and carefully jogged down the hill toward the back of Jeanette Carrell's house. When he reached the bottom of the hill, the figure slowed to a walk. The light above the back door of Katherine Hixson's house was lit, yet it was unable to illuminate anything on the far side of the five-foot wall between her and Carrell's backyard. Carrell's back door light was not on.

The figure moved to the door.

From where I was standing at the tree line, I heard a soft knock. For some unknown reason, I flashed on "The Raven," by Edgar Allen Poe.

While I nodded, nearly napping, suddenly there came a
  tapping,
As of someone gently rapping, rapping at my chamber
  door.
"'Tis some visitor," I muttered, "tapping at my chamber
  door—
"Only this and nothing more."

The door was pulled open and the light from inside the house revealed the figure in full.

Derek Carlson.

Jenny's husband.

I could not see Jeanette Carrell from where I was standing; only her hand as it reached out, grabbed Derek by the shirt, and pulled him inside.

The door was shut.

There was nothing more to see.

I climbed the hill again and walked across it to Evangeline's house. I was tempted to jump in my Mustang and simply drive away, only I promised her I would stop by. I knocked on her front door. She opened it. I was surprised to see that she was wearing the same clothes that she had on when we were lounging around the fire ring earlier. For some reason, I expected Evan to be dressed for bed. I glanced at my watch. Was it really only half past ten P.M.? How time slows down when you're having fun.

"What did Bethany have to say?" Evan asked.

"Nothing, really."

"Oh c'mon, McKenzie. You're not going to tell me? I thought we were partners. You Nancy Drew, me George Fayne. Or Bess. I could be Bess Marvin."

"Evan, what do you know about Derek Carlson?"

"Very little. I've seen him around, but we haven't really spent much time chatting."

"I was talking to both him and Jenny Carlson this morning. They don't seem to get along very well."

"It's the same old story, McKenzie; I could write a book based on my personal experiences. She loves him. He loves himself."

"Rebecca Westermeyer Wright says he likes to run without his shirt on."

Evan laughed at the image.

"Yeah," she said. "That pretty much describes him."

"What does Jeanette Carrell think about Derek, do you know?"

"Not really. Once, though, a few weeks ago, I was up at the gazebo. He was there along with Jenny and a few others who lived on the Circle plus Jeanette and he kept trying to joke with her and she kept trying to ignore him. My impression, she would have been more than happy to run him over with her car."

"Nothing is more dangerous than a friend without discretion."

(116)

"What?"

"Something a French poet named Jean de La Fontaine once said."

"Which you're repeating now because . . . ?"

"Something about the Circle keeps taking me back to my English lit classes."

EIGHT

Our condo in downtown Minneapolis had a master bedroom and guest room that Erica used whenever she was in town, plus a bathroom for visitors. Beyond that, we didn't have rooms so much as areas—dining area, living area, music area where Nina's Steinway stood, office area with a desk and computer, and a kitchen area that was elevated three steps above the rest. The south wall featured floor-to-ceiling bookcases that turned at the east wall and followed it to a large brick fireplace. The north wall was made entirely of tinted floor-to-ceiling glass with a dramatic view of the Mississippi River where it tumbled down St. Anthony Falls.

Nina was standing in front of the windows and sipping coffee from an oversize mug with the words YOU DO REALIZE ONE DAY I'LL SNAP, RIGHT? printed on it. Her head turned toward me when she heard my laughter.

"What?" she asked.

I spoke to her from behind my desk near the front door.

"An email I was expecting," I said.

"What?" she repeated.

I pointed at the computer screen.

"Come, take a look," I said.

She crossed the condo, positioned herself behind me, and read over my shoulder.

"Oh, my God," she said.

"This is a transcript of a meeting of the Chippewa Woods Homeowners Association. The woman calling Jeanette Carrell all those names is her neighbor."

"She doesn't like Carrell at all, does she?"

"She's also the chief witness against Carrell in her murder trial. Along with the transcript, the head of the HOA sent me a video file. Want to watch?"

"No, and if you do, please wear your headphones. I've already heard the C-word enough in my lifetime."

"If you were on the jury and you heard this woman testify that she saw Carrell committing a heinous crime, would you believe her?"

Nina took a long sip from her mug before answering.

"You'd have to give me a little more than her testimony, otherwise . . ."

She shook her head and drank more coffee.

"Yeah, that's what I was thinking, too," I said.

"Did Carrell commit a heinous crime?"

"Same as the last time you asked—I honestly don't know. I do know that the case isn't nearly as open and shut as the assistant county attorney thinks it is."

"Or you could be making it more complicated than it needs to be. You have been known to do that."

"I deeply resemble that remark."

As if on cue, my smartphone began playing "West End Blues." I glanced at the caller ID.

"Speak of the devil," I said.

Nina went to the kitchen area, where she rinsed her mug and set it next to the coffeemaker while I answered the phone.

"Mr. Brandt," I said.

"Mr. McKenzie. I just received notice that Ms. Carrell's trial date has been set. I've scheduled an appointment with her in my office this afternoon. I'd like you to be there."

"Okay."

"Please say you have something for me."

"A couple of somethings, although I don't know how helpful they'll be."

"Do I get a hint?"

"And ruin the surprise? For what it's worth, I'm hoping to meet with William Sainsbury this morning if his sister can arrange it. He became the majority owner of Sainsbury Construction after his father died; the one who'll be developing the Circle if he wins the civil suit. His sister, Bethany Gilman, doesn't believe that Jeanette Carrell killed her father, by the way. She's absolutely convinced that she's innocent."

"Will she testify to that in court?"

"She said she would."

"That would be helpful, very helpful, yes. All right, I'll see you this afternoon. Two P.M.?"

"I'll be there."

After watching me hang up the phone, Nina called from the kitchen area.

"Looks like your day is planned," she said.

"What about you?"

"I need to go in early. I have supply-chain issues."

"Anything I can do to help?"

"Mostly what I need is a vendor that doesn't treat a small business like it's a small business; who'll give us the same courtesy as his larger customers. I could also use a couple more people on my waitstaff. Know anyone?"

"Sorry."

"Have you ever waited tables?"

"No, but I'll try anything once."

Nina stared at me as if she was actually contemplating the possibility. Finally, she shook her head.

"As if I don't have problems enough," she said.

Sainsbury Construction was located in an aging, three-story office building in a St. Paul suburb overlooking a large man-made pond that it shared with a tech start-up and a medical device company. It was bordered by woods on one side and a park on the other that featured a picnic pavilion and three Little League baseball diamonds and I wondered if Charles had built it.

There was an elevator, only I ignored it, using the carpeted staircase to reach Sainsbury's offices on the third floor. A woman wearing a mask sat behind a reception desk and for a moment I felt guilty that I wasn't wearing mine. She didn't seem to mind, though, and after asking me who I was and what I wanted, she made a call. A few moments later, a man appeared who I assumed was William Sainsbury—we weren't introduced. He was about my age and dressed the same way I was in a sports jacket, jeans and Skechers; he wasn't wearing a mask, either.

"McKenzie," he said. He didn't offer his hand, but that might have been because of COVID. "This way."

I followed him down a corridor to a corner office; half of his large windows faced the pond and the other half faced the park. He moved around his desk and sat, pointing to a chair in front of his desk at the same time.

"Let me guess," Sainsbury said. "You're here because you wanted to see the evil developer"—he quoted the air—"in his natural habitat."

"Are you an evil developer?"

"We all are. Don't you watch the movies? Listen, Beth called this morning. Well, you know that; I told you when you called me. She seems to think that my business associates are somehow involved in my father's murder. I agreed to see you because I can't have that, man, c'mon; people making baseless accusations like that. I don't care if she is my sister."

Sainsbury sighed heavily and I remembered that Bethany said he loved to talk about himself.

"At least she's not blaming me," he said. "I know that some people on the Circle are and that pisses me off more than anything. The sheriff deputies blamed me, too, at first. They questioned me—where were you between the hours of nine A.M. and eleven A.M.? I told them, but they wouldn't take my word for it. They had to check with witnesses; had to subpoena the GPS information on my phone. They were doing their job; I get that. Still . . ."

"Bethany doesn't believe that Jeanette Carrell killed your father," I said.

"I get that, too. Jeanette has always been good to her, especially after my mother died. She was good to all the girls on the Circle. Only I'm not a girl and she wasn't good to me and she hated my father. That's why I can see things a little more clearly than Beth does. Personally, I'm not altogether sure Carrell isn't some kind of lesbian pervert the way she fawns on all those chicks."

There were a lot of ways to respond to that remark, except the investigator in me demanded that I remember why I was there.

"Why did Carrell hate your father?" I asked.

"Because he was an evil developer," Sainsbury replied. "That's the way we're always portrayed in the movies and on TV. You think I'm kidding? Go back to that Christmas movie that they rerun on TV every single year—*It's a Wonderful Life*. The wicked Mr. Potter wants to force the people in Bedford Falls to live in his slums instead of George Bailey's affordable, quality, suburban housing and will commit any crime to make that happen. Yeah, okay, fine. Potter was an asshole. Bailey, though, George Bailey, the guy Jimmy Stewart played, was a lousy businessman. Irresponsible. Twice his bank needed to be bailed out. Twice.

"Ever since then—what was it, 1946 when the movie came out? Ever since then developers have always been the bad guys trying to raze the orphanage, bulldoze the park, demolish the small town's beloved library or bookstore or bakery or whatever. It's a lousy trope that supposedly gives the heroes a clear-cut enemy to fight and something to fight for. Never, never, never do the movies talk about the benefits new developments provide in the form of housing, retail space, and offices that allow people and businesses and whole communities to grow and thrive. It's ridiculous.

"The demand for new homes has skyrocketed across the country," Sainsbury said, "yet the people who build them are constantly portrayed as Mr. Potters. People demand affordable housing at the same time that they're petitioning for more and more restrictive zoning codes and protesting new construction in their neighborhoods and, in the time of COVID, refusing to pay their rent. I mean, the Circle isn't even a park. It's a guy's backyard. Only the people who lived around it can actually use it. The guy who lived across the street from my old man, he wasn't even allowed to go up the hill. If he wanted to, he'd have to sneak through someone's yard and risk going to jail for trespassing. Yet I'm a scumbag because I want to build houses there; because my father wanted to build houses there."

Sainsbury stopped speaking and for a moment I wondered if he was waiting to catch his breath.

"Nice speech, don't you think?" he asked.

You could sell tickets, my inner voice said.

"I see your point," I said aloud.

"I gave a similar speech a couple years ago at the Minnesota

Construction Summit. That was a short version. McKenzie, I really mean it, though. Drug dealers get better treatment than we do."

"How did you convince Carson Vaneps to sell?"

"I asked him. I went up to his house, knocked on his door, and asked if he was ready to make a deal. He said no. Then he called me back the next day and said, yeah, maybe it was time. So we worked it out. Afterward, I went to see Jeanette Carrell."

"You did?"

"Didn't she tell you?" Sainsbury asked.

"No."

"I wanted her fifth of the hill, too. I told her about Vaneps; told her that once I started building, her strip of land would become worthless and she wouldn't be able to do anything except pay taxes on it for the rest of her life. She didn't say a word for a long time, like she was thinking it over, and then she told me to get lost. I didn't take it personally, though. The way I figured it, once I started bringing my machines up the hill and she was faced with the reality of the situation, she'd change her mind. You already know what happened afterward."

"You've been on hold for the past six months," I said.

"A decision could come any day. I'm amazed it's taking this long. Even if it goes against me, though, the decision, I'll go back to the Vaneps family and offer them the same deal; maybe sweeten the pot. What'll you bet that they'll see things my way?"

"Tell me about your business associate, the Polachek Companies."

"So, we're back to that. God, Beth, what were you thinking? Look, McKenzie, one thing has nothing to do with the other. Polachek—let me tell you what happened. I'll try to keep the story short."

I don't believe you.

"I was—am—developing an apartment complex in St. Paul, not at the old Ford plant, but near there," Sainsbury said. "A combination of low-to-moderate-cost housing. I already had several buyers interested before I even started. Then things went to hell, partly because of COVID, but mostly because of the shipping crisis; the supply crisis. Costs for building materials escalated. I mean they went bonkers. That's if you can get them. Plywood doubled in price. So did nails. Nails. Electrical panels, circuit breakers quadrupled. Copper—we had to hire security to keep thieves from invading our work site and stealing it. I ordered a hot water boiler; it's designed to provide central heat to all of the apartments. It should have arrived in six months. My supplier called me and said it'll take a year and a half now and, oh, by the way, the price has doubled.

"Costs were exceeding all expectations, not to mention our construction schedule was shot to hell. It hasn't been this bad in forty, fifty years. Not since the oil crisis in the mid-seventies, anyway. So I brought in a partner, Adam Berenson at the Polachek Companies. My father worked with him I don't know how many times in the past. For a certain percentage of the sales price, he agreed to help with financing. Except things then went from bad to worse because the City of St. Paul, in its infinite wisdom, decided it needed rent restrictions, rent control, because of evil developers, right? All of a sudden my buyers are saying, hey, wait a minute. Are we sure we can make money over the long haul?

"Something else," Sainsbury said. "McKenzie, there are three-point-four million people living in the greater Twin Cities area, yet only three hundred thousand in St. Paul. Ask yourself—why would you build in St. Paul when you could build in Roseville and not worry about rent control? Or Maplewood or Arden Hills or Richfield or Shoreview or—you get my point? If I knew this was going to happen, I would never have tried to build in St. Paul.

"This is starting to be a long story," Sainsbury said. "I'm sorry."

I didn't say anything because I didn't want him to stop.

"After a while, Berenson came to me and said, Hey, where's my money?" Sainsbury added. "He knew damn well where his money was but a contract is a contract. If I had completed the Circle project on time, I would have been able to hand him a check. Since we've been delayed, he's now saying, don't worry about it, you can pay what you owe me later, plus interest, and the interest—you'd think I was dealing with loan sharks or credit card companies it's so high. Or I could give him a bigger percentage of the sales price for the apartment complex, which means I'd be lucky to break even. Or he'd be happy to kick in a few more bucks than he already has and take the entire project off my hands. Polachek is much bigger than me; Berenson has more leverage. Probably he thinks he can use his clout to get a deferment when the rent control goes into effect or an exclusion from the St. Paul City Council. Probably he's right.

"The point is—it was to Berenson's advantage that the Circle project be delayed and if my father was the one doing the delaying, and he was, Berenson would have wanted him to live forever; I don't care what my sister says. So, please, don't go around accusing my business associates of murder."

"Okay," I said.

"Okay? We're on the same page here?"

"It's not my intention to accuse anyone of anything."

"No, it's the attorney's job to tell whatever lie he can think of if it'll get his client off."

"Actually, that only happens on TV and in the movies," I said. "What did you call it? A trope?"

"Yeah, all right, we'll see," Sainsbury said.

"Tell me something. You've known Jeanette Carrell for as long as your sister. Do you honestly believe that she killed your father?"

"I was surprised when she was arrested, but you know what? If that's what the deputies say, I have no reason to argue with them."

Sainsbury walked me to the door of his office. He actually shook my hand and said, "If you have any other questions, give me a call. I can answer them better than my sister."

I thanked him for his time and made my way out of the building. My Mustang was parked in the third row of the lot in front of the building. I needed to scurry around a black Mercedes-Benz S550 with tinted windows that was idling in front of the entrance to reach it.

The Mustang had all the latest electronics, so I didn't even need to take the key fob out of my pocket to unlock it. I was able to open the driver's side door only about half a foot, though, before a heavy hand slammed it shut. I pivoted toward the hand. It was attached to a young man wearing a suit and tie. He was about six feet tall, with blond hair, blue eyes, and an insolent smile and my first thought was to ask, Where the hell did he come from?

You're getting sloppy in your old age, McKenzie, my inner voice told me. *There was a time no one could have snuck up on you like that.*

My hand quickly moved to a spot just behind my right hip where I would have holstered my SIG Sauer P228 if I had thought to carry it.

Very, very sloppy.

The young man watched carefully as if he was waiting for me to make a move. When I didn't he pointed his chin at me.

"Yo, McKenzie," he said.

Yo?

"Boss wants to talk to you," he added. "Wants to talk to you now."

I took a tentative step backward.

"I said now," he told me.

The young man's gaze remained firm and his mouth set as if he thought his expression alone would be enough to dissuade any argument.

"Who's your boss?" I asked.

"He'll introduce himself."

"What if I don't feel like chatting with your boss?"

The insolent smiled turned into a bemused smirk.

"I'm sure Nina Truhler who owns Rickie's Jazz Club in St. Paul would want you to," he said.

Anger, like a jolt of electricity, instantly spread throughout my entire body. I tried mightily not to let it show. Instead, I gave the punk—he became nothing but a punk to me the moment he mentioned Nina's name—a nod and he gestured across the lot toward where the Mercedes was idling.

We walked toward it; I was two steps in front of him.

Just as we reached the car, I pivoted to my left and drove a fore fist just as hard as I could into his solar plexus. He gasped loudly and folded. He might even have fallen except I grabbed him by the back of his head and shoulder to keep him upright, and drove his face into the side of the Mercedes.

Then I did it again.

The third time I rammed him into the car, I held him there while I felt him up, checking for a gun under his arms, along his belt and between his legs. He was clean, so I threw him to the asphalt and stepped away from the black sedan.

Probably none of this was necessary; after all he was just a peon. But I wanted to make a point.

I folded my arms across my chest and waited.

The rear passenger window of the Mercedes was powered down and an older man peered out.

"Something my father taught me," I told him. "Good manners are how we show respect to one another. I have no idea what your father taught you, Mr. Berenson."

"You know who I am?"

"Call it an educated guess."

"Get in."

"No."

"No?" he asked.

"A man threatens my wife; that makes him my mortal enemy. I don't get into cars with my enemies."

"I didn't . . ." He rolled his eyes and gave me an exasperated sigh before asking, "Tony? What did you do?"

The young man on the ground started to get up. I pointed at him.

"Stay there," I said.

He stayed.

"Well?" Berenson asked.

"I told him that Nina Truhler would like it if he met with you, that's all."

"That's all? Why would you . . . ? Never mind. Get in the car. That is if it's all right with Mr. McKenzie."

I shrugged as if I didn't care one way or another. Tony scrambled to his feet, using the Mercedes for support, and climbed in behind the steering wheel. At the same time, Berenson exited the car, closing the rear passenger door behind him. He looked to be in his mid-sixties and was dressed in a dark blue double-breasted suit with a white silk shirt and blue silk tie. Somehow I didn't think he spent much time working from home. He gestured at the park and together we began walking toward it. We didn't speak to each together until we were seated on the bleachers alongside the third base line of a Little League base-ball diamond.

"Did you play ball, McKenzie?" Berenson asked.

"Second base for St. Paul Central. You?"

"Pitcher and outfielder for St. Louis Park. I tried to walk on at Wisconsin University"—he wiggled the fingers of his left hand to show me his class ring—"but I lasted only two weeks."

"High school was as far as I could go, too. Same with hockey. Did you play hockey?"

"I'm almost embarrassed to say since I grew up in the state of hockey, but no. I played basketball."

"There's nothing wrong with that."

"There are those who disagree. McKenzie, I apologize for Tony. I did not tell him to threaten your wife or even mention your wife's name. We checked you out, of course we did, after Sainsbury told us what you were up to; what he thought you were up to. That's why we know all about you. What I want you to understand; Tony is my sister's youngest son. He's been work-ing as my PA since he was graduated from college; nearly all of my nieces and nephews work for me in one capacity or another.

"Tony thinks he knows our family's history. He thinks that it's romantic; likes to play at being a gangster as if he's in the *Godfather* movies; the first one, anyway, before Michael Cor-leone started slaughtering his own family. That's because he doesn't know any better. Partly that's my fault; the fault of my sisters, too. We never told him the truth about who his grand-father was, what he was. Personally, I find it embarrassing. Something I don't like to talk about. I've had problems all my life, both personally and in business, because of who my father was; because of who his friends were; my family's true history. Now I hear you're trying to connect me to the murder of Sains-bury's father . . ."

"Honestly, I'm not," I said.

"Honestly?"

"If you had spoken to William Sainsbury in, say, the past ten minutes, you would have known that. Mr. Berenson, until yesterday I had never heard your father's name, much less yours. I'm not trying to mess with you. I'm just trying to help the lady."

"If you get her off, then what?"

"What do you mean?"

"If Jeanette Carrell didn't kill Charles Sainsbury, who did?"

"What do you care?"

"I care because that leaves people to speculate that someone else must have done it; that maybe I did it. I don't need that. It's not good for business. It's not good for my peace of mind. People say my father was a gangster so I must be one, too. It's not true. Quite frankly, I think it's all a bunch of anti-Semitic bullshit. It was okay for Joseph Kennedy, who claimed to be Roman Catholic, to make his family's fortune in bootlegging. No one was concerned with that when his kids John and Robert and Ted ran for public office. But for Jews to do it? I've been investigated by the FBI; by the Bureau of Criminal Apprehension so many times. The IRS audits me every other year, it seems. They think I'm Al Capone, for heaven's sake; they want to put me away for tax evasion like they tried to get my father. Now this."

"Honestly, all I can say—"

"There's that word again."

"If someone accuses you, it won't be me," I said.

"I'm going to hold you to that, McKenzie."

"Feel free."

Berenson studied me for a few beats before standing up.

"I apologize for what my nephew said," he told me. "I really am not that person."

Berenson stepped away from the bleachers and walked toward his Mercedes. Not once did he look back.

What do you think? my inner voice asked.

I don't believe a single word he said.

Me, neither.

I arrived at Carrey-Brandt Law in downtown St. Paul five minutes early and was immediately ushered into Alexander Brandt's office. He was sitting behind his desk and looking very tidy in a dark gray suit; his burgundy tie neatly knotted under his chin. I decided that Jeanette Carrell must have had something to do with his appearance. She was sitting in a chair in front of his desk and dressed for a matinee at the Ordway Center for the Performing Arts. Her legs were crossed; the black electronic GPS monitor strapped to her ankle contrasting nicely with her peach-colored skirt. Neither of them was wearing a mask so I removed mine.

"There he is," Jeanette said.

"I hope I didn't keep you waiting," I said.

"Not at all. Alexander was in the midst of a lecture, weren't you, Alex?"

"I'm afraid that Ms. Carrell fails to grasp the urgency of the situation," Brandt said.

"I assure you, Mr. Brandt, I am well aware of the urgency. Perhaps even more so than you are."

"Urgency?" I asked.

Brandt slipped a sheet of paper off his desk and handed it to me. It was a pretrial order that had been issued in the matter of the State of Minnesota, Plantiff, vs. Jeanette Lee Carrell, Defendant.

The above-entitled matter came on for a Scheduling Conference before the Honorable Mary Ann Randele, Judge of District Court; Ted Kaplan, Assistant Ramsey County Attorney, appearing for the State;

and Defender Alexander Brandt; appearing for and with Defendant Jeanette Lee Carrell.

ORDERED THAT:

1. This matter is set for **date-certain** Jury Trial beginning on **November 7 at 8:30 AM.** The trial is estimated to last two weeks.

2. No further amendments of the Complaint herein shall be permitted without leave of the court.

3. The parties shall serve and file complete and final lists of witnesses who will actually testify by no later than end of business on **October 24.** Unlisted witnesses, including rebuttal witnesses, shall not testify unless good cause exists for failing to timely disclose the witness.

4. The parties shall serve and file complete and final exhibit lists by no later than end of business on **October 24.** The parties shall comply with the relevant requirements of Minn. R. Crim. P. 9. Undisclosed and unlisted exhibits shall not be admitted unless good cause exists for failing to timely disclose the exhibit.

"Notice the reference to witnesses and exhibits not being admitted at trial unless they're disclosed by October twenty-fourth," Brandt said.

"United Nations Day," I said.

Both Brandt and Jeanette looked at me like they were amazed that I knew that.

"I read," I said.

"What's significant about the date is that it gives us just over two weeks to respond," Brandt said. "That doesn't leave us much time."

Jeanette sighed dramatically.

"Mr. Brandt, I've shared everything with you," she said. "I don't know how many times I need to say it."

"At least once more."

Brandt leaned back in his chair.

"Sit down, McKenzie," he said. "Tell me something interesting."

"Yes, McKenzie," Jeanette said. "I've been told that you have made yourself quite busy up on the Circle. You actually discussed possible scenarios with the Plot Whores, is that true?"

"Among other things."

I sat in a chair next to Jeanette, yet only after I retrieved a thumb drive from my pocket and set it on the desk in front of Brandt.

"What's this?" he asked.

"It's a transcript and actual video of Katherine Hixson addressing the Chippewa Woods Homeowners Association about the need for a very tall fence to prevent Jeanette from abusing her children."

"Abusing her children?" Jeanette's hand went to her mouth. "I had forgotten about that."

"It's a colorful performance," I said. "You two will enjoy it."

Brandt slipped the drive into a USB port on his computer and pulled up the video. Jeanette unfolded her legs and leaned forward. He angled his monitor so she could see.

It didn't take long before she leaned back again.

"What a foul mouth on that woman," she said. "I didn't know that she said those terrible things about me; that Kate thought those things. I had spoken to Mr. Hegarty for about five minutes over the phone; it must have been at least a year ago. He asked if I would be amenable to building a short wall between Kate's and my backyards, except he did not go into detail at the time. I wish he would have. No, no, perhaps it was for the best that he didn't, that he kept Kate's complaints to himself. It greatly reduced the animosity between us."

"Or not," Brandt said. "I suggest that it only increased her rancor to the point where Ms. Hixson's testimony cannot be relied upon."

"You're going to call her a liar in court?"

"We would not necessarily use that word."

"Far be it for me to tell you how to do your job."

Jeanette smiled as if she was looking forward to watching Brandt do his job.

"Anything else, McKenzie?" Brandt asked.

"I told you about Bethany Gilman," I reminded him, and then described in greater detail what the woman said. When I finished, Jeanette said, "Bethany," filling the word with affection.

"Unfortunately," I said, "Bethany's brother William Sainsbury is less than complimentary."

I related details of my conversation with the man. I also mentioned meeting with Adam Berenson that morning outside Sainsbury's offices. Brandt nodded, yet said nothing. The way he leaned back in his office chair and tapped his fingertips together while staring at the ceiling gave me the impression that he could see the future only he wasn't willing to commit to it.

"Then there's Linda Welch," I said.

I explained some more, emphasizing Charles Sainsbury's animosity toward the woman.

"I could call her," Brandt said. "Some defense lawyers label it Plan B. Blame it on someone else. I don't like to employ that defense unless I have no other options. Thanks, thanks for the heads-up, though."

"Now I'm going to tell you something you might not like." I was gazing at Carrell when I spoke. "William Sainsbury spoke to Jeanette immediately after he made his deal with Vaneps. He wanted to develop her one-fifth of the hill, too. She declined his offer."

"What are you suggesting, Mr. McKenzie?" Carrell asked.

"You knew what Sainsbury was up to well before anyone else, yet you didn't say a word."

"There was nothing I could do to dissuade Mr. Sainsbury," Carrell said. "Why make everyone miserable before it was necessary?"

Why, indeed?

"I wish you would have told me," Brandt said.

"Would it have made any difference?" Jeanette asked.

Brandt raised his hand and let it fall as if he wasn't sure.

"Now I'm going to tell you both something that I know you won't like," I said. "I'm only telling you because Sergeant Michael Swenson, he was the arresting officer, knows everything I know and he'll probably tell the ACA. It begins with a retired Ramsey County deputy named Dominic Belden."

"That odious man," Jeanette said.

"You know him?" Brandt asked.

"He accused me of murdering my husband."

"What?"

"It gets better," I said.

I told them everything about Belden and his accusations, including my conversation with Special Agent Brian Wilson concerning organized crime in Minnesota and, no, I didn't call him Harry.

"That's outrageous," Jeanette insisted.

"Clearly," I said.

"It's also immaterial," Brandt said. "If the ACA even whispered a word about David Carrell's disappearance twenty-seven years ago, much less speculated about who might be responsible, I'd immediately motion for a mistrial and I'd get it, too."

"Just so you know," I said.

"All right, thank you. Anything else?"

I pivoted in my chair so that I was looking directly at Jeanette.

"Is there anything else?" I asked.

"I don't know what you mean."

"From the very beginning you've been holding back information. Your attorney knows it. So do I."

"I haven't . . ."

"Tell me why."

"McKenzie . . ."

"I know the truth, Jeanette."

Actually, you're only guessing, my inner voice reminded me.

"Tell me why you didn't speak up six months ago," I said aloud.

I expected her to hem and haw, only she didn't. She spoke as if she had already answered the question a hundred times in her head.

"I know how things work, criminal investigations," Jeanette said. "How important the first forty-eight hours are. The first week. The first month. I know that the longer it takes for the police to make an arrest, the less likely they are to make an arrest. I wanted the police, the prosecutor to believe that I killed Charles because the longer they believed that, the better the chances were that the real killer would get away and I wanted the real killer to get away."

"You might change your mind if you're convicted," I said.

"Ms. Carrell, do you know who killed Charles Sainsbury?" Brandt asked.

"No, sir, I do not. I was being completely honest when I told the deputies I was in my house at the time the murder took place."

"You weren't alone, though, were you?" I said.

Jeanette didn't reply.

"Ms. Carrell," Brandt said.

She watched me intently, a poker player staring down a bluff. I decided to show her my cards.

"Derek Carlson," I said.

Jeanette stared some more.

"Ms. Carrell," Brandt repeated.

"It's not what you think," she said.

"Was Derek Carlson with you when . . . ?"

"Yes."

NINE

Alexander Brandt interviewed Derek Carlson extensively in his office the next day. Neither Jeanette Carrell nor I were present at the time. I was told later, though, that Carlson admitted that he had been seeing Carrell "off and on" during the months he had been forced to work at home because of COVID and yes, he was with her during those critical hours when the Ramsey County medical examiner estimated that Charles Sainsbury had been killed. He said he kept quiet about it all this time partly at the insistence of Jeanette, but mostly because he didn't want his wife, Jennifer, to learn that he had been cheating on her.

"You don't have to tell her, do you?" he kept asking.

Brandt included a transcript of Carlson's statement, along with the intelligence I had gathered concerning Katherine Hixson, in a package of information he sent to Ramsey County Assistant Attorney Ted Kaplan by overnight mail. He didn't need to be anywhere near that comprehensive. A proposed witness list and proposed exhibit list was all that the law required, only he wanted to send the ACA a message.

Apparently, the message was received because three days later, Kaplan interviewed Carlson himself in the Ramsey County attorney's offices. Or rather, Sergeant Michael Swenson conducted the interrogation, working him over pretty good,

I was told later, while Kaplan watched and listened. Carlson wasn't required to answer the ACA's questions, much less Swenson's. He agreed to do so in the hope that they would keep his testimony confidential if the ACA decided to dismiss the charges against Carrell.

By the following Thursday, the ACA did indeed drop the case against Ms. Jeanette Lee Carrell, stating that "the evidence does not support a charge of second-degree murder at this time."

I learned about it by reading a short story under the heading LOCAL BRIEFS in the Friday edition of the St. Paul *Pioneer Press*. It was only five paragraphs long and was attributed to the Associated Press instead of a local reporter. The name Derek Carlson was not mentioned.

Two hours later I received a call from Evangeline.

"You are the best," she told me. "I don't know what you did or how you did it but oh my God, what did you do? How did you do it?"

"I have no idea what you're talking about," I said.

"Stop it. You're worse than Jeanette. I just spoke to her. Instead of being absolutely ecstatic that she's a free woman, she's complaining about all the money she had to pay for that anklet they forced her to wear, which, by the way, they were removing when I called. She also complained about the interest she lost on the 250,000 dollars she posted for her bail that was returned to her this morning."

"So, everything is back to normal, then?"

"McKenzie, what did you do? All the people I called because you wanted to question them, the Plot Whores, they're all calling me now. They want to know the same thing. What did you do?"

"Very little, as it turns out."

"McKenzie."

"Evan, I really can't say. It would be unethical. People could get hurt."

"You're not actually a licensed private investigator, you know. You're not bound by a professional code of ethics."

"Let's pretend that I am."

"McKenzie . . ."

"I would hold your secrets just as tightly, Evan."

"Yes, you would. McKenzie, there'll be a gathering at the gazebo tonight. Everyone wants you to be there."

"Okay."

"I'm bringing the bourbon, a bottle of that Knob Creek Smoked Maple stuff that you like so much. If I ply you with alcohol, will that loosen your tongue?"

"Let's find out."

I parked my Mustang in Evangeline's driveway and rang her doorbell. She didn't answer and I decided she must already be partying with her friends. I rounded her house, passed through her yard, and climbed the hill. The sun was threatening to set as I approached the gazebo, yet there was enough daylight that I could easily see a dozen or more people gathered beneath the roof and leaning against the two-foot-high railings on all eight sides of the structure. Most of them were dressed in heavy coats against the forty-six degree temperatures. One of them was Carson Vaneps. He was wearing a black wool overcoat over a dark blue wool suit. Another was Sara Vaneps. She was dressed in blue jeans and a brown parka with an imitation fur collar. He seemed agitated. She was clearly alarmed by his agitation.

I heard their voices as I approached.

"Who are you people?" Carson wanted to know. "What are you doing in my gazebo?"

"Grandfather, they're friends," Sara said.

"I don't know any of them."

Ruth Krider rested a hand on Carson's arm and said, "I'm Ruth. Don't you remember me?"

Carson brushed her hand away.

"Ruth died years ago," he said.

For some reason, I attracted his attention. He watched carefully as I rounded the gazebo and climbed the brick steps.

"Carson, it's good to see you again," I said.

He pointed his finger like an accusation.

"I know you," he said. "You're Jacey's young man."

"J. C. says hi," I said, hoping her name would calm him. "She'll be coming up the hill to see you soon."

Carson began to wag his finger.

"Yes, yes, I remember. You and her were dancing in the gazebo. Well, better to be dancing in it than under it, am I right?"

He laughed at that and I laughed along even though I didn't get the joke.

"Where is she?" Carson asked. "Where is my Jacey?"

"I'm sure she'll be here soon," I said. "She's probably getting dressed for the occasion."

"Jacey and Patty, they always spent more time getting ready for a party than they did at the party."

Patty? my inner voice asked.

Carson laughed some more while I sought Sara's face. She mouthed "My grandmother" at me.

"I remember a party we had at General Mills," Carson said. "A Christmas party; I'm going to say five years ago. It was catered. Live orchestra. Black tie. All the bigwigs were there. Patty started getting ready at nine in the morning. I'm not kidding. Had to get her hair done, her nails. She refused to eat so much as a single Christmas cookie all day because she was afraid it would make her look fat. Finally, she put her dress on ten minutes before we got into the car. She didn't want to wear it before then for fear it would wrinkle, you see. Boy, that was some dress, too.

Made of silk and lace. Midnight blue. Fit her like a glove. Every once in a while she'll put it on just for me. Patty. Where is she, anyway?"

"She's down at the house," Sara said.

"We should go down there; hurry her up. You. I forgot your name."

"McKenzie," I said.

"Come with us. You'll want to meet my Patty."

I took Carson's arm; he seemed fine with that, and Sara and I escorted him down the hill toward his house. He began to tell a story about how Patty thought it was silly that Bugles corn chips were made to fit on a customer's finger like a fingernail, yet soon became distracted and distant. By the time we reached his back door, he was looking at me as if he had never seen me before.

"Who are you?" he asked.

"He's a friend," Sara told him.

"I remember. Your Sara's new boyfriend. The model. I don't know. Maybe you should think about a real job."

Carson disappeared inside the house. Sara stood in the doorway, her eyes shut.

"Christian," she said at last. "My boyfriend's name was Christian and he was a model, a fashion model and actor. That was awhile ago, though. I don't know what he's doing now. McKenzie, I want to thank you. Thank you for what you did up on the Circle just now and thank you for what you did for Jeanette Carrell. You'll never know how much it means to me that she won't be prosecuted. It's such a load off of my mind."

"I'm glad I could help," I said.

"I need to go inside now and find out what my grandfather is up to."

"I understand."

"Thank you, again."

Sara went inside the house and closed the door. I turned around and started back up the hill, thinking that what was happening to Carson Vaneps could easily one day happen to me, to anyone. Just considering the possibility made me anxious and depressed. Would someone as loving as Sara look after me? Would Nina? Would I want her to? Would I have a choice in the matter? At least I had some money, I told myself. That would help. But what about the people who don't? One in nine Americans older than sixty-five suffer from Alzheimer's and eighty percent of them are seventy-five years old or older, I told myself.

Maybe we live too damn long. Maybe we should stop worrying about living so damn long.

The number of people hanging around the gazebo had more than doubled by the time I returned. I recognized many of them, including members of the Plot Whores Book Club that I had seen only by firelight. Evangeline gave me a hug that reminded me of all those faux dates we had gone on when we were both young and impressionable.

"You're a good person, McKenzie," she told me.

"Practice makes perfect."

As promised, Evan poured me a very large glass of bourbon with one ice cube. I was grateful for the drink, although it forced me to remove my hand from the pocket of my brown leather jacket, the one that made me look like a World War II fighter pilot.

"Drink up," she told me. "There's plenty more."

I told Evan that if I did, she'd have to roll me down the hill.

She didn't think that would be a problem.

Jeanette Carrell had yet to make an appearance. From what her neighbors said, that was not unexpected.

"You know she's going to make a grand entrance," Rebecca said. "I mean grand."

"She wouldn't be the old J. C. if she didn't," Rachel added.

While we waited, I was barraged by the same question asked in different ways.

"What happened?"

"What did you do?"

"Did you find the real killer?"

I kept dodging them with vague answers.

"I don't know."

"The assistant Ramsey County attorney doesn't confide in me."

"Ask Jeanette."

Ruth Krider said, "It's because of what you found out about Kate Hixson, isn't it?"

I said I didn't know.

Everyone else asked, "What?"

Krider explained.

While she explained, I glanced around. Hixson wasn't at the gazebo, which didn't surprise me. Linda Welch was; which did surprise me. Jennifer and Derek Carlson were also present. He immersed himself in the festivities. She hovered at the edge with a smile that seemed affected.

We made eye contact. Jenny used her eyes to direct me to the edge of a gazebo near the steps. She spoke in a low voice.

"What happened with Jeanette," she asked, "is that because of Derek? Please, McKenzie, I need to know."

"Like I keep saying, the county attorney doesn't confide in me."

"McKenzie, the county attorneys questioned Derek for hours at their headquarters in downtown St. Paul. I wasn't allowed to go with him, to be there with him. Later, I asked what happened and Derek said they only wanted to know if he saw anyone on the Circle when Charles was killed. But, McKenzie, they had asked him those same questions months ago and when Derek answered them nothing came of it. Now, suddenly, he tells them the exact same thing and the charges against Jeanette are dropped? That doesn't make sense."

Do not get involved in this, my inner voice told me. *Do not, do not . . .*

"Perhaps he saw something that he didn't remember the first time he was questioned," I said aloud.

"What?"

"Ask Derek."

"He won't tell me. What's more, he made me promise not to tell anyone that he was interviewed by the deputies, again."

"The ACA might have sworn him to secrecy."

"I'm his wife."

"I can't give you any advice, sweetie," I said. "I'm sorry."

Yeah, I was being chicken.

"Meaning you won't say that Derek has been cheating on me with half the women on the Circle," Jenny said, "and that one of those women might have been Jeanette Carrell, and I should stop kidding myself and get the hell out."

"Has anyone told you that?"

"Just the woman I see every morning in the mirror. God, I hate COVID. I need to get back to my office. So does Derek. Our lives would be so much easier if we could just get back to the office."

She might have been onto something, I decided. What's the proverb? The devil makes work for idle hands? I might have actually said something along those lines, too, except I was distracted when the soft lights of the gazebo were turned on. Up until that moment, I didn't know the gazebo even had lights. They ran along the perimeter of the eight-sided structure and gave everything a warm, orange glow.

It was then that Jeanette Carrell made her appearance. She crested the hill almost like a character from Greek mythology, Circe perhaps, or maybe Calypso, women who knew how to keep what was theirs. She was wearing a black cape over her shoulders that brushed the ground behind her, a red skirt that swished when she walked, displaying her unshackled ankles, and a gray sweater over a white shirt, the shirt buttoned to the throat. Over her left breast she had pinned a gold and diamond brooch that spelled the initials J. C.

Some of her neighbors actually applauded when she approached the gazebo; the rest became intent on giving and receiving hugs as quickly as possible.

"It's over," someone said.

"Yes, finally," Jeanette replied.

"What happened? Why did they let you go?"

"Didn't McKenzie tell you?"

"No," echoed across the hill.

"I've known McKenzie for over twenty years," Evan said. "Apparently, he has ethics. I'm as surprised as you are."

Jeanette had reached the bottom step of the gazebo and looked up at me. In that light another mythological figure came to mind, Helen of Troy, whose face launched a thousand ships and started a ten-year war.

"I'm grateful to you," she said.

I showed her the tumbler of bourbon I had been sipping.

"You're welcome," I said.

"What happened?" a half-dozen voices asked nearly in unison.

Jeanette said, "Before a trial can begin, the court orders both the prosecutor and the defense to compile a list of all the evidence they intend to present and all the witnesses they intend to call—I found out about this last week in my lawyer's office. The county attorney looked at his list and then he looked at our list and then he looked at his list again and decided to drop all charges."

"What was on your list?" Jennifer Carlson asked.

Out of the corner of my eye, I could see Derek wincing at the question.

"McKenzie found out a couple of things that the prosecutor didn't know, that I didn't know," Jeanette said. "Is Katherine Hixson here?"

No, she was told.

"It turns out that her testimony that she saw me burying Charles Sainsbury's body was tainted," Jeanette said.

"What does that mean?" Linda Welch asked.

"She lied."

"Are they sure?"

"It would seem so," Jeanette said. "Of course, I claimed all along that I was innocent. Didn't you believe me?"

Linda didn't say if she did or didn't.

Jeanette glanced around, found Jenny in the crowd, and gave her an encouraging smile, an act I found almost courageous.

"That was the major development," she said. "There were a few other minor details that didn't amount to much and are hardly worth mentioning. At least I won't mention them. As for myself, I'm hoping to move forward as best I can and put all of this nonsense behind me."

"That sounds like good advice," Jenny said.

It was all fun and games and music coming from a smartphone and portable speakers after that. I kept expecting someone to ask, "If Jeanette didn't kill Sainsbury, who did?" Only the question was never asked, at least not out loud.

Eventually, Jeanette asked if anyone had seen Sara Vaneps. That's when the festivities took a turn. Between Evan and the Westermeyer sisters, she was told that Sara had brought Carson to the top of the hill earlier in the evening and Carson had become distraught, almost hysterical, because he didn't recognize anyone and somehow thought they were all there to vandalize his gazebo. Sara was forced to escort him back down the hill with my assistance.

"Carson Vaneps—such a kind and gracious man," Jeanette said. "How can God do this to him? To anyone?"

"Do you blame God?" Ruth Krider asked.

"Let's just say He has a lot of explaining to do and let it go at that."

Conversation about Carson Vaneps quickly turned to the Sainsbury family and the future of the gazebo and the hill.

Someone said, "The wrong Sainsbury was murdered, that's for sure."

A voice shouted, "Who said that?"

I spun toward the steps of the gazebo. Once again Bethany Gilman had managed to materialize out of the darkness.

"Who said that?" she repeated.

She was answered by silence; it was as if the entire party was holding its breath.

"How can you say that about my family?" Bethany wanted to know.

Jeanette Carrell stepped forward.

"I'm sure whoever said it didn't mean it," she said. "Beth, Beth." She wrapped her arms around the woman. "I am so sorry for your loss. I wish I could have told you sooner."

"I knew you didn't do it," Bethany replied. "I just knew you couldn't have done it."

"Thank you for that."

The two women released each other and a kind of calm settled over the gazebo.

"Thank you for coming," Jeanette said.

"Don't thank me, J. C. I'm afraid I'm bringing you very bad news; bad news for everyone."

Everyone leaned forward to listen.

"I found out late this afternoon, the court ruled in my brother's favor," Bethany said. "It declared that my brother legally owns the Circle and can do with it as he pleases."

The news was met with disappointment and more than a few obscenities.

"I knew it," Evan said.

"How can they do that?" Rebecca Westermeyer Sauer said.

"Will there be an appeal?" Ruth Krider asked.

"I don't think so and even if there is an appeal, I doubt it will come in time," Bethany said. "William is going to send his bulldozers up the hill the first thing Monday morning."

"I'm surprised he didn't send them already," Linda Welch said. "Or at least send them tomorrow."

"Tomorrow is Saturday," Bethany said. "He doesn't want to pay overtime if he can avoid it. This project has already cost him too much. I'm sorry, everybody."

"Well," Jeanette said. "Well, it looks like this will be our last gathering under these stars."

She hugged Bethany some more. And the Westermeyer sisters. And all of the rest of her girls who were present. She whispered into their ears and what she whispered made them smile or shed tears. Except for Jennifer Carlson. What she said to Jenny made her laugh.

"All good things must come to an end, mustn't they," Jeanette said. "McKenzie, isn't that what people say?"

"What some people say," I told her.

Jeanette stepped away from the gazebo and turned to face all of us standing there.

"My good friends," she said. "My circle of friends. I will always be grateful to every one of you for your friendship and your love no matter what Monday brings."

Jeanette turned again and started moving across the open

field. No one spoke to her; no one asked her to stay. Nor did they spend much time speaking to each other while they gathered their belongings. There was nothing more to say. The party was over, after all. They all knew what Monday would bring.

I continued to watch Jeanette's figure receding into the darkness, however. I thought I heard her call my name without turning around. She called it a second time and I hurried to her side.

"I told you that I liked you because you have an open mind," Jeanette told me. "Please, keep it open, McKenzie. I promise you; things are not what they seem."

"What things?"

"Good-bye, McKenzie."

Good-bye, my inner voice repeated. *Not good night.*

I stood in the darkness and watched as Jeanette Carrell slowly descended the hill toward her home.

They discovered the bodies three days later.

TEN

It was all very professionally done.

The Sainsbury Construction Company started by using white flags to delineate the excavation site. It followed that task by making what in Minnesota is known as a Gopher State One Call, which sent a small army of "locators" up the hill that used spray paint and various colored flags to mark the location of underground facilities such as electric power lines, telephone and internet cables, water and sewer pipes, and gas mains within the excavation site. While that was going on, a member of the firm carefully placed wooden stakes with orange ribbons attached to them along Ruth Krider's property line.

Despite what was threatened, William Sainsbury didn't actually send a bulldozer up the hill. Instead, he sent an excavator, what kids used to call a steam shovel. The excavator was unloaded from a flatbed trailer directly onto the front lawn of Charles Sainsbury's house, its steel tracks cutting into the turf as it was driven around the house, carefully avoiding Ruth's yard. There were trees to negotiate. Normally, I was told, they would have been knocked down first. Except Sainsbury wanted to make sure everyone knew who was in charge, so the driver of the excavator maneuvered around and past them, climbed the hill, and drove in a straight line at approximately twenty miles per hour toward the gazebo.

When he reached it, he extended the excavator's long arm and used the bucket at the end of it to knock the witch's hat off the top of the gazebo while neighbors, including Linda Welch, stood at a distance and watched. The walls came next, all of the wood pushed into a careless pile next to the concrete slab that used to be the gazebo floor. The driver hammered the concrete into pieces with the tip of his bucket and began digging it up, depositing the debris on the pile. Only something caught his eye, and he stopped.

With the excavator's engine still humming, he climbed out of the cab and off the undercarriage, approached the hole, and took a long, hard look.

The driver called his supervisor.

The supervisor was still at the bottom of the hill and it took him a few minutes to climb it and cross the huge lawn to where the excavator sat, its engine now turned off.

The driver showed the supervisor what he had found.

The supervisor made a call to the construction site manager.

The construction site manager had never come across anything like this before, so he called the boss.

I was told later that William Sainsbury's reaction was punctuated by a long string of volatile expletives.

Eventually, they called 911; what else were they going to do?

A Ramsey County sheriff's deputy was dispatched to the scene.

He took one look, told everyone to back the hell away from the rubble and called the Criminal Investigations Unit, which is what brought Sergeant Michael Swenson to the top of the hill.

Swenson contacted the sheriff's department, the Minnesota Bureau of Criminal Apprehension crime scene response team, and the Ramsey County medical examiner's office in that order.

At some point, he managed to call me.

"Hey, Mike," I said. "What's going on?"

"Come to the Circle," he said. "Come now."

"Why? What happened?"

He replied by hanging up the phone.

I parked in Evangeline's driveway and passed through her backyard on my way to the top of the hill. When I reached it, I found streams of yellow tape with the words CRIME SCENE DO NOT CROSS surrounding what used to be the gazebo, the excavator, and about thirty yards of empty lawn. Neighbors were standing behind the yellow tape and watching while a half-dozen men and women wearing white jumpsuits, gloves, goggles, and booties examined and dug in the dirt. A massive blue van with a satellite dish mounted on top and the words RAMSEY COUNTY MOBILE INCIDENT COMMAND CENTER painted in white on the side, somehow had managed to follow the excavator's track up the hill and was now parked outside the yellow tape.

I spotted Swenson standing on the far side of the crime scene, his hands in his pockets. I circled the yellow tape and the truck until I reached his side. I didn't say hello and neither did he. We just stood there side by side and watched the evidence techs at work.

Finally, Swenson said, "Two bodies, both badly decomposed. We haven't been able to identify the woman yet. The man still had his wallet in his pocket, though. David Carrell."

Sonuvabitch, my inner voice screamed. *That old rummy Dominic Belden had been right after all.*

"Have you taken Jeanette Carrell into custody yet?" I asked aloud.

Swenson's response was to stare at me for a few beats.

"Come with me," he said.

The sergeant spun slowly around and began walking toward Jeanette Carrell's house; I followed closely behind him. When we reached her backyard, we discovered Katherine Hixson standing on her side of the five-foot wooden wall; it was like she had been waiting for us.

"Are you happy?" she wanted to know. "Are you happy, now? I told you. Didn't I tell you? I told you about that bitch but you wouldn't believe me. You called me a liar. A liar."

Swenson ignored the woman. So did I. The deputy who was standing guard outside Carrell's back door gave us a shrug.

"She's been like that all morning," he said. "Guess she thinks we should give her a medal or something."

"Or at least an apology," Swenson said.

There were blue disposable gloves in a box outside the door. Swenson gave me a pair and we put them on before entering Carrell's house.

"I want to show you something," Swenson told me. "I don't have to tell you not to touch anything. We're considering the house part of the crime scene and the BCA hasn't processed it yet."

I followed him into the dining room. He gestured at the dining-room table. Very neatly arranged on top of the table I found Jeanette Carrell's driver's license, passport, Social Security card—I didn't even have a Social Security card, only the numbers—birth certificate, American Express, Visa, and Discover credit cards, bank debit card, health care insurance card, American Red Cross blood donor card—she was O-positive—Costco membership card, AARP membership card, auto insurance information, and cell phone.

"She left all of this for us to find," Swenson said.

"How courteous of her."

"Why, McKenzie, in your expert opinion, do you think she left all this for us to find?"

"She wants us to know that she doesn't need any of it. She wants us to know that Jeanette Carrell no longer exists."

"She's mocking us," Swenson said. "Catch me if you can, she's saying."

"That, too."

"BOLO's already been sent out and the county attorney is going to hold a press conference, get Carrell's face on the TV and in the newspapers, only I don't like our chances. We checked her bank account, she left her bank card, after all; checked the rest of her accounts. She very carefully, very systematically sold her stock, liquidated her IRAs, and drained her savings. She started doing it weeks before Sainsbury was killed; started at approximately the same time that she and her neighbors had learned that the Circle had been sold to him. The woman was worth well over three-point-five million dollars."

"She told me she was good with money," I said.

"Yes, but where did it all come from? Where did all that money go? Who knows? Maybe she's carrying it around in a shopping bag along with a dozen prepaid cell phones and credit cards."

"The last I saw of her was Friday night on the hill."

"The last time anyone saw her was Friday night on the hill," Swenson said. "The woman has a three-day head start because of us. Us. You and me, McKenzie. Mostly I blame you, but I'm partly to blame, too, for not countering your bullshit. If she still had that GPS monitor strapped to her ankle . . ."

"How long do you think she's had a go-bag ready, do you think?" I asked.

"At least six months, although . . ."

"Yeah."

"It could have been years," Swenson said. "Decades. At least we now know why Carrell was so desperate to keep Charles Sainsbury from developing the hill."

"For what it's worth, I still don't think that she killed Sainsbury."

"Why not?"

I gestured at the assorted IDs.

"It was a sloppy job," I said, "and this woman is not sloppy."

"Crime of passion," Swenson said. "She did Sainsbury in a moment of extreme anger; did it before she had a chance to think it through."

"What about Derek Carlson?"

"Yeah, what about him?"

Maybe he lied, maybe he didn't. Not that it matters, now.

"Geezus, Mike, I don't know what to say," I told him.

"Whether Carrell killed Charles Sainsbury or not, she most certainly killed her husband and the unidentified woman."

"We don't know that."

"C'mon, McKenzie. She knew what we would find when they took down the gazebo, that's why she ran. That's why she's been prepared to run for God knows how long. You're not still defending that bitch, are you?"

"You knew the woman. Five nine, one hundred and twenty-five pounds. How did she get the bodies up the hill?"

"Assuming that she didn't kill them on the hill, I'd say she had help."

We know where that help came from, too, don't we? my inner voice told me.

"Better to be dancing in the gazebo than under it," I said aloud.

"What's that supposed to mean?"

"Something Carson Vaneps told me."

"I should question him."

"Good luck with that. He thinks it's twenty-five years ago."

"Then the memory of what he did should be fresh in his mind," Swenson said.

Even as he said it though, both Swenson and I knew nothing good would come of it. Even if it could prove Carson had been involved in the crime, which was doubtful, what was Ramsey County going to do about it? Arrest him? Subject him to a Rule Twenty-five Competency Hearing and confine him to a mental facility until his Alzheimer's improved enough that he would be competent to stand trial?

"I'm sorry for my part in all this, Michael, I really am," I said. "I thought I was doing a good thing; helping a woman who looked like she had been falsely accused of murder. I should have—I don't know what I should have done. Taken Dominic Belden more seriously? I don't know."

"No good deed goes unpunished, isn't that what they say?"

"What are you going to do?" I asked.

"What do you mean, what am I going to do? Do you think I can do anything? Goddamn . . ."

Swenson launched into a vocal tirade that was so loud and vulgar that the deputy working the door was compelled to come inside and check on him. Swenson stared at the deputy with angry eyes.

"What?" he asked.

"Nothing, Sarge, I just . . ."

"Get back where you belong."

Swenson watched the deputy leave and then pressed the heels of both hands against his eyes.

"Dammit, McKenzie," he said. "Should I tell you what's going to happen? The county attorney is going to be embarrassed as hell over this; his office clearing a murder suspect three days before we discover that she's a mass murderer . . ."

"I don't think . . ."

"Three dead, McKenzie. That's a fucking mass. The county

attorney isn't going to take responsibility, either. Hell no, and he's not going to blame the ACA or anyone else in his office. He's going to lay the blame on the sheriff. He's going to call it a failure of the Ramsey County Sheriff's Department, which the sheriff will translate to mean my failure. Me personally. I'm the one they're going to point the finger at. Somehow I don't think I'm ever going to make lieutenant now."

Swenson smiled when he said that and laughed, an amazing thing to do, I thought, all things considered.

"I don't care about being promoted," he said. "What really pisses me off is that Carrell is going to get away with this. We had her and we let her go and I doubt we'll ever lay eyes on her again."

"You don't know that, Mike," I said.

"C'mon, McKenzie. She's not some dumb blonde who shot a john and is now couch surfing; bunking in a friend's basement thinking this will all blow over. She very carefully, very deliberately disappeared"—Swenson gestured at all the IDs on the dining-room table again—"and was proud enough of her accomplishment to advertise it.

"The other day you mentioned Sara Jane Olson," he added. "For twenty-five years she was in the wind. Hell, she even worked as an actress; how many people watched her perform? Yet they still couldn't catch her and they wouldn't have caught her except for a tip generated by the TV show *America's Most Wanted*. Is that even still on the air?"

"I don't know," I said. "I've never watched it."

"Now Jeanette Carrell is in the wind with a whole new identity, by the looks of it, and three days head start. She could literally be on the other side of the world by now."

"Île Saint-Paul," I said.

"What?"

"That's French for St. Paul Island, which is located in the

Indian Ocean. That's what's literally on the other side of the world from us."

"It really pisses me off that you know that."

"Carrell has to be somewhere, Mike. She can be found."

"By who? Me? The other guys in the CIU? Yeah, we'll search for her in between our other cases. Ramsey County doesn't have the resources and while the state of Minnesota is better than most . . . How many felons know they can escape the charges filed against them simply by crossing a state border because law enforcement and prosecutors have decided it's not worth the time and effort and expense to retrieve them; to extradite them if they're captured? A lot of times, fugitives aren't even entered into the National Crime Information Center."

"Jeanette Carrell will be entered."

"Yeah, and the U.S. Marshals and the BCA agents on the North Star Fugitive Task Force will be all over it until they find something better to do with their limited time and resources like hunt domestic terrorists. Then they'll just sit back and wait until Carrell screws up because, let's face it, that's what most fugitives do, why most get caught. I doubt Carrell will be one of them, though."

"The marshals do a good job," I said.

"They do a good job catching punks. I read where they scooped up over eighty thousand of them last year. Only there's a reason why the Fifteen Most Wanted list rarely changes; why some guys have been on it for thirty-some years. Do I sound bitter, McKenzie?"

"I'd say you had just cause."

"You know what? The FBI hunts fugitives, too. I'm going to call and ask that your friend Harry be assigned to the case. What do you think?"

"I think that'll just make one more person who'll be mad at me," I said.

"I'm not mad," Swenson said. "Well, maybe a little. But you didn't lie, you didn't cheat. Everything you did you did the right way. Who knows? Jeanette Carrell might actually be innocent of the Sainsbury killing. It's just now I wish you had never gotten involved."

You and me both, brother. You and me both.

We left Jeanette Carrell's house through the back door. Swenson circled it, heading to his squad car parked in front. He was scheduled to testify in court on a completely separate matter later that afternoon.

"Lucky me," he said.

I cut across Carrell's yard with the plan of climbing the hill and making my way to Evangeline's house, where I had parked my own car, only I was intercepted by Katherine Hixson. She was still standing on her side of the wooden wall, except she was no longer alone. Linda Welch had joined her. My first thought was, Why?

"I know what you did, McKenzie," Hixson said.

"I'm sorry, have we been introduced?" I asked.

"I know who you are. They told me what you did."

"Everyone knows what you did," Linda added.

I was just as upset by what had happened as Sergeant Swenson and my first instinct when confronted by the two women was to lash out. Only what would that accomplish, I asked myself.

"What did I do?" I said, speaking as calmly as I could.

"You told all those people that I was a liar and they believed you," Hixson said. "They let that bitch go because they believed you."

"No, I merely reported what you said about Carrell in front of the Chippewa Woods Homeowners Association, which, by the way, directly contradicted what you told the authorities about how you and Carrell were neighborly; that you got along just fine. That's not why they dropped the charges against her, though."

"Why did they drop the charges?"

I came *thisclose* to revealing the full truth, yet managed to catch myself in time. Jennifer Carlson had enough problems without me dropping her—or her husband's—name.

Assuming Derek Carlson told the truth, which is now open to debate.

"I proved that she couldn't have killed Charles Sainsbury which means that someone else on the Circle did it," I said aloud. "Any thoughts?"

"Bullshit," Linda said. "You helped that bitch get away with murder."

Hixson pointed at the hill.

"What's going on up there right now proves she's a killer," she said.

"Time will tell," I said.

"Go to hell, McKenzie," Linda said.

"Yes, ma'am. I'm on my way."

I spun around and made my way through the trees and up the hill. Along the way, my inner voice insisted on chiding me.

They're probably right, it said. *Jeanette Carrell probably is a killer. You did help her get away. And, oh yeah, you probably will go to hell.*

ELEVEN

Members of the media had gathered at Ramsey County's blue camper by the time I had crested the hill. I recognized some of them, including Kelly Bressandes, who was roundly reputed to have the best legs on local television. They were standing in a semicircle around the Ramsey County attorney, who was standing on a wooden platform behind a bank of microphones so the cameras would be filming him at an upward angle.

I hid my face as I followed the tree line the long way around the Circle for fear a reporter would recognize me. At the same time, my inner voice asked, *Does the Mobile Incident Command Center come equipped with a two-foot-high media platform just in case someone wants to conduct an impromptu press conference or do all politicians carry them in their back pockets?* I managed a third of the way before I heard a female voice call my name. The voice sounded weak and my name painful to speak, yet I flinched just the same. I turned my head, expecting to find a journalist stalking me, and discovered Bethany Gilman standing among the trees at the top of the hill behind her father's house.

"McKenzie."

She looked as if she was hiding. She looked as if she had been weeping.

"McKenzie, what happened?" Bethany asked the question

as if she didn't know the answer, yet I guessed that she did. "J. C.—she couldn't have done the terrible things they say. No, no, I won't believe it."

"For what it's worth, I'm still convinced that she didn't kill your father," I said.

"The others, though. Her husband? That woman? Both of them buried beneath the gazebo that she helped build?"

"I don't know."

"I knew J. C.'s husband," Bethany said. "David. I remember— I remember that he was handsome. I was just a girl at the time I met him and I remember thinking that it was like the movies because J. C. was so beautiful and David was so handsome. My mother told me at the time that it was what was inside that made us beautiful and handsome and I thought, whatever that was, J. C. and David must have had plenty of it because they were so nice to me and they seemed so nice to each other. They held hands. How many couples do you know that hold hands while they're just walking down the street or sitting on a bench? Then he was gone. Just like that. Gone. And he didn't die. That's what I was told, my mom told me. He didn't die, he just left. I couldn't wrap my head around it. How could you just leave? Then my mother died and that—that was harder to take but easier to understand. Now I know the truth. But it can't be true, McKenzie. It can't be. Everything J. C. said, all the things she taught me, the person she was, who I wanted to be, what I tried to be—if this is true, then all of that is a lie."

Tears filled Bethany's eyes and she brushed them away.

"I'm sorry if I seem emotional," she said. "I know men don't like it when women become emotional because they're so out of touch with their own feelings that it makes them feel uncomfortable or even inadequate—one of the truths J. C. tried to explain to us, to her girls."

I didn't know how to respond to that. Instead, I said the first thing that popped into my head—"Things are not what they seem."

"What the hell is that supposed to mean?"

"I don't know. It's something Jeanette told me. The very last thing that she told me."

"When?" Bethany wanted to know. "Friday night? I saw the two of you walking together to the edge of the hill."

"Yes."

"J. C. wanted you to know that—that things were not what they seem?"

"Yes."

"Why?"

I shook my head.

"Why you?" she asked.

"I don't know."

You say that a lot.

"She's hiding now—I heard them talking," Bethany said.

"Yes."

"Where?"

"The entire local, state, and federal law enforcement community would like to know the answer to that question, as well."

"Will they find her?"

"I don't know."

It's staggering how much you don't know.

"Can you find her? McKenzie, I'll pay you to find J. C."

"No."

"I have plenty of money, most of it from my father."

"Beth, I'm not a licensed private investigator. I just do favors for my friends."

"Then do a favor for me. Find her. Find J. C. for me. Evangeline said you can do anything; she said that you're kind of a genius when it comes to this stuff."

"Evangeline exaggerates."

"Please."

"I wouldn't even know where to begin looking."

"Understand, McKenzie—I don't want J. C. to go to jail. I just want to talk to her. I just want to ask—I want to know the truth. I want to know why things aren't the way they seem."

Me, too.

"Let's say for argument's sake that I do find Jeanette Carrell and you're able to ask your questions," I said. "What if the answers she gives aren't the ones you want to hear? What if you discovered that she really is a murderer? That she killed her husband and the woman they found and maybe even your father? Then what?"

Bethany gave it a few moments of thought. Her eyes filled with tears again, and again she brushed them away with the backs of her hands.

"Do you know who Gloria Steinem was?" she asked.

"Yes."

"Gloria Steinem wrote a book—*The Truth Will Set You Free, But First It Will Piss You Off.* The truth is what's important, McKenzie, not my feelings about it."

Bethany's answer surprised me. Given the massive amount of misinformation that her fellow citizens gleefully consume and just as gleefully spread every day as long as it defends or supports what they already believe, to actually seek unvarnished, perhaps even painful truth would make her both a strong and courageous individual.

The woman Jeanette Carrell wanted her to be.

"Let me think about it," I said.

"Are you thinking about it?" Evangeline asked.

"No, not really." I took a sip of the maple-flavored bourbon she had poured for me. "It was just something I told Bethany so

I could walk away without looking like I was dismissing everything she had to say. Ah, Evan, for a couple of days there I was feeling pretty good about myself."

"So was I for getting you involved in all of this. For what it's worth, I don't blame you for what happened and neither do the Westermeyer sisters or the Plot Whores or anybody else I've spoken to."

"I take it you haven't heard from Linda Welch and Katherine Hixson."

"Most people didn't even know what was going on until the county attorney held his press conference. Did you know it was carried live on three of the local TV stations?"

"No, I didn't," I said.

"After that people started calling, sending texts. No one blamed you, though. Mostly they were just trying to reconcile the Jeanette Carrell they knew and loved with the one who killed her husband and that woman and buried them under the gazebo."

"What about Carson Vaneps?"

"His name was mentioned," Evan said. "Everyone assumes that he helped her. What do you think will happen to him?"

"Nothing. First, Ramsey County would need to prove that he was involved in a crime that took place twenty-seven years ago and good luck with that. Plus, given his Alzheimer's, just the simple act of questioning him would cause all kinds of problems in court. I just don't see it. 'Course, I'm not a county attorney running for reelection."

"At least they stopped destroying the hill."

"Temporarily, at best," I said. "I'm sure Sainsbury is already screaming that they need to release the crime scene. It's possible the BCA will wander all over the hill with ground-penetrating radar to find out if there are any more bodies buried up there, but that shouldn't take too long."

"Unless there are more bodies buried up there," Evan said.

I raised my glass to her.

"Good point," I said.

"During the press conference, they kept cutting to a photograph of Jeanette; I don't know where they got it."

"Let me guess, a very pretty woman with whitish blond hair."

"Yes."

"She doesn't look like that now; I can all but guarantee it," I said. "Probably Carrell's already colored her hair black, brown, or even red. She could be wearing a long wig until her hair grows out. Not to mention hats and hoodies. She could be wearing glasses, too. You wouldn't think that would make that big a difference, yet it does. She left her cell phone behind, so the deputies can't use that against her. I expect they'll find her car in a shopping mall parking lot at any moment now so they won't be able to track her using traffic cameras. This is assuming Carrell's a smart woman. Do you think she's a smart woman?"

"Very smart," Evan said.

"Me, too. Plus, she's had God knows how long to prepare for this; to plan. She's not doing anything on the fly; she's not doing anything spontaneously."

"You seem to understand it so well."

"The U.S. Marshals and BCA agents that make up the North Star Fugitive Task Force understand it better. Let's leave it to them."

"Do you really mean that?" Nina Truhler asked.

"There's nothing I can do that the task force can't do better," I said.

We were drinking coffee from white mugs while sitting at a table for two in front of the stage she had built in the parking lot of Rickie's. Her people were preparing it for a concert that was scheduled to begin within two hours featuring one of my favorite jazz singers of all time, Connie Evingson.

"I'd like to commandeer this table, by the way; the one we're sitting at," I said.

Nina took a sip of her coffee.

"No," she said.

"No?"

"Paying customers come first and Connie always draws a nice crowd, so . . ."

"I'd be happy to pay the cover."

"McKenzie, you haven't paid a tab here since we started dating eight years ago."

"I've always left a tip big enough to cover the bill and then some."

"Which is why my waitstaff loves to serve you," Nina said. "Nonetheless . . ."

"You're not going to make me stand in the back, are you?"

"We'll see what kind of turnout we get. It's going to get down to thirty-six degrees tonight."

"Which is the average temperature for an October evening in the Cities," I said.

"After all the above average warm days we've had, too. McKenzie, you can't blame yourself for Jeanette Carrell."

"What makes you think I'm blaming myself?"

"Eight years, remember?"

"I keep telling myself she didn't kill Charles Sainsbury; that I was right about that."

Nina drank more coffee.

"Let's say for a minute that you weren't right; that you didn't get her off," she said. "What would have happened when Carrell heard that they were going to bulldoze the hill and she still had that GPS thing attached to her ankle?"

"Probably she would have cut it off; all she would have needed was a bolt cutter or even a sharp scissors. Then she would've run just as fast as she could. During the day, she would have had a head start of twenty minutes. She did it at night, though. The marshals aren't actively monitoring at night. The pretrial services officer would have had to alert them. That would have given her more time to disappear."

"What's the difference, then?" Nina wanted to know.

"The difference is that Carrell would have had only about a three-hour head start instead of three days."

"Now you're feeling used and abused because of those three days; a woman took advantage of you."

"Something like that."

Nina started laughing.

"You think that's funny?" I asked.

"I was just thinking of all the damsels in distress that you've helped over the years."

"There haven't been that many."

"Who are you kidding, McKenzie? I can think of a half dozen off the top of my head and that's not even counting Erica . . ."

"I've never thought of your daughter as a damsel."

"Now one of them has turned on you and it pisses you off. True?"

"True," I said.

"So, you're going to let the North Star Fugitive Task Force take it from here?"

"Also true."

"I don't believe you."

"Nina, I have never lied to you in all the time we've been together; not even once."

"You're not lying to me, you're lying to yourself."

"I am not. Look, maybe I would go after Carrell if I had any idea at all where to look. I don't. I haven't got a clue."

I looked away, first at the stage, and then at Rickie's, anywhere but at Nina. While I turned my head, I caught movement in the sky to my right. A large bird, its wings spread wide, glided through the air. I followed it as it soared to the top of the tent that enclosed the stage and perched there. Nina must have followed my eyes because she was able to see what I saw.

"Is that a hawk?" she asked.

"No. It's a prairie falcon."

"How can you tell?"

"Turtle shell–colored back, white-spotted front, white neck, the yellow beak."

"Suddenly, you know a lot about birds."

"Birds of prey. Raptors. You don't often see prairie falcons in the Cities. Mostly they're found in the western part of the state."

It came to me then, almost as a revelation, while I watched the falcon and sipped my coffee.

"The secret, Nina, to finding a fugitive is knowing who they were before they went on the run," I said. "To be successful, fugitives need to give up their entire past. Most people can't do that. You'd be surprised how many fugitives stay close to home; how many try to keep in touch with family, friends, and acquaintances; placing phone calls or using social media; how many simply cannot give up the things they most cared about."

Nina leaned forward, rested her chin in her hand, and smiled at me.

"Do tell," she said.

"Something Jeanette Carrell said the day I met her—before she became a Badger, she was a Falcon."

"I don't know what that means."

"Carrell graduated from the University of Wisconsin. Before

that, though, she told me that she lived in Faribault, Minnesota; that she went to Faribault High School, home of the Falcons."

"Faribault is what, an hour's drive from here?" Nina asked.

"Less, I think."

"When are you going?"

"What makes you think I'm going?" I asked.

Nina answered by tapping the back of her wedding ring on the brim of her coffee mug.

"Eight years," she said.

TWELVE

I had no idea where the North Star Fugitive Task Force had its offices. I could imagine a member of the task force, though, a U.S. marshal or a BCA agent, sitting at his or her desk and carefully filling out a fugitive information form while sipping their morning coffee. Once completed, the form would contain nearly every known fact about Jeanette Lee Carrell, from the style of her dress (conservative chic) to her hobbies (gardening) to the languages she spoke (English and Spanish) to her driving record to her spending habits (three credit cards, entire balances paid monthly) to her physical characteristics—height, weight, her body type, the color of her eyes, the shapes of her ears and nose, the quality of her walk.

Some of this information would come from her driver's license and passport applications. Most would come from making phone calls and knocking on doors. In many fugitive recovery cases, the paperwork that fugitives are required to fill out by bail bondsmen—current address, employment information, contact info for friends and family, etc.—would be accessed. Except Jeanette had posted her own bail and hadn't been forced to reveal anything of herself.

There was GPS tracking, yet without a cell phone or car to focus on, that wouldn't help them moving forward, although the task force would, I was convinced, carefully inspect every corner of every location Jeanette had visited in the past year or more to learn her habits and get a hint into where she might have escaped to. They'd be monitoring all of her social media sites, too, although Jeanette never struck me as a social media woman, as well as the phones and social media sites of all of her friends, her girls, whether they approved or not. They might even watch websites that carried information about her, such as online newspapers, in case she decided to look herself up.

Yet while the task force was searching for Jeannette Lee Carrell, I decided to employ a different strategy. I decided to look for Jeanette Lee Fitch.

I started by doing what I suspect everyone would do. I fired up my computer.

Truth is, while I have some skills and experience, I am not an expert with a computer. Or even a gifted amateur. I was merely tenacious. I wasn't going to stop after the first half-dozen pages. If the search engine listed 3,560,000 results, I was prepared to sift through them all. It wasn't like I had a real job to occupy my time.

I began by typing Jeanette Lee Fitch's full name into a search engine and immediately found Jeanette Lee, aka the Black Widow, possibly the greatest female pool shark of all time, although Jennifer Barretta and Allison Fisher might dispute that opinion.

I was also directed to Janet Fitch, the bestselling author of *White Oleander* and *Paint It Black*.

Next came an African-American woman with the correct spelling in New Orleans; a filmmaker in San Jose; an IT girl in LA; a baker in New Jersey; a nurse in New Britain, Connecticut; a set designer in New York City; a ninety-six-year-old who passed two years ago in Attica, Indiana; a woman with seventeen aliases, including Jeanette Lee, who was now doing time in the Women's Eastern Reception, Diagnostic and Correctional Center in Vandalia, Missouri; an MRI technologist in Peoria, Arizona; a sewing specialist in South Carolina; a financial consultant in Enterprise, Ontario; an assistant manager at Victoria's Secret in Oklahoma City; and on and on and on.

Eventually, I changed my search parameters to include anyone with the name Fitch living in or near Faribault, Minnesota, and discovered a half-dozen residents, including a woman who owned a clothing store on Central Avenue North.

I reached for my cell phone and stopped. In my experience, people were more inclined to answer questions in person than on a phone; it's easy to be rude and hang up a phone.

By then Nina was up and about; running a jazz club for the past couple of decades, she rarely went to bed before two A.M. and seldom rose before ten. She was pouring herself a cup of coffee from the French press I had prepared for her in the kitchen area when I called to her.

"I'm driving to Faribault," I told her.

"I figured you would."

"Nobody likes a know-it-all."

Nina thought that was funny.

"When will you be back?" she asked.

"I don't know."

"Have fun," she said.

Faribault was founded in 1826, thirty-two years before Minnesota became a state, by the son of a French-Canadian fur trader and a Dakotah woman that he had married. It started as a trading post perched on the banks of the Straight River, where it joined the Cannon River. Back in those days, rivers were the preferred means of travel. Then it became roads and highways, which were routed through the city. Only the government decided to build Interstate 35 on the western edge of Faribault—it was cheaper—allowing traffic to bypass the city. Before that event, the town experienced double-digit growth in every decade from 1880 through 1960. Afterward, growth declined to the point where Faribault actually lost population over a nearly thirty-year period, although it had been coming back recently. You wouldn't have known that, though, if you hadn't read Faribault's *Wikipedia* page. Its tree-lined streets seemed vibrant with energy, its businesses thriving; its downtown lively.

It took me forty minutes to get there, driving south on I-35. I parked across the street from a three-story brick building that looked as if it had been built during the Roaring Twenties, if not earlier. In fact, the entire downtown area appeared as if it should be placed on the list of National Historic Landmarks. A name was painted across the huge glass window of the storefront located on the ground floor of the building—FITCH'S FASHIONS. I walked inside. A bell above the door announced my presence. A woman, who could have been ten years older or ten years younger than me, threaded past racks of brightly colored women's clothing until she reached my side.

"May I help you?" she asked.

Her smiled seemed as cheerful and genuine as the clothes surrounding us.

"I'd like to speak to the owner," I told her.

"Please tell me that you're going to make her an offer on this place that will make her independently wealthy."

The request caught me by surprise and I stammered my reply, "Umm, no."

"Pity." The woman extended her hand. "I'm the owner. Angela Fitch."

I took her hand.

"McKenzie," I said.

"You don't have a first name?"

"Rushmore."

"No kidding?"

I told her the story I nearly always told when my name received that reaction.

"According to my parents, I was conceived in a motor lodge in the shadow of the Mount Rushmore monument during a vacation they took through the Badlands of South Dakota. It could have been worse, though. It could have been Deadwood."

Angela thought that was funny. Most people did.

"How can I help you, McKenzie?" she asked.

"I'm hoping you can tell me about a woman named Jeanette Lee Fitch."

"Never heard of her."

"Are you sure? A distant cousin, perhaps?"

The look of concentration on her face suggested that she actually thought about it before she shook her head.

"Sorry," she said. "Can I ask why?"

I gave her the answer I had already prepared.

"She disappeared a few days ago," I said. "We know very little about her except that her name was Jeanette Lee Fitch and that she was from Faribault."

Angela shook her head some more.

"I'm sorry to hear that," she said. "I wish I could help you. I'm not actually from Faribault myself. I moved here ten years ago from Austin."

"Austin, Texas?"

"Austin, Minnesota, home of the Spam Museum. There's a woman, the only other person I've met in Faribault named Fitch. What's her name? It was an odd name. I sold her a blue dress, mother of the bride, actually mother of the groom—Vina. Vina Fitch."

Vina Fitch, not among the names you discovered during your computer search, my inner voice told me.

"You think you have a story, ask her where her name came from," Angela told me.

"Do you know where I can find her?" I asked.

"Hang on."

She didn't ask me to, yet I followed Angela as she made her way across the store to a lighted glass display case loaded with jewelry. Behind the display case was a desk. She sat on a chair and accessed a computer on top of the desk. After a few minutes, she wrote an address on a small sheet of yellow notepaper, tore it off, and handed it to me.

"Nice woman, Vina; I liked her," Angela said. "I hope this won't cause her any trouble."

"Me, too."

Like the old song, Vina Fitch was five foot two with eyes of blue and had a turned-up nose. She stared when she found me standing at her front door as if she was convinced I was there to cause her trouble.

"Mrs. Fitch," I said.

"Ms. Fitch."

"Excuse me, Ms. Fitch. My name is McKenzie. I was hoping . . ."

"What do you want, Mr. McKenzie?"

"I was hoping . . ."

"If you wish to speak to my husband, he's at the high school."

"Is your husband a teacher?"

The question seemed to catch Vina by surprise. She took a full step backward.

"It's possible I might have misjudged you, Mr. McKenzie," she said. "I apologize. My husband is Ken Haines. He's the principal at Faribault High School. Usually, when I find a stranger knocking on my door it's because they want to complain about how poorly their children are being treated or to demand that a book that they're expected to read be banned from the library."

"Does that happen a lot?" I asked.

"The first ten years we lived here, it hardly ever happened. The last couple of years, though, it seems to happen all the time."

"I'm very sorry to hear that."

"More and more, it seems, people are searching for things to be outraged about. Partly it's because so many are frustrated because of the coronavirus, but mostly I think it's about politics. I'm sorry. Mr. McKenzie, would you care to come in? May I offer you a cup of coffee?"

I answered yes to both questions—the Code of Minnesota Nice was followed even more vigorously in small towns than in the Cities, although I doubted that the twenty-five thousand people who lived there considered Faribault to be small. A few minutes later, I was drinking black coffee at Vina Fitch's kitchen table. It wasn't nearly as good as the coffee Jennifer Carlson had poured me, still . . .

"Your husband's name is Ken Haines," I said. "But yours is Fitch."

"Are you one of those people who believe that women should give up their names, their identities, when they marry?"

"Not at all. My wife kept hers."

"Did she?"

"Nina Truhler."

"Good for her. And you. It's surprising how many people don't approve. Both my mother and mother-in-law still send Christmas cards addressed to Mr. and Mrs. Kenneth Haines no matter how many times I tell them not to. Nina—that's a name you don't hear very often."

"A little more common than Vina, I think."

"In Scottish Gaelic it means 'beloved' or 'friend.' In Spanish it means 'vineyard.'"

"Angela Fitch told me your name comes with a story," I said.

"You met Angela?"

"She's the one who gave me your address."

"Did she also tell you that my extended family was Spanish? They didn't name me Beloved or Friend, they named me Vineyard. I've been trying to wrap my head around that since I was six years old. I asked my mother about it and she told me that my father's grandmother's name was Vina and his mother talked him into giving it to me after my great-grandmother died, which happened well before I was born."

"I like it, though—Vina."

"I do, too. What can I do for you, McKenzie?"

"I am looking for any information you can give me about a woman named Jeanette Lee Fitch."

"Why?"

"She disappeared in the Cities a few days ago," I said. "We know very little about her except her name and that she was originally from Faribault."

"You're an investigator?"

"Yes."

"I understand."

Like Angela, Vina didn't require any more information than that.

"I've never heard the name," she said. "I don't think any of the students at the high school are named Fitch, either. It's just me and Angela."

"Are you from Faribault?"

"No, I'm from East Lansing, Michigan. That's where I met Ken; we both went to Michigan State. We moved around for a while and then came to Faribault when he was hired as principal. Like I said, as far as I know, Angela and I are the only Fitchs in town."

"Are you sure?"

I pulled out my notebook and showed Vina the names I had written there.

"I don't know any of these people," she said. "Sorry."

It took me an hour and five minutes to cross the next two names off my list, and that included a pit stop for a grilled clubhouse sandwich and a craft beer at the Crooked Pint Ale House. Both names belonged to men. One was an African-American who had moved to the city ten years earlier chasing a job at Faribo Manufacturing, a company that made outdoor lighting covers and plastic storage containers for the food industry. The other moved to Faribault more recently to work for Faribault Foods, which sold canned beans, vegetables, pasta sauce, and chili, among other things.

A short time later I knocked on the door of a woman whose Facebook page identified her as a "Christian, birdwatcher, book reader, cat fancier, hammock enthusiast by day, knitter by night." She opened her front door wide yet kept her storm door closed. She seemed to shiver, which I assumed was caused by the fifty-degree temperature and not my face. She spoke with a timid voice through the door.

"Yes?"

"Daphne Fitch?" I asked.

"Yes."

"My name is McKenzie. I'm hoping you can help me. I'm trying to gather information about a woman named Jeanette Lee Fitch."

I didn't need to ask if she knew her; I could see the flash of recognition in her eyes. I asked anyway.

"Do you know her?"

"What is this?" Daphne asked.

"Ma'am, if you can help me . . ."

"Is this some kind of scam? If you're trying to . . ." She moved to close her door. "I will not be taken advantage of again."

"Ma'am, please." I placed my hand flat against my heart. "It's important."

Daphne paused.

"Why is it important?" she wanted to know.

"A woman disappeared in the Cities a couple of days ago and we're trying to find out about her. All we know for sure is that her name was Jeanette Lee Fitch and she claimed to be from Faribault."

"Well, it sure wasn't my sister, I can tell you that."

"Your sister is named Jeanette Lee Fitch? Can you tell me how to find her?"

"Mister, my sister has been dead for thirty-three years."

That's all Daphne Fitch would give me before she slammed her door shut.

I stood staring at it while a million thoughts raced through my mind. I managed to get control of the most prominent one.

The woman I had known as Jeanette Lee Carrell had been ghosting.

She had been pretending to be Jeanette Lee Fitch. Daphne said her sister had been dead for thirty-three years, which meant she'd passed—I quickly did the math—in 1989. Jeanette had married David Carrell—wait, wait, what were the dates? Carrell disappeared in 1995. Jeanette told me it was three years after they married. That meant she was pretending to be Jeanette Lee Fitch since at least 1992.

She had been ghosting for at least thirty years.

Probably longer, my inner voice told me. *As long as thirty-three years.*

My God.

No wonder she had done such a masterful job of disappearing once William Sainsbury announced he was sending his bulldozers up the hill.

She had done it before.

Whoever she was.

I considered my options. One was to pound on Daphne's front door until she opened it again and demand that she answer my questions or I'd send the U.S. Marshals to arrest her and what would her neighbors think about that?

Yeah, that's pretty lame even by your standards.

Instead, I retreated to my Mustang and started working my smartphone. I called up the website for the *Faribault Daily News* and accessed its obituaries link. Unfortunately, its archives only reached back to 2002.

Now what?

THIRTEEN

The Thomas Scott Buckham Memorial Library was built over ninety years ago by someone who loved both Art Deco architecture and Greek literature. The outside was all yellowish dolomite limestone with rectangular windows filled with pastel-colored glass and a four-story central tower with a huge arched stained-glass window and a clock that actually told the correct time. The inside featured four large murals depicting life in Sparta, Athens, Delphi, and Olympia, Greece, during the fourth century B.C.

It also had a Local History Room, which included microfilm of every edition of the *Faribault Daily News* dating back to 1948. I found a librarian. She was wearing a mask because the county demanded face coverings inside all government buildings. Her eyes told me she was smiling, though, when she asked how she could help me—I love librarians. She led me to the History Room after I explained what I needed and helped set up a microfilm scanner that looked as if it had been built a full century before the internet. I started surfing the newspapers starting with Sunday, January 1, 1989.

It took me ninety minutes before I reached Wednesday, November 22, and found:

Faribault—Jeanette Lee Fitch died peacefully in her sleep of an undiagnosed brain aneurysm at the home of her parents, Donald and Susan (Lucas) Fitch. Known as "Lee" by her family and friends, she graduated from Faribault High School in 1974, where she played softball and volleyball. She continued her education at the University of Wisconsin, where she earned a business degree in 1978. She is survived by her parents and her sister, Daphne. Private services were held at Eden Funeral and Cremation Services.

Not much there, my inner voice told me. *Do the math and we know that she was thirty-three years old and living at home. It doesn't mention if she had a job. Private services were held—does that mean no friends were invited to say good-bye?*

I looked up the obituaries for her parents. Susan Lucas Fitch died in 2006 and her husband Donald died almost exactly one year later. The causes of their deaths were not listed nor were public funeral services held in either case. Daphne was mentioned as the only survivor.

Again, I was tempted to go back to her house and pound on her door. What was I going to ask her, though—who do you know who might be pretending to be your sister? Truth was, it could be anyone.

Couldn't it?

I thanked the librarian for her help. Before I left the library, though, I used the map app on my smartphone to locate Eden Funeral and Cremation Services.

I found the funeral home not too far from the Shattuck-St. Mary's boarding school. There were only a couple of cars in the parking lot, which told me that there were no services being conducted that midafternoon.

Business must be dead, my inner voice said.

It was a poor joke and not nearly as funny as the billboard that had been erected by a funeral home on Highway 36 in Roseville when I was a kid—DRIVE CAREFULLY. WE CAN WAIT.

I found an office just inside the doorway. A woman dressed in a business suit was sitting behind a desk in the office. She stood up and smiled. It was an odd sort of smile that suggested goodwill but not joy or happiness and I wondered if it was something a funeral director might practice.

"May I help you?" she asked.

"Good afternoon. Yes, thank you. I'm hoping you can give me some information on a funeral that your people conducted in 1989."

"Nineteen eighty-nine? That would be my people. My father."

"The name would be Jeanette Lee Fitch," I told her.

The woman watched me for a few beats as if she was wondering if I could perform any other tricks. I was impressed by how businesslike her voice sounded.

"What is this pertaining to?" she asked.

"A woman disappeared in the Cities a couple of days ago and we're trying to find out about her. All we know for sure is that her name was Jeanette Lee Fitch and she claimed to be from Faribault. We tracked down her sister, Daphne, and she told us that Jeanette had passed in 1989."

The woman nodded her head as if it was a tale she had heard many times before.

"Identity theft," she said.

"It looks that way."

"We get a lot of that these days. Used to be thieves would rob the home of the deceased during scheduled funeral services or steal their Social Security numbers or request duplicate driver's licenses so they could apply for loans under the deceased's name, open credit cards, file false tax returns. A newer scheme has thieves filing a change of address order with the post office to reroute the deceased's mail, providing them with access to bank and credit account numbers, banking and investment statements, even allowing them to receive the death certificate instead of the family. It's a sad world sometimes."

"Yes, it is," I agreed.

The woman sat behind her desk and accessed her computer, talking to me as she did.

"Nineteen eighty-nine," she said. "That's a long time ago. These days we offer all kinds of services to the family of the deceased to help them prevent identity theft. We tell them to restrict the information they put in obituaries like a birth date, city of birth, mother's maiden name. We tell them to have the death certificate sent to us or someone they trust instead of their own address. Once they have the death certificate, we tell them to contact the national credit bureaus to prevent thieves from opening new credit lines. This is taking longer than I thought. Give me a second."

"Sure," I said.

"What else?" the funeral director asked. "We tell them to contact the postal service and check to make sure the deceased's mail is being delivered to the correct address. We tell them to notify organizations the deceased belonged to like the Veterans Affairs, U.S. Citizenship and Immigration Services, Social Security Administration—we offer to do a lot of that for them, contact Social Security; part of the services we provide."

"Did you do that for Jeanette Fitch?"

"Hang on a sec. This was input long before we installed our new system so it's not as specific, mostly just the notes my father made at the time. Here we go. Jeanette Lee Fitch, age thirty-three, daughter to Donald and Susan Fitch. They're the ones who paid the bills. It was a very bare-bones funeral. Not even a visitation. The body was cremated."

"Cremated?" I asked.

"That was unusual back then. In the nineteen-eighties, the cremation rate was only about one in ten. Today it's over fifty percent. Umm, according to my dad's notes, we didn't contact the Social Security Administration. 'Course, people weren't anywhere near as concerned about identity theft back then as they are now."

"If Jeanette was cremated, there would be no grave, no tombstone."

"Yes, well, that's why people do it."

"I'm sorry," I said. "I was just thinking out loud."

I returned to my Mustang and sat in the parking lot.

If Jeanette was cremated, there would be no grave, no tombstone, my inner voice repeated. *Whoever stole her identity didn't do the cemetery thing, strolling among the headstones until she found the name of a woman who would have been roughly the same age that she was when she died.*

That's the way it was done; how "ghosting" got its name. A person could become the ghost of a dead person simply by obtaining the individual's birth certificate and using it to create a false identity by obtaining a new Social Security card or hijacking the old one, acquiring a driver's license, what else?

It isn't as easy now because a county clerk usually can quickly access a search engine to learn if a death certificate had ever been issued to a person listed on a birth certificate. Yet, back before the widespread use of computers, when birth certificates were kept in huge file drawers in a large room on the second floor of the old county courthouse while death certificates were kept in a cabinet in a smaller room on the third floor, it wasn't that difficult at all. Especially for women.

A woman could steal the identity of a dead female who was *married* and who used her husband's name, something that was quite common in the eighties. That way the birth certificate and the death certificate would have two different surnames, which made detection tougher. If she then took a husband herself, adopting his name—going from Fitch to Carrell, for example—discovery would be nearly impossible. Plus, the gaps in the ghost's employment history would have caused less suspicion by an employer or the IRS than it would today because the ghost could claim that she spent those years working as a housewife, as a stay-at-home mom who made no wages.

Except . . .

Yeah.

If Jeanette was cremated, there would be no grave, no tombstone, for the ghost to find.

Yeah.

So how did she manage it?

She must have known Jeanette personally, I told myself. Or read the obituary in the paper, which suggested that she was in Faribault when Jeanette died.

The words flowed back to me—*Before I became a Badger, I was a Falcon.*

I returned to the Thomas Scott Buckham Memorial Library. The librarian I had met earlier was still working the front desk. Her voice was only slightly muffled by her mask.

"More microfilm?" she asked.

"High school yearbooks," I replied behind mine.

"Faribault High School yearbooks?"

"Yes, ma'am."

"This way."

I followed her back to the Local History Room and watched as she waved at a bookcase filled with large, thin hardback volumes. She set a long index finger on the spine of an olive green book.

"The *Voyageur* of 1941," she said.

She moved her finger across the books until she reached the end.

"The *Voyageur* of 2022," she added.

"Thank you," I said.

"Are you working on some kind of history?"

"Some kind."

"Good luck."

"Thank you."

As she was leaving the room, I stepped to the bookcase. I found *Voyageur* 1974, sat at the square table in the center of the room, and opened it. I easily found Jeanette Lee Fitch's class photo, plus a few action shots of her playing softball and volleyball. She was tall and she was slender and she was a blonde, yet no one would have mistaken her for the woman who had been living under her name for the past three decades.

I wasn't actually searching for her photo, though. I wanted to see the face of every female who had gone to Faribault High School with her. I reviewed them carefully, knowing that people could have changed an awful lot in the nearly fifty years that had passed since the "real" Jeanette Lee Fitch had been graduated. I found no one who even came close.

I went to the 1975 *Voyageur*.

And 1976.

And 1977.

I kept reminding myself not to be influenced by hair length and color or glasses or clothes or anything else that wasn't permanent. Concentrate on the eyes, I reminded myself. That's what I was taught at the police academy. The eyes are considered to be one of the most reliable body parts for human identification. And the width of the mouth. And the chin.

I went through *Voyageur* 1978, 1979, and 1980.

Several times I found a young woman who maybe, possibly, could have been the woman I knew as Carrell, only to dismiss her, then go back and check a second time and a third.

1981.

1982.

1983.

After reviewing the 1984 *Voyageur*, I decided to go backward, starting with the 1973 yearbook.

People have been flirting with automated facial recognition programs since the 1960s and have yet to figure it out. Even the best technologies have been criticized for commonly making inaccurate identifications, not to mention encouraging gender discrimination and racial profiling. Yet I was thinking that an app might be useful right about now.

1972.

1971.

1970.

I remembered when I was with the St. Paul Police Department and I'd have witnesses browsing mug books. Well, not actual books, but computer databases loaded with the photographs of repeat offenders. I'd become impatient when they couldn't ID a suspect. What a jerk.

1969.

1968.

1967.

I stopped and rubbed my eyes. I was tired and I was hungry. I glanced at my watch. It wasn't even five P.M. yet.

I returned the yearbooks to the shelf, thanked the librarian for her kindness, and returned to my Mustang. I sat in the car, the driver's side window rolled down despite the crisp air. It was so quiet I could hear the three flags flapping in the slight breeze from poles in front of the library and the zipper on my brown leather coat as I pulled it up.

I was convinced that the woman who had been ghosting as Jeanette Lee Fitch for the past thirty years had not attended Faribault High School between 1967 and 1983. Yet that didn't mean she wasn't living in Faribault when Jeanette passed. I had met four residents just that afternoon who had moved there from somewhere else.

Could the ghost have been a friend? A co-worker? A neighbor?

I decided there was nothing for it but to return to Daphne Fitch's house and find out if she would help me.

"Please, go away," she told me.

"Ma'am, it's important. I wouldn't bother you if it wasn't important."

"If you don't leave I will have you arrested for trespassing," Daphne said. "I've done it before. The police department is only a mile away on the other side of the Straight River."

I told her that was a good idea; to go ahead.

"I'll wait," I said.

"You'll what?" Daphne wanted to know.

"Ma'am, a woman who claims to be your sister—at least I'm pretty sure she was claiming to be your sister—hurt some people in the Twin Cities. We're trying to find her. Not just me, but the FBI and the U.S. Marshals and the Minnesota Bureau of Criminal Apprehension. I'm sure the Faribault Police Department would be interested, too."

Daphne Fitch didn't have anything to say to that. I noticed, however, that she didn't reach for her phone.

"Ma'am, I am so sorry for the inconvenience," I added. "I promise you're not in any trouble yourself. Only we need your help." I flashed on her Facebook bio. "It would be the Christian thing to do."

"I won't invite you in," Daphne said.

"That's fine."

"A man claiming to be from the IRS stole thousands of dollars from me just a few months ago."

"I'm so sorry, ma'am."

"It won't happen again," Daphne vowed.

"You are absolutely right to be careful."

"What do you want to know?"

"Anything you can tell me about your sister before she passed," I said. "Where did she work?"

"She was some kind of manager at Cannon River Manufacturing; got the job when she came back from college."

I pulled out my notebook and wrote the name down.

"Where is it located?" I asked.

"Oh, it was closed twenty years ago. They built a different business in its place and that was closed, too."

The IRS requires that a business that ceases operation must keep its records, including employment files, for only seven years, my inner voice reminded me. *Meaning you're only thirteen years late. Swell.*

"Did she have any close friends?" I asked.

"I didn't know Lee's friends. She pretty much kept to herself after—after—she had a boyfriend who promised to marry her so she gave him things that a good girl shouldn't give a man before they were married and then he abandoned her, moved to the Cities with a woman that he also promised to marry and didn't. Lee moved back in with Mom and Dad so she wouldn't have to be alone. She didn't date after that."

"I'm sorry," I said.

I asked more questions; asked about clubs and church groups and her college friends.

"Lee should never have gone so far away to college," Daphne said. "She should have stayed in Minnesota. Going to Wisconsin for four years, that's what ruined her, if you ask me."

I didn't.

After a few more questions, I thanked Daphne for her time and returned to my car.

Well, that was helpful.

I drove off even though I had no idea where I was driving to. I just wanted to get away from Daphne's house.

I started talking to myself.

You know, you may be going about this all wrong.

In what way?

Instead of looking for Jeanette Fitch, you should be looking for the person who is pretending to be Jeanette Fitch.

I thought that's what I was doing.

Yes, but, ask yourself—why do people ghost?

To escape.

To escape what?

The police, the courts, for a crime they committed.

What else?

Debts owed to an unforgiving lender.

What else?

A dysfunctional family.

And?

A bad marriage.

So?

So, there would be drama. A crime would have been committed and the police would be on the lookout for a suspect.

That would be in the newspaper, especially decades ago when it was the chief means of communicating with an entire city. Or debt collectors or an abusive husband or family and friends would want to know where she was; they'd want to have her declared a missing person and say to the cops, "Find the girl." That would probably be in the paper, too.

Yes, it would.

I took up my smartphone again and used it to access the Minnesota Missing and Unidentified Persons Clearinghouse maintained by the BCA. There were nearly a hundred names listed, some going as far back as the sixties. Most were clearly unsolved homicides—a woman was last seen leaving a party, leaving a casino, leaving with a male friend, getting into a car with an unidentified male, arguing with her ex-husband. Others were not so clear—a woman disappeared after expressing a desire to move to a warmer climate, or after she left a note telling her parents that she was going to Texas with her boyfriend, or after she was released from jail.

No one came close to resembling the woman I knew as Jeanette Lee Fitch.

Just because she wasn't on the list, though, didn't mean she hadn't gone missing.

I returned to the public library.

"I can tell by your expression that you're not having much luck," the librarian told me.

"Even though I'm wearing a mask?"

"Even though."

"It's starting to be a long day," I admitted.

"More yearbooks?"

"More microfilm."

I started rereading the *Faribault Daily News* starting once again at January 1, 1989. This time I didn't skip forward to the obituaries, but studied the headlines, the news briefs; looking for anything that might explain why a woman living in Faribault might suddenly disappear.

Only nothing fit.

Nothing even came close to fitting.

By August 1991 I decided that Faribault was the quietest town in America.

Hours later, the librarian startled me by tapping my shoulder.

"Excuse me," she said.

"What?"

"I'm sorry, we close at eight P.M."

I automatically glanced at my watch. It was eight ten.

"You don't have to go home," she added. "But you can't stay here."

FOURTEEN

The next morning I again woke before Nina. I didn't bother to get dressed. Instead, I threw on a robe and went directly to my desk. Well, not directly. I needed to make coffee first.

Once fortified, I fired up my computer. I used it, and my cell phone, to search for missing persons or fleeing fugitives in Rice County, where Faribault was located. When that proved unsuccessful, as expected, I contacted every county circling Rice, starting with Steele County, where the City of Owatonna was located, followed by Waseca, Le Sueur, Scott, Dakota, Goodhue, and Dodge Counties—any place where a copy of the *Faribault Daily News* might be read; Jeanette Lee Fitch's obituary was not printed anywhere else that I could find.

Always, I searched the county's sheriff department website first. It was about fifty-fifty on how helpful they were. Many didn't provide much more information than the name of the sheriff. Others were remarkably useful. Dakota County, for example, listed 164 names on its most wanted list including photographs. Steele County provided, in alphabetical order, the names of over 275 miscreants who were fleeing the arrest warrants it issued, while Le Sueur County provided 150 and Goodhue County listed a whopping 859—all without photographs—and, unfortunately, all issued in just the past twenty years or so.

That's when I used my cell phone. After I explained what I wanted to whoever answered my call, I was always directed to someone in the records department. Sometimes they answered my questions cheerfully, sometimes not so much. Always they were suspicious. Usually they were apologetic when they failed to provide the information I was seeking—the name of a woman, any woman, who had gone missing or was fleeing the authorities for any infraction whatsoever between January 1, 1989, and December 31, 1990, who could have plausibly, possibly, conceivably been ghosting as Jeanette Carrell.

Imagine my frustration.

Maybe there wasn't any drama; that's why we can't ID her, my inner voice told me. *Maybe our ghost didn't just disappear, making family, friends, neighbors, and co-workers wonder what had happened to her, if she was kidnapped or murdered. Maybe she wasn't hiding from an abusive husband; maybe she didn't leave a pile of debts. Maybe she didn't commit a heinous crime for which she was wanted by the whole of the United States justice apparatus, either. Maybe she became Jeanette Lee Fitch simply because she wanted to be someone other than the woman she was.*

She left two dead bodies on the hill, I reminded myself. Whether she killed them or not, she certainly knew they were there.

Yes, but that came later. One thing might not have anything to do with the other.

Or it might have everything to do with it. The problem is, we won't know until we find the woman.

So, find the woman.

Don't talk to me anymore unless you have something constructive to say.

How 'bout this—where the hell are the U.S. Marshals?

It was a good question. At no point during my investigation were the marshals or the North Star Fugitive Task Force mentioned by anyone. Weren't they working the case, too? A front page story in my online edition of the St. Paul *Pioneer Press* said they were. Except you'd think we would have tripped over each other by now.

I read the newspaper story carefully. It didn't state any facts that I didn't already know. A photograph of Jeanette Carrell was included. She was smiling in the photo.

"Who are you?" I asked.

"The love of your life?" Nina asked in return.

By then she had entered the kitchen area and was pouring herself a mug of coffee. Unlike me, she was dressed to impress.

"Not you," I said.

"Not me?"

"I meant Jeanette Carrell."

"Jeanette Carrell is the love of your life? Since when?"

"I was speaking to her photograph."

"You speak to her photograph but not to mine? What's that about?"

"Nina . . ."

"Does her photograph answer you?" Nina asked.

"Stop it."

Nina's smile suggested that she was done teasing me, at least for the present.

"So, how goes the investigation?" she asked.

"It has not improved any since we spoke last night."

"I was listening to Minnesota Public Radio while I was getting dressed. They said the woman they found buried with David Carrell has not yet been identified."

"I find that hard to believe," I said. "A woman disappears at a specific time in a specific place; there should be a missing person's report somewhere. It's possible that the victim has been IDed but the sheriff's department decided to keep her name to itself for now."

"Have you identified your missing person yet?"

"No."

"Well, then."

"It's an entirely different set of circumstances. My ghost was actively hiding; is actively hiding. The woman buried beneath the gazebo clearly didn't mean to disappear. Someone must have wondered what happened to her. Someone must have gone looking for her."

"Why?" Nina asked.

"What do you mean, why? If Erica disappeared, you'd move heaven and earth to learn what happened to her."

"That's because I'm her mother and I love her. This woman—what if she didn't have a mother, what if she didn't have someone who loved her? No family. No friends. What if no one was waiting for her to come home?"

"She'd have a job . . ."

"Not necessarily."

"A house or an apartment, a car, money in the bank, a telephone bill to pay; electricity."

"Does Xcel Energy file a missing person's report when a customer fails to pay a bill?" Nina asked.

"Probably not, but sooner or later someone would have knocked on her door. A landlord. A debt collector. A mail carrier wondering why she hadn't picked up her letters. Someone."

"If she didn't answer?"

"Eventually, the police would be called. Someone would be sent to her house; they call it a welfare check. If she didn't answer, an officer would gain entry."

"If she wasn't there?"

I flashed on a bulletin posted on the BCA's Missing and Un-identified Persons Clearinghouse I had read the day before. It consisted of a photograph of a woman, obviously taken from her driver's license, above a list of vital statistics, also taken from her driver's license, and a single line: "The circumstances under which she went missing are unknown." It depressed me then and thinking about it now only depressed me more. How empty must your life be that you could literally disappear, just go "poof," and no one would care where you went or wonder why.

"My point is, she would be in the system," I said.

"On that happy note, don't forget we have Bobby and Shelby Dunston tonight," Nina said.

"Here or there?"

"There."

"Okay."

"Are you going to pick me up at Rickie's or meet me at their place?"

"I'll pick you up."

"I'll believe it when I see it."

"What do you mean?"

"I know how you get when you're in one of these moods. You know what? I'll call you later."

"Fine."

Nina waved her hand at me.

"You might want to get cleaned up before you leave the condo. I don't want you frightening the children."

"I wish you would stop talking like that. You know I have serious self-esteem issues."

"You are going outside, though, right? I know it's cold, but the sun is shining, the birds are singing . . ."

"I'll be leaving the condo, yes."

"Just out of curiosity, where will you be going? Back to Faribault?"

The Minnesota History Center is an enormous sparkling gem of a building located on a high hill overlooking the sprawling State Capitol Complex to the north, the Xcel Energy Center, where the Wild play hockey to the south and much of downtown St. Paul to the south and east. If you study its architecture closely, you'll see elements of the State Capitol building, the majestic St. Paul Cathedral located just to the west, and even Fort Snelling.

The center is home to the Minnesota Historical Society and houses a museum that possesses more than one million artifacts, including archaeological objects, books, photographs, maps, paintings, prints, drawings, manuscripts, government records, periodicals, and newspapers. When I say "newspapers," I mean digitized copies of nearly every edition of every newspaper ever printed in Minnesota from 1849 to, well, now.

The newspapers were stored in the Gale Family Library on the second floor, the library consisting of two rooms—the Weyerhaeuser Reference Room and the Ronald M. Hubbs Microfilm Reading Room. Most of the newspapers printed since 2010 were available in print or were freely accessible online. The papers I wanted to read, however, were printed between January 1, 1989, and December 31, 1990. That put me in front of a microfilm scanner in the Hubbs Room.

Yet another pleasant librarian helped me out. If there was a difference, the woman in Faribault acted as if aiding my microfilm search happened only occasionally while the woman at the History Center behaved as if she did this thirty times a day.

I started with the *Owatonna People's Press,* Owatonna located nineteen miles due south of Faribault. When that proved unhelpful, I tried the *Dakota County Tribune* in Burnsville thirty-five miles north, the *Northfield News* fourteen miles northeast, the *Kenyon Leader* fourteen miles east, the *Dodge County Independent* out of Kasson forty miles southeast, the *Waseca County News* twenty-five miles southwest, and the *Montgomery Messenger* in Le Sueur County twenty-two miles northwest.

By the time I was finished, I was pretty sure that if there were a *Jeopardy!*-like Minnesota trivia contest somewhere, I would win it. Beyond that, all I had to show for my research was a bad headache. And a sour mood. When my cell began vibrating and the caller ID said that Nina was calling, I answered with a surly "What?"

"Oh, someone's having a good day," she said.

"I'm sorry. What did— Oh, I'm supposed to pick you up and take you to the Dunstons', aren't I?"

"Well, since I'm already there . . ."

"Wait. What time is it?"

Bobby Dunston was the best cop I had ever known; much better than I had been. We started together at the St. Paul Police Department nearly twenty-five years ago. He stayed on after I retired, eventually moving up to commander in the Major Crimes Division, mostly running the Homicide Unit. The thing about him that bugged me, even when we were kids running around the Merriam Park Community Center just across the street from his house, was his grin that made him appear as if he already knew the ending to a movie the rest of us had just started watching.

"Something on your mind, Bobby?" I asked.

I was sitting on a sofa in the rec room I had helped him build in his basement. The basement was in the house where he grew up, where I practically grew up, Bobby's mother all but adopting me after my own mother passed because, she said, there were things my jarhead father simply couldn't teach me, jarhead being a reference to the fact that the old man was a former marine and therefore devoid of human feeling, which wasn't even close to being true, although he was a stern and taciturn fellow. Bobby bought the house from his parents when they retired to their lake home in Wisconsin and Nina and I were frequent visitors, coming for dinner at least once during the even-numbered months while Bobby and Shelby came to our place at least once in the odd-numbered months.

Bobby took a long sip from his Summit Extra Pale Ale and grinned some more while he watched the Minnesota Timberwolves playing basketball on his big-screen TV. We were watching the Wolves because the Wild weren't playing. Bobby and I were both hockey guys and had played together at Merriam Park and Central High School and now in pickup games at the Charles M. Schulz Arena in Highland Park.

"You just can't help yourself, can you?" he said.

"You're referring to . . ."

"I had a chat with Mike Swenson this morning. We're both part of a SPPD-Ramsey County violent crimes task force."

"Uh-huh."

"Guess whose name came up."

"I can't imagine," I said.

"He's really pissed at you."

"I didn't do anything wrong."

"He didn't say you did," Bobby told me.

"I'm convinced that Jeanette Carrell did not kill Charles Sainsbury."

"So is Mike. Well, at least half convinced, anyway. He kept pointing out, though, that he now has two dead bodies and a suspect in the wind, so . . ."

"I'm trying to fix that," I said.

"I gathered."

"Should I tell you what I've been doing?"

"Sure. I haven't had a good laugh since this morning."

I gave him a condensed version.

"Jeanette Lee Fitch died in 1989," Bobby repeated. "Did you tell Mike? Did you tell the U.S. Marshals?"

"Not yet."

"Why not?"

"You know how the Feds work," I said. "They're very good at taking in information yet very poor at dispensing it. I'll wait until I have something worth trading with them."

"Does the term 'obstruction of justice' mean anything to you?"

"Hmm, what?"

"Yeah, that's what I thought. You're just being the same old McKenzie that we all know and love, aren't you?"

"I do not know what you mean, Commander Dunston."

"You're going to find the woman before everyone else does just to prove that you can."

"That would suggest I'm doing all this out of ego."

"Aren't you?"

"Let's just say I'm doing a favor for your sister-in-law."

"Sure you are."

"Okay, I'm going upstairs now because you're being mean to me."

Bobby thought that was worth laughing at.

"If you see my daughter, encourage her to go to the U, would you?" he said.

"She got in?"

"She got in everywhere she applied—Stanford, Tulane, Northwestern, Boston College. Do you know how much it costs to send a kid to a decent school these days? At the U, though, the tuition would be a quarter of what Northwestern charges, plus they offered her a half-ride academic scholarship."

"I remember when we went there. It was considered a backup school; anyone could get in."

"Times have changed," Bobby said. "Now they only take the best students, probably because the in-state tuition is so low. They can pick and choose."

Victoria Dunston was sitting in the center of her bed surrounded by letters, pamphlets, student handbooks, magazines, and other materials from the nine colleges and universities that had accepted her.

"Look at all this stuff," she told me. "Everybody sent me thick packages filled with information about their schools."

I reminded her of our bet.

"Don't you owe me five bucks?" I asked.

"Swear to God, McKenzie, I didn't think I would get accepted by *every* school I applied to. Most of them, sure, but not all of them. Not only that, they all offered me scholarship money. Everyone except Northwestern University. They told me they would help me get a low-interest student loan, so . . ."

Victoria picked up a glossy periodical with the name *Northwestern Magazine* printed across the top and tossed it on the floor.

"Have you made a decision yet?" I asked.

Victoria put an index finger to her lips and pointed at her bedroom door. I closed the door. She gestured at me to come close and whispered.

"I'm going to the U but I don't want Mom and Dad to know it yet," she said.

"Why not?"

"I have a plan. I'm going to talk up Tulane, where Erica is going, and Stanford and Notre Dame; get them all anxious about the tuition and room and board and travel expenses and then I'll spring it on them. I'll say 'I suppose I could go to the University of Minnesota, but . . . if I did, would I have to live at home?'"

I had to laugh at that.

"Shh," Victoria told me.

"I can't speak for your mother, but I suspect your dad will do the math very quickly and say, 'Why no, dear. No, you don't.'"

"I love my parents, McKenzie, but I gotta get out of here."

"I felt the same way when I was your age. So did your mom and dad. Neither of them lived at home when they went to school. That might help boost your argument."

"You think?"

"'Course, if things don't work out, I know where you can get a zero interest student loan and about fifty years to pay it off."

"Mom says you spoil me and Katie."

"Nina says the same thing about Erica. But you are my heirs."

"Thank you."

I picked up another magazine, this one with the title *Badger Insider*.

"Did you actually apply to the University of Wisconsin?" I asked.

"Yes, but only to annoy Dad. Although, they did offer me fifteen thousand dollars a year."

"It pays to be a good student."

"What my parents always told me."

I paged through the glossy magazine. It contained the kinds of articles you'd expect in a publication dedicated to the University of Wisconsin and its alumni, including . . .

I stopped and stared.

Badger Insider had a section with the title *Remembering Those We've Lost.*

Obituaries.

Once again, I heard Jeanette Carrell's words echoing inside my head: *Before I became a Badger, I was a Falcon.*

Before I became a Badger . . .

A Badger . . .

I actually spoke the words aloud. "Before I became a Badger . . ."

Victoria glanced up at me.

"What are you talking about?" she asked.

"I've been searching the wrong yearbooks."

I was anxious to get home. I tried not to show it, but probably I did.

Ten minutes after Nina and I entered the condominium, I was at my computer. I searched the online copies of *Badger Insider* and the more glossy *On Wisconsin* magazines. Jeanette Lee Fitch's obituary was printed in the winter 1989–1990 edition and it was even shorter than the Faribault obit:

> Jeanette Lee Fitch, Class of '78, died peacefully in her sleep
> of an undiagnosed brain aneurysm at the home of her parents
> in Faribault, Minn. She attended UW-Madison, where she
> earned a Bachelor of Business Administration degree.

I went directly to the University of Wisconsin–Madison website. The website had a portal for the UW-Libraries and I clicked on that.

That led me to yet another portal for yearbooks.

The Wisconsin University yearbooks were all available online dating back to 1886, when it was called *Trochos*. By 1889 it had been renamed *Badger*. I clicked on *Badger 1978*, the year Jeanette Lee Fitch had graduated.

The table of contents directed me to *Chapter 11. Graduates.* I clicked through until I found a section dedicated to business majors.

There she was, Jeanette L. Fitch, located right between Debra S. Fish and Daniel A. Foulks.

I started moving slowly after that, carefully examining the photographs of her fellow female students. I stayed in the business section since I knew that Jeanette Carrell had worked in business. The site had a zoom function and that helped.

When I finished with 1978, I moved on to *Badger 1979*.

And 1980.

1981.

1982.

When I reached 1986, I decided one more yearbook and then I'd go back and examine the photographs of all of the students, not just the business grads.

One more was all I needed.

There she was, Class of '87, page one hundred and forty-five, fifth row, second from the left—Luna Cifuentes.

She had long auburn hair and eyes the color of dark chocolate. Perhaps I was influenced by her name because I actually attempted to talk myself out of it. She looked Hispanic, I told myself. Jeanette Carrell with her blond hair seemed Scandinavian.

Only there was no mistake, it was her.

The shape of her eyes, the width of her mouth, her chin—it was her.

Forget her name.

It was her.

No wonder you look so damn good for your age, my inner voice said. *You aren't the age you give people. You're nine years younger.*

I did not celebrate my discovery. Instead, I quickly printed out the page because I was afraid—I don't know what I was afraid of. That the page would disappear just as she had, I suppose.

By then Nina was sound asleep in the bedroom so jumping

up and down and screaming "I got you, I got you" didn't seem appropriate. I decided to continue my hunt, typing the name Luna Cifuentes into the computer's search engine.

This time I couldn't contain myself. I half expected Nina to explode from the bedroom, but being such a sound sleeper she didn't wake when I screamed "Sonuvabitch!"

The first result the search engine found—a newspaper article that had been printed by the Cedar Rapids *Gazette* in Iowa on June 8, 2015.

25 YEARS LATER, THE GREATEST BANK ROBBERY IN CEDAR RAPIDS HISTORY REMAINS UNSOLVED
Female teller got away with $385,000

Just before closing on Friday, June 8, 1990, a bank teller named Luna Cifuentes walked into the vault of the First Trust Bank here in Cedar Rapids, filled a paper bag with $385,000 in cash, and walked out again, telling the security guard *¡Buenas noches!*

No one has seen the young woman—or the cash—since.

It was one of the biggest bank heists in Iowa lore: Cifuentes's loot would be worth $820,000 in today's dollars. The fact that no one noticed that either she or the money had gone missing until the following Monday gave Cifuentes more than a 48-hour head start on law enforcement that would spend over a quarter of a century searching for the woman.

They haven't stopped looking.

"We will find her," said Deputy United States Marshal Elliot Kane. "It has taken longer than usual, I admit. But we will find her. It's just a matter of time."

Kane pointed out that a federal grand jury had indicted Cifuentes not long after the robbery was committed. That meant the statute of limitations no longer applied in her case.

"Six years or sixty," Kane said. "We will find her and she will go to prison."

Included with the story was a photograph of Cifuentes, apparently taken from her employee ID badge. She looked exactly as she had in her college yearbook picture taken a year earlier except the angle was different and that difference proved to me without a doubt that she was Jeanette Carrell.

I had all my notes laid out on the desk in front of me. I started working the math.

Jeanette Lee Fitch died on Wednesday, November 15, 1989.

Her obituary appeared shortly after in the University of Wisconsin alumni magazine, which Luna would receive.

Luna robbed the bank on June 8, 1990, exactly five months and twenty-three days later.

I went back to the newspaper story.

Cifuentes had been well liked by her fellow employees. One co-worker said, "Luna was one of the nicest people I had ever met. She was always very kind."

This caused speculation at the time that the robbery was a spontaneous, spur-of-the-moment crime. However, when authorities raided her apartment the Monday afternoon following the robbery, they discovered that Cifuentes had not only disappeared, she had left behind her wallet containing her driver's license, credit cards, and other forms of identification.

"She had planned the crime well in advance," Kane said. "She knew exactly what she was doing."

"Luna," I said aloud, "Jeanette, J. C., whoever you are, I have to admit it—you're a clever girl."

FIFTEEN

Deputy U.S. Marshal Amy DeVries Linabery didn't care for me at all, even though we had never met before that morning; even though I had sprung for the cappuccino she was drinking at Caribou Coffee on Cedar Street in downtown St. Paul. It caused me to speculate that, in the course of checking me out, she might have heard scurrilous and inaccurate reports about my character from someone who was jealous of my many investigative successes.

Nah, that can't be it, my inner voice told me. *You're so universally loved and respected.*

The coffeehouse was virtually empty; most of the customers who had stopped in to grab a quick cup of joe before work were already at work. We were sitting at a tall table in the corner with even taller windows on two sides of us. Marshal Linabery had chosen the location; apparently Mike Swenson and I weren't welcome in her office in the Warren E. Burger Federal Building. Or at least I wasn't.

Marshal Linabery drummed her fingers lightly on the tabletop.

"It's your meeting," she said.

"May I ask what progress you've made in the killings on the

Circle?" I asked. "Have you identified the woman who was buried alongside David Carrell?"

Marshal Linabery quickly glanced at Deputy Swenson, her expression suggesting that I had grievously insulted her and she was having a hard time believing it.

"I'm not working a homicide," she said. "That's his job. If you have questions, I suggest you ask him."

"Well, in searching for Jeanette Carrell . . ."

"What do you want, McKenzie? Why was I brought here? Deputy Swenson told me that you have something important to say. Do you?"

Geez, lady, lighten up.

I gave her a long, deep theatrical sigh because—why not?— and reached for the manila envelope that I had brought to the coffeehouse. I opened it, and slid out the photograph of Jeanette Carrell taken from yesterday's St. Paul *Pioneer Press* that I had printed out. I pushed the photo in front of Linabery. I did this instead of showing her the pic on my phone because it was more dramatic.

"And?" she said.

I pulled the second photograph from the envelope, this one taken from the June 8, 2015, edition of the Cedar Rapids *Gazette* and set it next to the pic of Carrell.

Linabery and Swenson both stared at the two photographs.

After a full minute, the deputy marshal's eyes found mine.

"Talk to me," she said.

"The woman on the right is Luna Cifuentes. The photo was taken in 1990, the year she robbed a bank in Cedar Rapids, Iowa, and disappeared without a trace."

"Wait," Swenson said. "What did you say?"

Marshal Linabery stared at the photographs some more. Swenson stared at me. I had been somewhat less than forthcoming about the reason I had wanted him to arrange a meeting with a member of the North Star Fugitive Task Force and I detected that he was slightly miffed at me for keeping it a surprise.

"Are you saying that this woman and Carrell are one and the same person?" he asked. "Is that what you're telling us?"

Before I could answer, the deputy marshal muttered a few obscenities that Swenson and I weren't meant to hear followed by a couple more that we were.

"How the hell did you manage this?" she wanted to know.

I explained, emphasizing more than was probably necessary that Cifuentes had been in the wind for over thirty-two years without the U.S. Marshals catching so much as a whiff of her.

"I didn't work this case," Marshal Linabery said. "It was never on my desk."

Is she trying to explain why she hadn't IDed Cifuentes before you did?

"What about Elliot Kane?" I asked.

"He retired in 2018."

"Did you know him?"

"We met when I was coming up. He was kind of a mentor to me. He was—he was a little obsessed with this case. The one that got away, you know what I mean."

"Yes, I do," Swenson said.

Marshal Linabery gazed at him as if she wasn't sure that he did.

"So do I," I told her.

"Cifuentes was an assistant bank manager," Linabery said.

"The newspaper said she was a teller."

"No, she had a higher clearance than that, not that it mattered. The security at First Trust Bank was pretty loose. Cifuentes wasn't even fingerprinted . . ."

Which explained why her name didn't pop up when Jeanette

Carrell was fingerprinted after she was arrested for killing Charles Sainsbury; her prints weren't in the system.

"She walked into the vault right after lunch, put the money in a shopping bag, and set the bag beneath her desk," Linabery added. "There it sat all afternoon until Cifuentes walked out at closing. We have video. You say that Jeanette Fitch died five months before the robbery?"

"Closer to six," I said.

"Cifuentes obviously used that time to assume Fitch's identity and only when it was firmly in place did she make her move. That coincides with what Kane thought when he discovered that she had left her driver's license and Social Security card; that she had purposely left her life behind when she disappeared. She had obviously planned the heist well in advance. I didn't notice the similarities between that disappearance and our girl in Shoreview until now. Sonuvabitch."

"You know, I said the exact same thing," I told her.

"Carrell, Fitch, Cifuentes—she's a clever girl," Swenson said.

"Yeah, I said that, too. Marshal Linabery, I have to assume that Kane and the Marshals Service learned everything there was to know about Cifuentes prior to the robbery; where she was from, who her people were."

"Yes."

"Can you tell me?"

Linabery stared again, only there was no rancor in her eyes this time, only resignation.

"No," she said.

"No?"

"There are rules."

"So?"

"There are rules about what I can and cannot share with the public. I'm sure your friend Special Agent Wilson has explained it to you."

"On occasion."

He couldn't have been the one who poisoned Welch against you, could he? Maybe you had better stop calling him Harry, after all.

"I appreciate that you brought this to me," Marshal Linabery said. "At the same time, I don't want to see it in a newspaper. I don't want to see it on Twitter or as a Facebook post."

"You're saying I can't share information with the public, either?" I asked.

"McKenzie, please."

"I promise."

"Thank you."

"I will keep trying to find her, though."

Linabery's response was to snatch the manila envelope off the tabletop and fill it with the two photographs.

"I'm going to keep these," she said.

"Sure."

Marshal Linabery rose from her chair, gathered her belongings, and rested a hand oh so briefly on my wrist.

"Thank you for the coffee, McKenzie," she said.

Does that mean we're friends now?

After Linabery left the Caribou, I spoke to Swenson.

"That should have gone better," I told him.

"What did you think was going to happen? The marshals had been searching for this woman for thirty-two years and you found her in three days. Did you think they would be thrilled?"

"Two days and, yeah, I thought they'd be pleased. Wouldn't you?"

"Professional pride, ever hear of it?"

"Once or twice. Speaking of which—Mike?"

"What?"

"Have you identified the woman who was buried with David Carrell?"

Swenson gave me a stern look, pointed a finger in my face, and slowly let both fall.

"No," he said.

"No?"

"I've already heard everything you're going to say, okay? We have nothing, no missing persons; nothing that suggests a woman approximately five foot four with blond hair went missing on or around June eighth, 1995."

"June eighth, '95?" I asked.

"What about it?"

"That's the date David Carrell went missing?"

"Yeah."

"I didn't know the exact date."

"What difference does it make?"

"It was the fifth anniversary of the bank job in Cedar Rapids."

"Oh, man. You're right."

"Coincidence?"

Swenson shook his head.

"Probably not," he told me. "But when I say we have no woman who went missing on or around that date, I don't just mean Minnesota. I mean everywhere in the country."

"Which means she wasn't reported missing."

"You think? We decided to try using forensic genetic genealogies searching, you know, upload the vic's DNA on the various ancestry databases. I don't know if that'll lead anywhere or even if the sites will accept our request. We'll see."

"What about David Carrell?" I asked.

"Jeanette reported him missing late in the morning on June ninth."

"Not the day of?"

"According to Dominic Belden's report, she said the fact that David didn't return home immediately after work didn't mean he was missing."

"Uh-huh."

"All we know for sure is that no one reports seeing him since he left his office on the eighth," Swenson said.

"Where did he work?"

"Where Dominic Belden said he worked, North Country Properties."

"Which was owned at the time by Adam Berenson, the son of that well-known gangster Omer Berenson," I said.

"The way it was explained to me, old man Berenson founded North Country. It's what they call an LLC, a limited liability company, and he used it to finance the projects he developed at the Polachek Companies. North Country also occasionally financed projects by other developers, including our good friends the Sainsburys. Berenson kept North Country and Polachek separate so he could reduce his tax liability and protect both Polachek and his own personal assets in case someone sued him, and he was sued often."

"Uh-huh."

"If you like that . . ."

"What?"

"The medical examiner has determined a cause of death." Deputy Swenson used the fingers on his right hand to form a gun and pretended to fire it twice. "Double tap to the back of the head. Downward angle like they were kneeling. Both of them. We found the bullets with the remains. Thirty-twos. Very professional."

"A mob hit?"

Swenson shrugged.

"Geez," I said. "What the hell happened?"

"What I would like to know."

"Have you been able to contact any of Carrell's co-workers at North Country?"

"We're working the problem, the problem being that Berenson folded the company in 2001. His business and employee records were disposed of seven years later."

I leaned back in my chair and stared at the ceiling.

"Find the girl," I said.

"Find the girl and then find a way to make her talk," Swenson said. "Right now I don't know what else to do."

I found myself repeating the same words I told Nina three days earlier—the secret to finding a fugitive is knowing their past. Except the U.S. Marshals probably knew every aspect of Luna Cifuentes's personal history yet had not been able to find her. What made me think I could do better, I mean, besides my immense ego?

You can try, can't you? my inner voice said. *You can at least do that.*

Why should I?

She's in the wind because of you.

No. She was prepared to run months, perhaps even decades before I came along. She was going to run the moment that William Sainsbury won his court case and sent his excavator up the hill.

You made it easier by getting that GPS tracker off her ankle.

Don't put that on me. One thing had nothing to do with the other.

Still . . .

Still, I told myself.

What about Bethany Gilman . . . ?

What about her?

And all the other women on the Circle, J. C.'s girls? They need answers.

Doesn't mean it's on me to provide them.

I spent a lot of time wandering around my condominium after that. I watched a little ESPN. I stared though the tall windows at St. Anthony Falls; microwaved and ate a couple of Polish sausages; started reading William Kent Krueger's new book. Only the pull was too much to resist and eventually I ended up sitting in front of my computer.

I used the search engines to find whatever was available about Luna Cifuentes. I discovered an influencer on Instagram, a manager on LinkedIn, a graphic designer on Facebook, a high school girl with a few hundred followers on Twitter, and someone named Gerson Luna Cifuentes, who posted a music playlist on SoundCloud. Nearly all of the other results were about a woman who robbed a bank in Iowa thirty-two years ago.

Most of them came from media outlets ranging from *U.S. News & World Report* to *The New York Times* to *The Des Moines Register*. Nearly all of their stories merely rehashed the details found in the news articles printed by the Cedar Rapids *Gazette*. One of the details was a woman identified as either a co-worker, a longtime friend, or a college classmate named either LuAnne Kinney or LuAnne Pederson who had insisted that Luna was "kind," "a devoted friend," "an honest woman who never bent the rules," and "one of the nicest people I had ever met."

I looked her up—she still lived in Cedar Rapids—found a phone number and gave her a call.

"My name is McKenzie," I said when she answered. "I wonder if you can help me?"

"What do you need, hon?" she asked.

"It's about Luna Cifuentes."

LuAnne thought that was funny.

"Already?" she said. "I usually get asked about her around June and then only when there's an anniversary of the bank robbery coming up."

"It's a little more complicated than that this time," I said.

"In what way?"

I flashed on Deputy U.S. Marshal Amy DeVries Linabery and her insistence that information about Luna not get out to the public and wondered how much I could tell LuAnne without getting into trouble.

"We think we found her . . ." I said.

"You did?"

"Then lost her again."

LuAnne thought that was funny, too.

"Butterfingers," she said.

"I'm hoping you can answer some questions," I said.

"Sure, why not? Luna's become my chief claim to fame even though I built one of the first woman-owned financial planning firms in Iowa. You'd think she was Martha Place or something."

"Martha Place? I don't know who that is."

"She was the first woman to die in the electric chair. Female criminals have gotten to be a hobby with me. Tell you what, hon, why don't you come on over?"

"It'll take awhile," I said. "I'm in the Twin Cities."

"Really? Are you saying that's where Luna ran off to? I'll be. Well, come on down. Call before you get here so I have time to get home and put the coffee on."

Google maps predicted it would take me four hours and eleven minutes to drive to Cedar Rapids, yet I managed to do it in three hours and thirty-nine minutes. It had helped that I had driven there before. Cedar Rapids was the second-largest city in Iowa and among its 138,000 residents lived the Minnesota Twins Class A minor league baseball team. The Cedar Rapids Kernels played in Veterans Memorial Stadium, which was only a ten-minute drive from LuAnne Kinney Pederson's house on Old Orchard Road. The house was large, made of brick, and had a garage built for two cars and a boat, which made me wonder, where would you use a boat in Iowa? There weren't any lakes that I had noticed.

When I met her, Jeanette Carrell told me that she was pushing sixty-five, although she was actually fifty-six and looked even younger than that. LuAnne was, in fact, fifty-six years old and looked her age. Except when she smiled. When she smiled she looked like she was fourteen. And she smiled all the time.

She answered the door before I knocked and bade me come inside. I noticed two things right off. The first was that while the house had an expertly-landscaped-be-sure-to-wipe-your-feet-affluent-people-live-here vibe on the outside, inside it was all about creature comfort, with furniture that people actually used instead of admired from afar. The second was an autographed photograph of LuAnne standing with Byron Buxton, the Minnesota Twins All-Star centerfielder and former Kernel, Buxton dressed in the team's white and green home uniform. The photograph was framed and hanging on the wall just inside the doorway so that a visitor couldn't possibly miss it. Buxton had autographed it: *To sweet Lu from Byron.*

I like her already, my inner voice advised me.

"You made good time," LuAnne told me.

"The traffic was light."

"I have coffee brewing. I told you I would make coffee, but considering how fast you drive, I bet you'd rather have a beer."

"I'll have what you're having," I said.

"Well, then . . ."

She pulled two bottles from her refrigerator, popped the caps, and handed one to me—an IPA bottled by the Iowa Brewing Company with the unlikely name Surf Zombies. And we talk about Minnesota Nice.

LuAnne took a long pull from her beer bottle and sat at her kitchen table. She was dressed in a blue business suit, the skirt ending several inches below her knees, and I remembered what she said about building a financial planning firm.

"Thank you for taking time off from your business," I told her.

"One of the advantages of being the boss," she said. "So, what do you want to know, McKenzie? Why did you drive all the way to Cedar Rapids?"

"First, tell me what to call you. The newspaper stories don't seem to agree."

"When I was a kid it was LuAnne Kinney. After I married it became LuAnne Kinney Pederson. When I started my own business, I evolved into Ms. Pederson. Sitting at my kitchen table, though, I'm just plain old Lu."

"Neither plain nor old, I think."

"Listen to you. Are you going to try to sell me something, now? Want me to invest in crypto?"

"None of that," I said.

"Well, then . . ."

"Something else the newspapers don't agree on, your relationship with Luna Cifuentes."

"We were friends. We met in school, the University of Wisconsin, both of us business majors. We hung out together. Partied. There was a lot of partying going on in Madison. When I enrolled my parents freaked. They kept telling me that Wisconsin had a reputation for being a party school. Well, yeah. One of the reasons I went there. Luna, she partied with the best of us.

The difference was, she had discipline. If she said she was going to stop drinking after two beers, she stopped drinking after two beers. The woman never gave in to temptation. Except for that one time when she robbed a bank."

LuAnne laughed at her joke and I joined along.

"So, hon, you said you found Luna and then you lost her, again?" she asked. "Tell me about that."

I told her Jeanette Carrell's story; told LuAnne everything that she could learn herself simply by searching the internet for Carrell's name. I ended the story by suggesting, in as vague a manner as possible, that after she disappeared we uncovered additional evidence suggesting that Jeanette might actually be Luna.

"Honey, I think you made a mistake," LuAnne said. "Luna would never hurt-hurt anyone, not like that. She might steal all your hard-earned cash, but murder someone? No, no, not my girl."

"She hasn't been your girl for a very long time," I reminded her.

"People don't change, not like that."

I could have given LuAnne twenty minutes on how people sometimes do change and exactly like that, only what would be the point?

"Tell me about your girl," I said instead.

"You tell me. How did she look?"

"She looks terrific. She has short blond hair now. At least she did."

LuAnne laughed at that.

"That's funny," she said. "I'll tell you why in a minute. What else?"

"She was well loved by most of her neighbors, especially the girls who grew up on the Circle. Apparently, she inspired them."

"Yeah, that's my Luna. She was the same way in school. She

was all about being your own woman and not letting anything keep you from being the person you want to be. That's why she became so frustrated."

"In what way?"

"She graduated with a business degree from Wisconsin; her grades were a lot better than mine, I can tell you that, and I was in the top ten percent. Only she couldn't land a decent job. She'd get plenty of interviews based on her résumé, but when the interviews were done it was don't call us, we'll call you. This was the late eighties, you need to understand. Women simply were not taken seriously in business, in finance; it didn't matter where you graduated from. We're still not, except it was far worse back then. Especially for women of color. Luna's skin was no darker than mine, but her name was, if you know what I mean."

I said I did.

"Look at the statistics," LuAnne added. "Women comprise over half of the entry-level financial services workforce, yet we fill only one-quarter of all management positions and of that number only one in twenty-five is a woman of color. That's today. Imagine what it was like thirty years ago.

"It was hard," LuAnne added. "It was hard for me and even harder for Luna. I remember her telling me more than once that if she had blond hair and blue eyes she'd be running General Motors. That's why I laughed before. I told her she should dye her hair and get contact lenses. She thought life should be fairer than that. From what you told me, she must have changed her mind."

"How did she come to work in Cedar Rapids?" I asked.

"That was on me. I'm from here. When I graduated, I came back home and looked for work and couldn't find any until I landed an assistant manager gig at a bank."

"First Trust Bank?"

"The one and only," LuAnne said. "I had kept in touch with Luna after graduating and I knew she was having a tough time so when another assistant manager position opened, I recommended her. Why the manager needed two assistants, I didn't know. Anyway, Luna got the gig, but I knew she wasn't happy about it. She thought she should be doing better. So did I. We both kept sending out résumés, sometimes applying for the same job; covering for each other so we could sneak away for interviews. Nothing ever came of it. I decided that the only way to get ahead was to start my own business. Luna decided to rob a bank."

"None of what you told me was ever reported in the newspapers," I said.

"That would have made her a role model for little girls everywhere, wouldn't it? Can't have that, McKenzie. A Robin Hood–like woman sticking it to the man? Better to portray her as a greedy thief than a frustrated feminist."

"Where was Luna from?" I asked.

"Well, hon, that's where things get a little complicated. The U.S. Marshals—they interview me every couple of years. For all I know, they've also had my phone tapped in case Luna decided to call me. Anyway, they've always thought that I might have been an accomplice because she and I were close in those days. They thought that I might have helped her in some way. They never actually came out and said that, but it was always the impression that they gave me. Partly it was my fault, I suppose. Once I recovered from the shock of what Luna had done, I found myself hoping that she would get away with it. I might even have said so out loud.

"In the beginning, it wasn't the marshals, though," LuAnne added. "It was the FBI asking questions. They wanted to know where Luna was from. I told them. They called me a liar. I asked what they were talking about. They told me that Luna was not born in Stevens Point, Wisconsin. That there was no birth certificate issued in her name in Portage County and I'm telling them I don't know what county she was born in, I only know that she told me that she was from Stevens Point. What was I supposed to have done when she told me that? Argue with her? McKenzie, I saw Luna's driver's license. Back in those days we would get carded when we went into a bar. Yet the feds kept insisting that no one by Luna's name ever lived in Stevens Point or the entire state of Wisconsin, for that matter."

"Wait, Lu," I said. "Are you saying that Luna Cifuentes was a ghost, too?"

"A ghost?"

I explained.

"What can I say, McKenzie? That's what the U.S. Marshals, after they took over the case, that's what the marshals told me."

I drank most of my Surf Zombie while I digested that bit of information. LuAnne allowed me to do it in silence.

"Tell me a story about Luna," I said.

"A story?"

"Things you've done together. What you learned about her while doing those things."

We drank a second beer while LuAnne told me several tales, most of them funny. One in particular stood out.

"Spring break, our junior year," she said. "Instead of going south, going to Florida with all the knot heads, guess where we went? We went north. We went to Toronto in Canada. There were seven or eight of us. Eight. We had just the best time. It helped that the drinking age was nineteen and we didn't drive anywhere. It was all public transportation.

"I remember we went to the top of the space needle, not that the Canadians would ever call it that. They call it the CN Tower. It's over eighteen-hundred-feet high. At the very top, they have a glass floor. You can stand on the floor and look down and it's as scary as hell. I couldn't do it. I couldn't make myself stand on the glass floor. All my friends could do it. Luna was hopping up and down like she was trying to break the glass and laughing and I'm like, would you please stop doing that. She told me that I was just like her grandmother. She said her grandmother had taken her to the top of the tower when she was just a child and she did the same thing, jumped up and down on the glass, and her grandmother nearly had a heart attack. I don't blame her."

LuAnne told a couple more stories, yet it was clear that I was starting to wear out my welcome. We finished our Surf Zombies and I thanked her for her time.

"I'm not sure what to tell you, McKenzie," LuAnne said. "Part of me, a very large part, hopes that you never find Luna. At the same time—she's not a murderer, McKenzie, but . . . I don't know. I only know that I liked Luna very much. She was my friend. Is my friend. If there is any way I can help her, I will."

I drove home. It took me longer than the drive down to Cedar Rapids because night had fallen. I have a laminated card that I keep next to my driver's license in my wallet proclaiming I was a proud member of the St. Paul Police Department—"retired"— and that was usually enough to get me out of speeding tickets. However, I ignored the traffic laws only when I could see what was directly in front of me and driving back to the Cities all I could make out was that part of the freeway illuminated by my headlights and the face of Luna Cifuentes at twenty-five and Jeanette Carrell at sixty-four.

I parked in the ramp in the basement of the building in downtown Minneapolis where my condominium was located and took the elevator to the lobby where I would switch to a different set of elevators that would take me to my place. I understood the security concerns that went into this arrangement. On the other hand, if you were trying to muscle, say, a Steinway grand piano upstairs, you might be less than thrilled by it.

As I stepped off the elevator, a security guard called my name.

"Hey, McKenzie."

The pair of security guards working the two P.M. to midnight shift four days a week were friends of mine. Smith and Jones had explained when Nina and I first moved into the building that they had checked me out—acting under building management's orders, of course; it was SOP for all new tenants—and they knew who I was and what I did. They had also made it clear that they were ready, willing, and able to assist me should ever the need arise—"The job can get so boring," they told me—and sometimes they did in exchange for Wild tickets or a case of very good Scotch or some other form of contraband that I would "find" in the hallway or on an elevator that I dutifully turned in to the Lost and Found because the firm Smith and Jones worked for had a strict policy against employees accepting gratuities of any kind from tenants.

For the longest time, I couldn't tell Smith and Jones apart without reading their name tags; they were always dressed in the identical dark blue suits, crisp white shirts, and dark blue ties of their profession. Now I could but sometimes pretended not to. It was a running gag between us, only tonight I wasn't in the mood.

"Guys," I said. "What's going on?"

"You tell us," Jones said.

"Did something happen that I should know about?"

"You had a visitor. Man walked into the lobby claiming to be a friend of yours and demanded that we let him upstairs."

"We didn't, of course," Smith said. "Especially since he refused to leave his name."

"We did call up, though," Jones said. "You didn't answer, so we told him you weren't home. He didn't take the news graciously."

"No," Smith said. "He didn't. Before he left he said, 'We know who you are, we know what you're doing, and we want it to stop.'"

"He said 'we,' not 'I'?"

"Yep."

"He didn't leave a name?"

"Nope."

"Can you describe him?"

Jones gestured for me to walk around the reception desk. They had several computer screens there displaying what the security cameras picked up in and around the building. He punched a couple of buttons and the large screen directly in front of me began to show taped footage of a well-dressed young man walking through the building's lobby doors and marching to the reception desk. He was about six feet tall, with blond hair, blue eyes, and a smile that suggested he knew things that you didn't. When he reached the desk, he stopped, looked straight up at the security camera above it, and smiled as if he knew it was there and wanted to make sure it caught his best side.

Jones hit another button and the image froze on the screen.

"His name is Tony," I said. "I have no idea what his last name is. He's the nephew of Adam Berenson, the real estate tycoon, who is the son of Omer Berenson, that well-known gangster."

"Gangster?" Jones said.

He and Smith glanced at each other and back at me.

"I didn't know there was organized crime in Minnesota," Smith said.

"Guys, don't get me started."

Tony was a nitwit; I had no doubt of that. Time and experience had taught me, though, that nitwits can cause an awful lot of damage. That's why, instead of going upstairs, I drove to Rickie's. I searched the parking lot and didn't find him or a black Mercedes-Benz S550 with tinted windows. I went inside and looked some more.

It wasn't until I was sure Tony wasn't there that I sat at the downstairs bar. The bartender knew me.

"Summit EPA or Maker's Mark?" she asked.

I went with Summit Ale.

A moment later, Nina found me.

She set a hand on my shoulder and said, "I didn't expect to see you here tonight. Something going on?"

"Just my usual paranoia."

"Your usual paranoia has kept me out of harm's way on numerous occasions."

"Only fair since my usual meddling in other people's business is what puts you in harm's way."

Nina sat on the stool next to mine.

"I'll let you know if I have a complaint. Should I have a complaint?"

I told her about Tony.

"So, I don't have a complaint," Nina said.

"A man doesn't want me to find Jeanette Carrell or Luna Cifuentes or whatever she calls herself now. The man might be dangerous. At the same time, Bobby Dunston, and probably the U.S. Marshals Service, claim that the only reason I'm chasing

Carrell in the first place is to satisfy my ego, which, let's face it, is a pretty stupid reason to do anything."

"Your point is?"

"Nina, the more I learn about the woman, the more I like her. This is a woman who robbed a bank. This is a woman who might have killed three human beings, plus God knows what other crimes she might have committed under her various disguises. Yet I like her. Nearly everyone I've met who knows her personally, they like her, too. I don't know if I want to find her anymore."

"But you will."

"Will I?"

"It's like watching a bad movie—you stick with it because you want to see how it ends."

SIXTEEN

The woman in question had at least two histories. Luna Cifuentes's history must not have led anywhere or the U.S. Marshals would have scooped her up long before now—they really are very good at what they do. I decided to concentrate on Jeanette Carrell's past instead. I had a list of all the people who knew her on the Circle; her girls. Only I wasn't sure that they could give me any more than I already had.

So, early the next morning, I studied all the news articles about Carrell in the online editions of the St. Paul *Pioneer Press*, Minneapolis *StarTribune*, and *MinnPost*, not to mention the newsfeed on the website of *Minnesota Public Radio*. A reporter for the *Strib* had interviewed the "elderly' sister of David Carrell at her home in White Bear Lake. I also knocked on her door, hoping she could tell me more than she had the reporter. Maybe when I was about ten years old I might have thought being sixty-three was elderly, yet at the tender age of forty-five I now knew better.

Her name was Danielle Carrell-Mowry, although she insisted that I call her Dani. I mentioned the "elderly" reference as a joke; an attempt to get her on my side. She didn't so much as crack a smile.

"It's just another example of age discrimination," she said.

Dani is a serious woman, my inner voice told me. *Treat her that way.*

"I apologize for intruding on you," I said. "I realize that this must be a difficult time."

"At least I now know what happened to my brother. My parents died without ever knowing. 'Course it was probably all explained to them when they got to heaven. Isn't that how it's supposed to work? All of our questions will be answered when we get to heaven?"

"So we've been told."

"I never actually believed that David was dead," Dani said. "Not once in all these years. Not until last week. Instead, I believed that J. C. had been right all along. I was sure of it."

"Sure about what?"

"After he disappeared, J. C. kept insisting that David had abandoned her; that she had driven him away, somehow. That she was too selfish. That she was too demanding. That she wasn't a good wife. I remember arguing with her at the time, telling her that David had probably been killed for the money in his pockets and his body thrown into the Mississippi River or something. Yet I had always believed she was right, that David had deserted her."

The expression on my face must have suggested my confusion.

"Ever since they found David's body and the police and reporters started coming around I've been wondering what to tell them," Dani said. "I suppose after all this time it doesn't really matter. My brother was killed. J. C. killed him. That's all that matters."

"I don't understand," I said. "Why did you believe Jeanette when she said that she drove David away? Why did you try to talk her out it?"

"I tried to talk her out of it because I didn't want her to know the truth, what I thought was the truth. McKenzie, I loved J. C. She was the sister I never had. Smart and strong and loyal—she was so loyal to me. When I was having trouble in my first marriage, my parents took my husband's side. I wasn't attentive enough to his needs, they said. J. C. wouldn't hear it. She stood up for me against all comers, including her own husband."

Dani told me more; told me how Jeanette remained steadfast during the divorce proceedings and later encouraged her to pursue a relationship with her current husband, who was ten years Dani's junior. She told me other stories, too. I had a burning question to ask, yet I put it on simmer while Dani told me her stories because, after all, that's why I had come, to hear her stories.

"J. C. never really spoke about her family," Dani said. "Never told us about her childhood except to say that she was from Faribault and that her people came from somewhere in Canada that I never heard of."

"Sault Ste. Marie?" I asked.

"Yes. Do you know where that is?"

"Near where Lake Superior, Michigan, and Huron join together."

"I had always thought that J. C. must have had a terrible childhood. Whenever it came up in conversation, she always changed the subject. It made me think that her family was, well, messed up. I remember the first Christmas we shared together; everyone gathering at my grandmother's house. It was absolute chaos. My aunts and uncles were there. My cousins. Children running around. Family members squabbling even as they were giving gifts to each other. My grandfather arguing with my grandmother over whether we should have had turkey or ham; my grandmother telling him if he had wanted turkey so bad, he should have cooked it. J. C. was standing there in the center of it all with tears in her eyes. She was actually weeping and I was sure that we had ruined her Christmas. Except the opposite was true. She told us that this was what she had always imagined Christmas should be like, family being a family. That night we all gathered around Grandma's tree and sang carols. We had never done that before, yet it became a tradition because of J. C. and we kept doing it even after David disappeared. After that, after David disappeared . . . J. C. and I stayed close for a few years, yet gradually we drifted apart. I hadn't seen or spoken to her for the longest time."

The burning question was starting to singe my brain. Finally, I asked it.

"Dani," I said, "you told me that when Jeanette claimed that she drove David away, you tried to talk her out of it because you didn't want her to know the truth, or at least what you thought was the truth at the time. What was the truth?"

"That David really did desert her for another woman and I didn't want J. C. to blame herself."

"What made you so sure?"

"He was cheating on her," Dani said. "I knew it. My parents knew it. We tried to talk him out of it. 'Are you insane? Where are you going to find a woman who's better for you than she is?' Before they were married, she was called Jeanette. Afterward, because of his last name, she became J. C. She had changed her identity because of him. What more did he want?

"At the time, I was sure that J. C. knew what was going on, too; knew that David was cheating on her. I changed my mind after he disappeared because of the way she behaved; the way she seemed so lost, so alone. Now, of course, I know that she knew exactly what David was doing. That's why she killed him and the woman he was with."

"What can you tell me about this?" I asked.

"There's not much to say," Dani told me. "It's like I told the deputies—David was a cheater. It was a chronic thing with him. As soon as he became involved with one woman, he'd have to get involved with someone else. He never had one girlfriend. It was always two or more. I don't know if it was insecurity or the simple fact that he was so good-looking he could have anyone he wanted and therefore he felt he was allowed to have anyone he wanted. Perhaps not anyone, but quite a few."

Bethany said he looked like a movie star, my inner voice reminded me.

"Even my girlfriends from high school and college wanted to sleep with him," Dani said. "His first wife, Lauren, lasted two years. David started cheating on her the week after they returned from their honeymoon. Then J. C. came along and she was so beautiful and so smart and so kind and everyone thought he had hit the jackpot, that he couldn't possibly want anything more. For three years, he didn't. He stayed faithful. At least as far as we knew. Only what do they say about leopards and spots? It's like he couldn't help himself."

"Who was the woman?" I asked. "Do you know?"

"No. I never met her. I only saw her that one time sitting in his car. Another blonde. She was pretty. She wasn't J. C., though. Not even close. I think she was older, too. When I asked David about it, he told me to mind my own business. God, what was he thinking?"

"When did you learn . . . ?"

"You're asking the same questions that the deputies asked," Dani told me. "The reason I went to his house, J. C. was on a business trip and she said she couldn't trust David to water her gardens. She loved to garden. Her plants, my God. As I pulled into the driveway, David and the woman were pulling out. The SOB had screwed his girlfriend in his wife's house. How low was that? A month later, he was gone."

"You never suspected Jeanette?" I said.

"Never. Even though they found the bodies under the gazebo—I had been to the gazebo so many times, too. Even though they found the bodies there, I still have a hard time believing J. C. is guilty."

You and me both.

I asked more questions, mostly about Jeanette's background—"Anything you can remember; anything you can tell me," I said.

Dani did the best that she could.

"It's funny," she said. "You think you know someone and then you learn that you don't know them at all."

I thanked her for her time and Dani led me to her front door. I left her house and started walking toward my Mustang. Dani stood in the doorway and watched. When I was halfway there, she opened the doorway and called to me.

"McKenzie," she said. "Hey, McKenzie."

Dani walked quickly from her doorway to where I was standing.

"I don't know where it came from, but I just remembered—Sue."

"What?"

"The woman's name. It's Sue. I know because—I just remembered when I was arguing with David about his cheating, he said 'What Sue and I do is none of your damn business.'"

"Sue?"

"Yes."

"Short for Susan?"

"He just said Sue."

"David didn't mention her last name?"

"No. Not to me, anyway. Sorry."

"Maybe it'll come to you."

"I'm going to call the deputy. He said I should call him if I remembered anything."

"So will I."

I called Ramsey County Sheriff's Deputy Sergeant Michael Swenson from my Mustang and told him what I had learned.

"Sue something," he repeated.

"According to Dani Carrell-Mowry," I said.

"The woman just called and told me the same thing."

"She said she would. I just wanted to make sure."

"Why?" Swenson said. "So you could annoy me as much as you did the U.S. Marshals?"

"Mike . . . ?"

"No, it's okay. I'm glad you called. This might help us, assuming the woman remembered correctly. It has been awhile, after all."

"Perhaps Adam Berenson would remember a Sue something who worked for him," I suggested.

"Berenson doesn't remember crap."

"You've already interviewed him, I take it."

"He gave us all of ten minutes of his valuable time," Swenson said, "and only, I suppose, because he didn't want his name appearing in the newspaper along with a story saying that he wasn't cooperating fully with the investigation."

"Was he cooperating?" I asked.

"He said he didn't know Jeanette Carrell, barely remembered David Carrell, and had almost nothing to do with North Country Properties, that he closed it down twenty-five years ago—if you call that cooperation. He also said he only kept the company's records for the seven years required by the IRS before dumping them. Sorry, he said."

"And yet . . ."

"And yet, what?" Swenson asked.

I explained that Berenson's nephew Tony had come to my condominium the evening before; I recited the message he had left with the security detail.

"I wonder," Swenson said.

"Wonder what?"

"I'm going to call Berenson and ask if he remembers a Sue something working for North Country Properties and when he says he doesn't, I'm going to mention that we have video footage of his nephew coming to your condominium to threaten you. I wonder what he'll say."

"He'll say he doesn't know what the hell you're talking about."

"Let's find out."

"Mike," I said. Only he didn't hear me. He had already hung up.

I returned to my condominium and slipped outside onto the balcony. I was frightened by heights; the idea of stepping onto the glass floor at the CN Tower in Toronto would have freaked me out at least as much as it had LuAnne Kinney Pederson. To lessen the freak, I sat in a chair pressed hard against the building's wall as far away from the railing as possible so I couldn't see the ground. Except for a perceptible increase in my heart rate, I was able to cope.

It was only ten in the morning, yet I found myself sipping from a bottle of Summit Extra Pale Ale, brewed in St. Paul, Minnesota, my hometown, thank you very much. In my head, I kept repeating the line I had been reciting lately to anyone who would listen—the secret to finding a fugitive is knowing their past.

What do you know about Luna Cifuentes?

She isn't afraid of heights.

Besides that?

She had a Wisconsin driver's license, but she wasn't born in Wisconsin, according to what the FBI told Hixson.

Where was she born?

I don't know, but . . . She spoke Spanish and had a Hispanic-sounding name, so—Mexico?

She told LuAnne she had danced on the glass floor of the CN Tower when she was a child. Could her family have been from Canada?

It's possible, if what she told LuAnne was true. On the other hand, I've been to Toronto a couple of times and I'm not from Canada.

Or Mexico.

I sipped more Summit Ale.

What do we know about Jeanette Carrell?

People liked and trusted her.

Besides that?

She loved to garden.

And?

Sault Ste. Marie. She told me that her grandmother was from Sault Ste. Marie. She told Danielle Carrell-Mowry that her family was from Sault Ste. Marie, too.

According to LuAnne, Luna's grandmother nearly had a heart attack while she jumped up and down on the glass of the CN Tower.

Her grandmother from Sault Ste. Marie?

Could Luna-slash-Jeanette have gone back there?

Why?

Why not? Most fugitives stay close to home, or so you've always been told.

Sault Ste. Marie hasn't been her home for at least thirty-five years, assuming we have Luna-slash-Jeanette's age correct, which is iffy at best.

So, no one would be looking for her there.

We don't know that. We don't know why she would have left in the first place. Besides, what would she be going back to?

A house.

A house?

The woman loves to garden. Wherever she went, she'd buy a house so she could garden to her heart's content.

Carrell was worth more than three million when she went on the run. She could easily afford to buy a house, even in this market.

Hell, she might already have closed. You can buy a house over the internet, can't you?

I pulled my cell phone from my pocket and scrolled through my contacts until I found a female realtor with the unlikely name of Moose Giannetti. On her business cards and literature she had printed the tagline: IF YOU HAVE TO VAMOOSE, CALL MOOSE! I called. She answered a few moments later.

"McKenzie, it's nice to hear from you," she said. "Have I thanked you for sending that nice couple to me that was looking for a house in Woodbury?"

"Yes, you did, and so did they. They love their new place, although I haven't actually been invited to see it, so . . ."

"So, what can I do for you?" Moose asked.

"Let's say, for argument's sake, I wanted to learn the names of everyone who bought a house in the past three months in Sault Ste. Marie, how would I go about it?"

"The names of the owners?"

"Yes."

"I don't think you can," Moose said. "Well, you can. You can go to the county property tax records and look up the addresses of the houses you want and that'll give you the names of the owners and their tax records. You'll need to wait until the tax records are updated, though, however long that takes. I don't know how long that takes. Sault Ste. Marie, is that even in Minnesota?"

"It's in Canada."

"I have no idea how it works in Canada, but I'd be surprised if it's that much different than how it works down here. I know, for example—I have access to the local MLS. MLS means multiple listing service. It gives me—it gives all licensed realtors access to the addresses and sales prices of all the homes that are bought and sold in the Twin Cities area so we can have an understanding of what's going on in our market. I know they have the same thing in Canada. Only individual names, that's not something that's easily accessible."

"Yes, well, if it was easy everyone would do it."

"Do what?"

"Moose, is it possible to buy a house over the internet?"

"The title company would need proof of identification, something that could be confirmed by a notary, but if the buyer had the proper financing and they were able to close using one of those companies that allows you to sign documents electronically, I don't see why not."

I returned to my computer yet again and quickly discovered that there were actually two Sault Ste. Maries, one a city of about 14,000 people on the Upper Peninsula of Michigan and the other a city of 75,000 directly across the St. Marys River in Ontario, Canada.

By visiting this website and that, I managed to learn the addresses and sales prices of just over one hundred houses that had been sold in the past six months on both sides of the border. Concentrating on small houses with big yards in less urban neighborhoods, I managed to whittle that number down to thirty-two possibilities that I thought might appeal to a woman who wanted to be left more or less alone.

Now what?

You need to go up there.

To do what, knock on doors?

Yes.

Nina isn't going to like it.

As it turned out, Nina didn't care.

"If that's what you want to do, go 'head," she told me.

"Seriously?"

"Did you think I was going to argue with you?"

"A little bit, yeah."

"McKenzie, I know better than to interfere when you're on a mission. You are on a mission, aren't you?"

"I think of it more as a quest."

"Of course you do. How far is Sault Ste. Marie, anyway?"

"About five hundred and fifty miles."

"Are you going to fly?" Nina asked.

"With all the COVID restrictions airlines are imposing these days, not to mention Canada, plus I'm going to need a car when I get there . . ."

"You're going to drive?"

"Yeah, I think so. It'll only take eight and a half hours."

"When are you leaving?"

"I'm already packed."

Nina thought that was funny.

"Drive carefully," she told me.

I stopped at the first hotel I came to just inside the city limits of the Michigan version of Sault Ste. Marie, a Best Western located at I-75 and Three Mile Road. It was surrounded by a Wendy's, Burger King, Arby's, and Domino's Pizza joint, only I had already consumed enough fast food at that point that my heart felt like it had grown three sizes larger and not in a good way, like the Grinch who stole Christmas. Fortunately, there was an Applebee's just down the road, and while that wasn't a vast improvement, they at least served alcohol.

I was drinking a Killian's Irish Red while I sat at the bar and mapped my route for the next morning. There were nine addresses I needed to check out on the Michigan side of the border and while I was hoping for the best, I was also planning for the worst. To cross the border into Canada, I not only needed my passport and proof of at least two vaccinations, which I had, I also needed a negative COVID test taken within the past seventy-two hours. I asked the bartender where I could get one. He directed me to a pharmacy that he said had done well by him. It was open until ten P.M. and after I finished my Bourbon Street Steak I headed over there. The woman wearing a KN-95 mask who swabbed my nose was both efficient and gracious. She told me I should have a result by the next afternoon.

I thanked her.

The Best Western's complimentary breakfast the next morning proved to be just as unappetizing as you'd expect during COVID. I had my choice of prepackaged breakfast sandwiches, burritos, dry cereals, muffins, pastry, yogurt, and fruit. Instead, I ordered an Egg McMuffin from the drive-thru at McDonald's. At least it was warm, I told myself, and not far from the first address on my list, a split-level near the intersection of Marquette and Kimbell Street.

The house was owned by a young couple, both of them literally walking to their car parked in their driveway when I arrived. I told them I was looking for a woman named Luna Cifuentes who I thought might live there. They told me they had moved into the house two months ago and had no idea who I was talking about. I thanked them for their time and drove off.

It was pretty much the same scenario at the second address near the Memorial Athletic Field except that the husband had already left for work even though it was a Saturday morning, leaving his wife to shake her head at my questions.

No one was home at a house that looked like a small church complete with bell tower on the east side of the Lake Superior State University campus or on the west side at a delightfully quirky two-bedroom, one-and-a-half-bath cottage that appeared as if it had been designed by a kid with an Etch A Sketch. I gave both addresses a check mark in my notebook, telling myself that I'd need to return later that afternoon.

Which gave me nearly the entire day to kill because learning that Luna-slash-Jeanette wasn't living at any of the other five addresses on my list took all of ninety minutes. I returned to the Best Western.

I was watching ESPN because what else was I going to do, when I received an email from the pharmacy I had visited the evening before. Apparently, I was COVID-free. Armed with that information, my vaccination card, and passport, I rushed to my Mustang. I jumped back on I-75 and followed it across the Sault Ste. Marie International Bridge to the port of entry on the Canadian side of the St. Marys River. All the while a line from Henry Wadsworth Longfellow repeated in my head—*Let us, then, be up and doing, With a heart for any fate; Still achieving, still pursuing, Learn to labor and to wait.*

Thirty minutes later, I was having a late lunch at an Indian restaurant called Mom's Kitchen and planning my route. It turned out to be a long afternoon. People were home at only eight of the first fifteen newly bought houses that I visited.

There was no one at number sixteen, either, a two-bedroom, redbrick bungalow sitting on one-point-three acres just off Fourth Line West.

I was sitting in my car, setting the coordinates on my map app for the next address, when I looked up.

She appeared before me like an oasis to a man dying of thirst in the desert; she seemed to shimmer in the light of the setting sun.

She was walking along the sidewalk, wearing a navy blue down jacket against the fifty-two degree temperature yet no hat. She wasn't allowing her hair to grow out as I had predicted; instead she had cut it even shorter. It was no longer whitish blonde, though, but a deep red. She was carrying a small purse on a long strap and a plastic bag, swinging both as she walked; the purse was light blue and the bag was white with the name Bootlegger printed across it.

She stopped when she spotted my Mustang with its Minnesota license plates parked in front of her house and stared.

There was no fear in her expression, nor anger or surprise, for that matter. She looked at me as if she had expected me to be there all along.

I wondered briefly if she would attempt to run.

No, my inner voice said. *She's much too smart for that.*

She continued to walk toward me.

I slid out of the car and circled it. I was leaning against the passenger door when she halted in front of me.

"You've impressed me, McKenzie," she said. "Please believe me when I say that I am not easily impressed."

"What do I call you?" I asked.

"Reese. My name is Amanda Reese."

SEVENTEEN

Amanda turned and strolled—strolled!—up the sidewalk to her front door. I followed. When she reached the door she handed the bag to me.

"Hold this," she said.

While she pulled her keys from her purse and unlocked the door, I looked inside the bag. It contained a scarf with the name and logo of the Soo Greyhounds, a junior hockey team playing in the Ontario Hockey League.

"I didn't know that you were a hockey fan," I said.

"The Greyhounds have a fan club. I thought I'd join; make new friends."

Amanda opened the door and we stepped inside. She locked the door behind us, which alerted all of my fight-or-flight defense mechanisms.

Be careful.

Amanda removed her coat and hung it in a closet.

"Take your coat?" she asked.

"I'm good."

"This way."

There wasn't a single piece of furniture in Amanda's living and dining rooms. We passed through them as we made our way to her kitchen. The kitchen had a table, chairs, and a coffee machine similar to mine sitting on the counter.

"Have a seat," she said.

I sat.

Amanda pulled open a drawer and hesitated as she looked inside it.

My fists clenched and I found myself preparing to leap off the chair toward her.

"Sault Ste. Marie," she said. "I told you my grandmother was from Sault Ste. Marie."

"You said the same thing to your sister-in-law Danielle Carrell-Mowry," I told her. "You also gave LuAnne Kinney Pederson the impression that your people were from Canada, too."

"That was careless of me. I'll not make the same mistake again. Pederson, you say? Lu married her boyfriend. Good for her."

"LuAnne and Danielle both miss you," I said. "They both love you. Neither of them believes that you killed your husband and his mistress."

Amanda reached inside the drawer.

I called her name louder than was probably necessary.

"Amanda," I said.

She paused.

"Please keep your hands in plain sight."

Amanda very slowly and very cautiously removed her hand from the drawer. She was holding two K-Cup coffee pods.

"Coffee?" she asked.

"Yes, thank you."

Amanda armed her coffee machine with a pod and pushed the flashing blue button, which immediately turned red.

"You don't need to worry, McKenzie," she said. "I didn't kill David and that woman."

"Yet you buried them both."

"Yes, I did do that. It seemed like a good idea at the time. That doesn't mean I killed them, though."

"You have a lot of explaining to do, Amanda."

She finished making one mug of coffee and set it in front of me.

"I don't have any cream," she said.

"Black is fine."

"The cupboard is pretty bare. I just moved in last week. Fortunately, I haven't bought furniture, yet."

"Fortunately?"

Amanda returned to the coffee machine and brewed another cup.

"I noticed that you're alone," she said. "No U.S. Marshals, no Royal Canadian Mounted Police, no Ontario Provincial Police, or even an officer from the Sault Ste. Marie Police Service. That means I have time. Not much, but enough. Ten minutes after you leave, I'll be gone. Amanda Reese will cease to exist and I will become, well, the next woman on the list."

"Is it a long list?"

"Long enough. I'm upset with you, McKenzie, make no mistake. I liked it here. I liked being Amanda. Only you have nothing to fear from me, unless you attempt to get between me and the door. Please don't try."

Well, you found her. And she's already prepared to run, again. Now what?

I took a sip of my coffee while Amanda took her mug and sat at the table across from me.

You've been spending a lot of time drinking coffee with women in their kitchens these past few weeks, haven't you— only not with someone like her.

"Like I said, you have a lot of explaining to do," I spoke aloud.

"To whom? You?"

"Why not?"

"I haven't explained myself to a single human being in my entire life," Amanda said. "I've had several long conversations with God, but they've all been one-sided."

I drank more coffee. Amanda did the same.

"Who knows?" she said. "It might be cathartic. Ask your questions."

"Did you kill your husband and Sue?"

"Sue? Was that her name?"

"We think so."

"I didn't know that. I didn't recognize her. Her face was—damaged—and I didn't spend a great deal of time staring at it. No, McKenzie, as I keep repeating, I didn't kill David or Sue. I didn't kill Charles Sainsbury, either. What else do you want to know?"

"If you didn't kill them, David and Sue, why did you bury them under the gazebo?"

"If you know LuAnne Kinney, then you know about Luna Cifuentes. She robbed a bank. That was a mistake, by the way. I wish now that I hadn't done it because then I would have been able to call the police when I found David's car parked in our driveway; when I found him and Sue dead in the backseat. Instead, I was too frightened of going to prison for twenty years for the one crime that I truly did commit."

"Did Carson Vaneps help you bury them?"

"Who?"

"Carson . . ."

She's not going to answer that question, dummy.

"Never mind," I said. "If you didn't kill David and Sue, who did?"

"Why do you care? Why did you go to all the trouble to find me?"

"I want to help you get clear of this."

"Again, McKenzie, why do you care?"

"The last time I spoke to her, Bethany Gilman was weeping. She asked me to find you. She said she wanted to know the truth about you. So do all the girls you left on the Circle. All the things you taught them, all the things that you meant to them; the women they're all trying to be because of you—it's in jeopardy because of what the deputies found under the gazebo. They believe if that is true, that you killed them, then all of the rest is a lie. Bethany even quoted Gloria Steinem at me. I came here to learn the truth."

Tears filled Amanda's eyes and she turned her head so I wouldn't see her brush them away.

"I've only cried once since I was sixteen years old, and that was the night I left the Circle," she said. "Fuck."

"You have a lot of explaining to do, Amanda."

"You keep saying that. Fuck."

She spun out of her chair and carried her coffee mug to the kitchen counter. I watched her open a cupboard; relieved when she pulled out a bottle of Jameson Irish Whiskey. She opened the bottle and poured a generous amount into the coffee mug. Afterward, she held the bottle up and asked if I wanted some. I shook my head.

Best to keep your wits about you.

Amanda set down the bottle and leaned against the kitchen counter while she sipped her beverage.

"Have you ever read *Alice's Adventures in Wonderland* by Lewis Carroll?" she asked.

"When I was a kid."

"I read it when I was twenty-two. In the final scene, where Alice is on trial, the White Rabbit presents evidence in her defense. *'Where shall I begin, please your Majesty?' he asked. 'Begin at the beginning,' the King said gravely, 'and go on till you come to the end: then stop.'* To begin at the beginning, McKenzie, I have no idea what my real name is. I have no idea who my parents were or where I came from. My earliest memories are of growing up in my grandmother's house or, rather, I should say, in the house of the woman who claimed to be my grandmother. It's not too far from here, actually. About ten miles."

"The woman who claimed to be your grandmother?" I asked.

"I have never told this story to anyone before. Please, don't interrupt."

Amanda took a long pull from her drink.

"To begin at the beginning," she said, "my earliest memories were of abuse—physical, emotional, eventually sexual as well . . ."

Jesus.

"I didn't rebel against this because I was too young; I didn't understand it. All I understood was that the people who came to visit my grandmother kept telling me how lucky I was that she took me in when no one else wanted me, so I felt lucky. At the same time, I was never told who my parents were or what their relationship was to my grandmother. I was never told what had happened to them, although, one of my grandmother's male friends, whom I was required to entertain, once made a vague reference to a car accident . . ."

Jesus Christ.

"Along with the abuse, growing up I was treated as an indentured servant," Amanda added. "All I did was work. Clean the house, cook the meals, wash the dishes, mow the lawn; serve my grandmother. I was not allowed to watch TV or listen to the radio and the books I read late at night were the ones my grandmother chose for me. I was sent to school solely because the law demanded it. At the same time, I was expected to return home within just a few minutes after the school day concluded. I was beaten if I was late. I was not allowed to attend sporting events or join clubs; I was not allowed to have friends. Still, school changed everything for me. I began to see how other children lived. It allowed me to question the life I was living and I began to question it a great deal when I entered my teens.

"One day, my grandmother was hit by a car and forced to go to hospital. Her injuries weren't life threatening, but bones were broken—a hip, a leg, several ribs. That meant she was required to remain in hospital for a time. During that time, it was left to me to maintain the household; pay the bills. I went through my grandmother's papers and discovered—well, it was what I didn't find that finally girded me to action. There was no birth certificate in my name. No adoption papers. Nothing to indicate that she was my legal guardian or that we were related in any way. I wasn't listed in her will or on her insurance policies or her financial statements or anywhere else. There was nothing that might identify any other family members, hers or mine, either.

"It became clear to me that I was taken in solely to be her servant and sex toy. How she came to possess me, I have no idea. Perhaps I was kidnapped; who's to say? I presumed that, eventually, she was going to kick me out of her house. So, I forged my grandmother's signature on a few financial documents, a few withdrawal slips, and stole every penny of hers that I could get my hands on, over forty-five thousand in U.S. dollars. I drove her car across the border into the United States. You could do that in 1983; do it with nothing more than a driver's license, which I was allowed to acquire only so I could run errands for my grandmother. I kept driving south until I reached Stevens Point in Wisconsin. The only reason I stopped there was because the sun was setting and I needed somewhere to spend the night. I was sixteen years old. Are you sure I can't offer you a drink?"

Amanda held up the bottle of Jameson again.

"Yes," I said. "I think I'd like one."

Amanda crossed the kitchen and poured a few ounces into

my coffee mug while I stood and removed my jacket. I hung the jacket on the back of the chair and took a long pull of the drink. She held the bottle in front of me.

"More?" she asked.

"Please."

She added more whiskey to my coffee, although it was pretty much all alcohol by then.

Look at her. For all of those terrible things to happen to her, to any girl . . . Yet look at her now. My God, she's strong.

Amanda wasn't finished with her story, though.

"There was a boardinghouse, what they used to have before bed-and-breakfasts," she said. "An old woman owned it. She called me 'dear,' wondered why a 'sweet little thing like me was traveling all alone' and rented me a room. I cried that night, cried in the room, the best, most comfortable room I had ever been in in my entire life. I had never been so frightened, yet never felt so liberated. A contradiction, I know. At the same time, I was blessed with a kind of clarity. I realized that I needed two things desperately. A place to live and a place to hide the money I had stolen from my so-called grandmother.

"The next morning the old woman fed me breakfast. I asked if I could stay longer. She said that would be fine. She called me 'dear' again. I think she suspected that I was on the run, yet she didn't know from what or whom and she never asked. Not once in the two and a half months I remained with her. I'd pay my rent in cash and she'd say 'Thank you, dear' and then I'd help her with her gardening and she'd help me in ways that she couldn't possibly imagine simply by being kind to me.

"While this was going on, I manufactured my future," Amanda added. "The first step was stealing a wallet from a girl a few years older than I was who worked at the café down the block from the boardinghouse. In case you're wondering, McKenzie, I returned the wallet a few days later, after I used her driver's license and other ID to secure a copy of her birth certificate. I whited-out her name and the names of her parents, ran off a copy on an old offset printing press, and then copied the copies one at a time until the whited-out area disappeared. I filled in the now-blank spaces with the names I had chosen, ran off a few more copies, and left them outside for three days to age. When it was ready, I sent the most authentic-looking birth certificate to the Social Security Administration, along with a note written in longhand explaining that my daddy was making me get a job to help pay for my college education. Two weeks later, I had a bona fide Social Security number.

"Next, I applied to take a driver's education course in order to get a Wisconsin driver's license with the name I had chosen. That was actually the hardest part, taking driver's ed, classroom and behind the wheel; nearly fifty hours all told. Somehow I managed to charm the instructor . . ."

"I bet you did," I said.

"And earned my license sooner instead of later. Armed with that, I opened a checking account, and a savings account, and deposited my money a little at a time. Given today's growing cashless society, it's hard for people to comprehend that there was a time when cash was king; when there were no debit cards, no PayPal or Venmo; when you didn't need to use a credit card to rent a motel room or buy an airline ticket."

"The name . . ."

"Yes."

"Luna Cifuentes."

"Yes."

"Why?" I asked.

"I was sixteen years old; at least I think I was sixteen . . ."

My God . . .

"I honestly don't know my own birthday," Amanda said. "It's hard to express how vulnerable that made me. I had no one I could turn to for help. The old woman was kind; she took my cash without question. Only I couldn't, wouldn't depend on her. I also knew that, sooner or later, I would need to leave the boardinghouse. Given my situation, where do you think was the best place for a young woman to hide, where she could learn; where she could grow up in comparative safety?"

I knew the answer only because I also knew what came next.

"A college campus," I said.

"Unfortunately, a fake ID stating that you're eighteen isn't enough to get into a college," Amanda told me. "You also need high school transcripts, ACT or SAT scores. Luna Cifuentes was the smartest girl at the Sir James Dunn Collegiate and Vocational School, the high school in Sault Ste. Marie. She was going to the University of Toronto, so I thought it would be safe to pretend to be her. I requested that Sir James send her transcripts and scores to the colleges that I applied to. I know it was risky. A couple of the schools never replied, which made me exceedingly anxious. However, the University of Wisconsin in Madison said they would be delighted to admit Luna that fall.

"So, I went to university," Amanda said. "It was hard. The hardest thing I've ever done. A sixteen-year-old taking courses designed for college freshmen. What's more, I looked like I was sixteen. At least for the first year. After that, I experienced a growth spurt. That first year, though. Fortunately, I had two things going for me. Immense discipline was one."

"LuAnne Kinney said the same thing," I told her.

"Don't ask me where it came from. The second thing was fear. I couldn't allow myself to be kicked out of school for academic underachievement, McKenzie. I simply had nowhere else to go. That kept me focused. It forced me to become older and wiser than my years."

"Why a business major?"

"Business and economics," Amanda said. "It taught me

about money. At the time, I thought it was the most important thing in the world. I have since learned that it is not the most important thing. It is, however, in the top three."

"Spanish?"

"The University of Wisconsin has a foreign language requirement and my name was Luna Cifuentes, after all."

"Are the Mounties or the OPP still looking for you?" I asked.

"I don't know. I don't know if they were ever looking for me. I have no idea what happened after I escaped my grandmother's home. As a wise man once said, never look back . . ."

"Satchel Paige," I said.

"Who?"

"Satchel Paige, the baseball player. He said, *Don't look back, something might be gaining on you.*"

"I was thinking of Henry David Thoreau—*Never look back unless you're planning to go that way.* In any case, even at the tender age of sixteen, I knew better than to return to the scene of the crime. I was convinced that the mere act of looking myself up could be enough to help the authorities find me."

Clever, clever girl.

"Do you want another drink?" Amanda asked me.

"No, thank you."

"Me, neither." Amanda rose from the table, crossed the kitchen again, and set the Jameson on the counter. "I don't like to drink and drive."

"Are you going to drive somewhere?" I asked.

"My plans haven't changed, McKenzie."

"If I promise . . ."

"Don't take it personally," Amanda said. "It's not a matter of trust. Your car is parked in front of my house. Your cell phone is in your pocket as you sit in my kitchen. If the U.S. Marshals suspected for a second that you found me, they would follow your GPS coordinates directly to where I'm standing. Hell, they may already be on their way."

"Why did you rob that bank?" I asked.

"For the money, of course. Also, a little payback."

"Payback?"

"Despite the heinous crimes committed against me when I was a child, I had lived a relatively sheltered life," Amanda said. "I took Luna Cifuentes's name because she was the smartest girl I knew. I had no appreciation of the discrimination I would face because of that name. A Hispanic name. I doubt you can imagine the way I was treated, the racist things I was called because of that name while I was in school and in the years that followed. Some of the bigotry was subtle, much of it was not, yet every day I felt it. I found it shocking. I had been teased and bullied my entire life in Sault Ste. Marie because of my clothes—they came from the Salvation Army Family Store; never in my life was I allowed to wear anything new—and because of the bruises on my arms and legs that those clothes couldn't hide. Yet still I was shocked by this. Even now I am amazed at how hateful people can be. Except, I could escape that hate. Hispanics, Blacks, Asians, Native Americans—all the people of color who have been discriminated against in the United States since the beginning of the United States—they're stuck with it. They can't change the color of their skin. However, a white girl from Canada, if I didn't like it, I could always quit. One day I decided to do just that. I decided to become someone else. Why not? It's been done before.

"I began searching for a new identity," she added. "Jeanette Lee Fitch was just one on my list, yet I liked her best because, although she was much older than I was, my research suggested that she was a loner, like me; she had been a business major at Wisconsin, like me; and she was a blonde. Getting her birth certificate, her social—that wasn't difficult. The hardest part, once again, was securing a driver's license in her name. I was forced to commute between Cedar Rapids and Austin, Minnesota, to retake driver's ed, yet again. Five hours round trip. Finally, I was ready. Everything was in place. I was going to tell LuAnne that I found a job in Minnesota, give my two weeks' notice to First Trust, and quietly become someone else."

"Why didn't you?" I asked.

"I discovered that Lu, who was working the exact same job that I was, had been making nearly a third more money. This wasn't a secret that she kept from me, McKenzie. We never discussed our salaries. Why would we? When I learned the truth, however, I went to our boss and asked why. He told me that LuAnne was worth a third more than I was. The only reason that could possibly be true, I concluded, was because, in his eyes, Lu was white and I wasn't. You could say that I robbed the bank in a moment of pique. It's something I have come to regret."

I was starting to think that another drink wasn't a bad idea, after all.

"You went to Minnesota," I said.

"I went to Minnesota and began working for a firm that supplied building materials to construction firms."

"Is that how you met David Carrell?"

"Yes, about a year later. He was with North Country Properties and part of his job was to secure reliable vendors for construction projects."

Amanda laughed at the memory.

"He was so easy," she said. "David believed that he was God's gift to the female population and I let him believe that. In some ways he actually was. A gift. At least to me. I had been badly used sexually when I was a child. I won't go into details except to say that, in my experience, sex was solely about what some man or woman could take from me in any manner that they wished. Until David. David gave as much as he took. He made me laugh. He made me feel"—she paused as if she was searching for the perfect word—"warm. Before him it had always been so cold. He was funny, too. Like I said, he made me laugh, and not just in bed. I deliberately made myself attractive to him; deliberately massaged his ego. He thought I was thirty-six, but I was actually twenty-five and looked it. He liked that I looked so young. We married and I vowed to stand by him even though I knew that he was not likely to remain faithful to me. I was Jeanette Carrell now. I was J. C. For the first time in my life, I felt safe."

Amanda closed her eyes and exhaled slowly, as if she was remembering that feeling of safety.

"What happened?" I asked.

"I don't know," she told me.

How can you not know?

"Your sister-in-law, Danielle, told me that David had been cheating on you," I said.

"I suspected as much, yet I didn't have any suspects. Did she?"

"The only name we have is Sue."

"Yes, you mentioned her," Amanda said. "I didn't know Sue. The night he disappeared—David had never done that before. Stayed out all night. I was genuinely concerned. I woke early the next morning and saw his car parked in our driveway. I called out to him. I thought he was in the house; asleep on the couch, perhaps. He wasn't. I went outside and found him and Sue in the backseat."

"You and Carson Vaneps were building the gazebo on the hill . . ."

"Leave him out of this."

"J. C. . . ."

"My name is Amanda."

"Amanda, you buried them both, David and Sue, under the floor of the gazebo and poured concrete over their graves."

"Yes."

"You didn't contact the police because . . ."

"I was wanted by the U.S. Marshals for robbing a bank and I was certain that an investigation would reveal my hiding place and I'd spend the next twenty years in prison."

"David's family, the woman's—they never knew what happened to them."

"It was a selfish act on my part, is that what you want to hear?" Amanda asked.

"David disappeared on the fifth anniversary of the bank robbery in Cedar Rapids."

"Not more than a few days pass at a time when I don't think about that."

"It suggests that whoever killed him and Sue knew who you were and what you did," I said.

"Unless it was the coincidence of all coincidences; God's idea of a prank."

"What do you think?"

"It depends on when you ask me. McKenzie, I kept waiting for the worst. Kept waiting for the marshals or the police to come knocking on my door. It never happened. The authorities decided to forget all about David and Sue. I'm still surprised by that. Shocked, actually. At the same time, I began assembling new identities. I eventually created four and maintained them all these years against the day when someone would discover the bodies. All the while, I've been asking myself the same questions—why? Why they were killed. Who killed them. Now . . ."

"Now everyone believes it was you."

"Possibly that's why David and Sue were left in my driveway

in the first place, so people would think that I killed them. That was my first thought. Something that Carson—something that a friend of mine also suggested at the time."

"Who?" I asked. "Who could have tried to frame you for the murder of your own husband?"

"Another question that I cannot answer."

"Someone living on the Circle?"

"It wasn't the Circle back then. It was a hill and only Carson Vaneps, Ruth Krider, Charles Sainsbury, and I lived on it."

"Adam Berenson?" I asked.

Where did that come from?

"Adam Berenson," Amanda repeated. "Why does that name sound so familiar?"

"He was upset when I was trying to prove that you didn't kill Charles Sainsbury," I said. "Apparently, he was also very annoyed when he learned that I was trying to find you after you skipped town once the bodies were unearthed."

Amanda closed her eyes and slowly opened them.

"This man wanted to see me convicted of Charles's murder, yet now wants me to escape arrest for killing David and Sue," she said. "Seems somewhat contradictory."

I shrugged at my ignorance.

"What does he have to do with anything?" Amanda asked.

"Charles and William Sainsbury had been involved in several building projects with him and the development company he owns, the Polachek Companies. Apparently, they owed him a lot of money . . ."

"Wait, I do know him," she said. "As you say, Adam Berenson owns the Polachek Companies; the firm I worked for was one of its vendors. He also owned North Country Properties, the firm that employed David. I met him only once, though; it was at our wedding reception. David had been married before, so his family thought it would be best to keep the wedding small and since I didn't have any family . . . The reception was held at Columbia Manor in Minneapolis. Only about one hundred and twenty-five guests. Berenson dropped in to say his congratulations. David was impressed that Berenson would do that, although I don't think he stayed for more than an hour. David was also impressed that his boss, the director of operations at— okay, okay . . ."

"What?"

"David's boss, the director of operations at North Country Properties, came to the reception with Berenson. I only saw her that one time. Her name was Suzanne Costello."

Not "Sue," my inner voice said. *"Suz."*

Amanda sat at the kitchen table across from me.

"Could that have been her in the backseat with David?" she asked.

"If it was, that might explain Berenson's interest in all of this."

"It doesn't make sense, McKenzie. If he had left the bodies in my driveway to frame me, why would he want me to escape? I'm the one the authorities are blaming for the murders."

"Another unanswered question," I said.

"Why would he want to kill them in the first place?"

"And another."

Amanda went silent for a few beats; I knew better than to interrupt her silence.

"In the basement of my house on the Circle there's a cabinet," she said. "Inside the cabinet is a photo album filled with wedding pictures; my sister-in-law, Dani, put it together for me. I don't think I've looked at it for—I don't know how long. Not since David disappeared, anyway. Suzanne Costello's photo might be in there. Possibly you can use it to confirm whether or not it was her in the backseat. David kept some papers in the cabinet, too. From North Country. He rarely spoke about what he did for them; mostly it was just gossip about his fellow employees, especially the female employees, although—I don't recall that he ever discussed Suzanne."

"I'll try to gain access to your house," I said. "I have friends with the Ramsey County Sheriff's Department."

"I know."

"Amanda, for what it's worth, I promise I'll keep trying to prove that you didn't kill your husband and the woman he was with."

"Thank you," she said.

"I promise that I'll also find out who actually did kill Charles Sainsbury."

"I wish you wouldn't."

"You know who did it, don't you?" I said.

"No, I don't."

"You have your suspicions."

Amanda didn't say if she did or didn't.

"It would be helpful if I could ask you questions along the way," I said.

"About David and Sue? I'll answer questions about them, although I'm sure I've already told you everything I know."

"It's been a long time. There are details you might have forgotten."

"I have your cell phone number and a bag filled with burner phones," Amanda told me. "What do they say? Don't call me, I'll call you?"

"Amanda, have you ever considered turning yourself in?" I asked.

"According to the Good Conduct Time provisions under the Prison Litigation Reform Act of 2006, inmates serving a sentence for offenses committed on or after November first, 1987, but before September thirteenth, 1994, will be awarded fifty-four days credit for good behavior, described in law as exemplary compliance with institutional disciplinary regulations, for each year served. That would mean I'd be incarcerated by the Federal Bureau of Prisons for a minimum of seventeen years and fifteen days. No, McKenzie, I haven't considered turning myself in."

"You could make a deal," I suggested.

Amanda shook her head.

"You can't live your entire life in the wind," I said.

"So far, so good."

"Amanda, I promise I won't tell anyone that you're here. You don't need to leave your home."

"Home? I don't have a home. There is no place for me in this world except for what I make for myself and it's always filled with longing and regret. I have paid for my sins, McKenzie. Maybe not in the eyes of the authorities, but . . . All the people I love and who might have loved me are beyond my reach. That's the sentence I serve."

We were both on our feet. She opened her arms and I stepped into them.

"Good-bye, Amanda," I said.

We embraced. I had never felt more sorry for any one person in my life.

"McKenzie, please," she said, "if you can manage it discreetly, tell the girls my story. Tell them that I love them."

EIGHTEEN

I took my own sweet time driving home; I didn't even speed. Well, at least not as much as usual.

First, I spent the night at the Best Western on the U.S. side of the border. The next morning, I started the long drive south along Lake Michigan to just north of Green Bay, hung a right, and drove west across Wisconsin to Minnesota. I stopped twice along the way to eat meals in actual restaurants instead of surrendering to fast food. As I neared Wausau, I saw a sign that told me I could take Interstate 39 south to Stevens Point and for a brief moment I considered it, only my inner voice asked a simple question—*Why would you do that?* I couldn't answer the question, so I continued on my way.

Other questions came to mind that I couldn't answer as well. Specifically, how was I going to prove that Amanda didn't kill her husband and the woman who might be Suzanne Costello as promised and how was I going to uncover the identity of the person who killed Charles Sainsbury, as I had also promised?

Assuming Amanda was telling you the truth, that she didn't kill them herself.

Why would she lie?

Gee, I don't know. Habit? If nothing else, the woman has been lying every day of her life since she was sixteen. Assuming she wasn't also lying about her daring escape from her so-called grandmother.

I decided I wasn't fond of the word "assuming" and spent several miles attempting to come up with an adequate synonym—presuming, supposing, surmising, imagining, accepting. I wondered if Rebecca Westermeyer Sauer could help me out. She was good at inventing words.

The Plot Whores Book Club.

What about it?

Just wondering if the members were as forthcoming as they could have been.

They all presumed, supposed, surmised, imagined, accepted that J. C. had committed the crime. Now that they know she didn't, perhaps they'll see the events surround Sainsbury's death in a different light.

You're assuming—there's that word again—that whoever killed him actually lives on the Circle.

Yes, I am.

What about David Carrell and Suzanne Costello?

The key is the woman, I decided. If I could learn her story . . .

Wait a second. This was a substantial woman; a woman who ran a finance company in 1995. How could she possibly have gone missing without the world noticing?

I followed I-94 across the St. Croix River, driving from Wisconsin into Minnesota. I considered using my Mustang's hands-free cell phone option to call Ramsey County Deputy Sergeant Michael Swenson and decided against it. He would ask me questions that I didn't want to answer. He would be angry with me for not answering. I decided to avoid the drama until later and continued driving I-94 through St. Paul to Highway 280, heading north toward the exit that would lead me to Dominic Belden's place in Lauderdale.

It was half past seven and dark outside; the sun had set a good hour earlier. I parked on the street and followed the low cyclone fence surrounding his house to the gate, opened the latch, and stepped inside, careful to lock the gate behind me. Belden's black Labrador retrievers were roaming freely inside the fence. They seemed delighted that I was there, greeting me with loud barks and wagging tails; jumping at me, too, as I made my way to the front door. Belden must have been alerted by the barking. The light above his front door snapped on and he pulled open the door just as I reached it.

"What the hell do you want?" Belden's eyes seemed blurry to me, or maybe that's what I expected. "Oh, McKenzie. I thought you were a Jehovah's Witness or something."

"Do you get a lot of that?"

"Now that you mention it . . . Hey, come on in, come in."

Belden opened the door wide enough to let me pass.

"Is Swenson with you?" he asked. "I expected to see him; expected to see both of you long before now."

I stepped inside his house expecting that it would be littered with spent beer bottles and empty pizza boxes. Instead, it was immaculate. The floors were vacuumed and swept; the furniture neat and orderly; the only mess, if you wanted to call it that, was in the corner where Belden had kept food bowls, beds, and toys for his dogs.

"I was watching football," he said. "Cowboys and the Vikings. Kickoff in a few minutes. Can I get you something? Wanna beer? I'm drinking iced tea."

Iced tea? Where are we? Who is this man?

"Tea will be fine," I said.

I followed Belden into his kitchen. It was bright, spacious, and even tidier than his living room. He filled a glass from a pitcher he kept in his refrigerator and handed it to me.

"I was right, wasn't I?" Belden said. "You thought I was wrong, some old drunk doesn't know shit. Didn't change the facts, though, did it? I was right. Fuckin' Carrell offed her husband and buried him just like she did the other vic, although . . . The woman buried with him, now that came as a surprise. Not a surprise surprise. I mean, a wife catches her ol' man cheating so she does both him and his girlfriend, that's nothing new. Have you IDed the female vic yet?"

"That's why I'm here," I said.

"Oh, so you didn't come to apologize?"

I had learned a long time ago that when it came to questioning people, it was best to go along to get along. Besides, Belden was close to being right about everything so far.

"I do apologize," I said. "I shouldn't have blown you off like I did."

"Nah, that's on me. Sometimes I imbibe a little more than I should. My advice, McKenzie—don't retire 'less you have somethin' better to do with your time than walk the dogs."

"It appears that you were right, though, only we still don't know how right."

"What do you mean?"

"You mentioned North Country Properties . . ."

"Owned by Adam Berenson."

"You told us Omer," I reminded him.

"Did I?" Belden said. "That alcohol messes with you, doesn't it? I meant Adam. Omer died, I want to say ninety, ninety-one."

"Nineteen ninety-one."

"The kid, though, Adam, he's just as bad as his old man."

"Apparently, the FBI agrees."

Belden smiled brightly. I didn't blame him. It's always nice when your opinions are validated.

"About North Country Properties," I said. "Did you interview the people who worked there, Carrell's co-workers?"

"'Course, I did. Whaddaya think?"

"What did they tell you?"

"Nothin' much. Some left the office before Carrell did; some left after he did; nobody mentioned seeing or hearing any drama. It was just another day in the workweek as far as they were concerned."

"Do you remember any names?"

"Names?" Belden asked. "Nah. I woulda written 'em down, though. They'd be in my sups."

Which means you're going to have to talk to Swenson whether you want to or not, my inner voice told me.

"Do you remember meeting with a woman named Suzanne Costello?" I asked.

"No. Who's she?"

"Costello was the director of operations at North Country Properties."

"The director . . ." Belden thought long and hard before waving his finger at me. "No, now that you mention it. She wasn't there. It was the day after Carrell went missing when we went over to North Country. I don't remember hearing her name. I do remember, though; I remember the guy who was in charge saying his boss hadn't shown up yet. Something Harper, Barber, whatever; the guy's name. He kept saying he wasn't sure what he should do when we asked him for permission to interview him and his staff; he kept saying we should wait for his boss. Finally he gave in. He said, 'I guess it'll be all right.' You're saying that his boss was this Suzanne Costello?"

"Did her name come up at all during your interviews?" I asked.

"No."

"No one mentioned that she and David Carrell might have had a relationship?"

"You're telling me that the woman buried on the hill with David Carrell was Suzanne Costello?"

"No one mentioned that she had gone missing, too?"

"Stop," Belden said. "If this woman had gone missing at the same time as Carrell, we would have known."

"You'd think so."

"Fuck. Fuck, fuck, fuck, it was that goddamn county attorney, little fucking Jerry Empson, covering for the mob, wasn't it?"

"You know," I said, "we could always ask."

Except little Jerry Empson was dead. According to a newspaper report I called up on my smartphone, the former Ramsey County attorney died of a heart attack seven months after losing his bid for a third term in office some two decades earlier. Belden's reaction to the story came with a snort.

"Do you believe that?" he asked. "A heart attack?"

"It's happened before," I said. At the same time, Belden's allegations had me wondering.

I chatted with him some more just to be polite. Afterward, I drove to Rickie's on Cathedral Hill in St. Paul. It took me fourteen minutes.

At the eleven-minute mark, Louis Armstrong began playing his trumpet for me. My caller ID suggested that I was in trouble.

"Hi, Mike," I said.

"What the hell, McKenzie?" Swenson said.

"Michael, whatever do you mean?"

"I just received a phone call from Dominic Belden. He said you were over to his place asking about a woman named Suzanne Costello."

"About that. Suzanne was—"

"He told me who she was. How did you come up with that name? Why didn't you call me first?"

I didn't answer.

"McKenzie?"

I didn't answer again.

"You found her, didn't you? Sonuvabitch, you found her. Jeanette Carrell, Luna Cifuentes, whatever the hell her name was. Where is she?"

"Mike, I'm in a kind of gray area here."

"What's gray about it?"

"Promises were made," I said.

"Promises were made to me, too. That day in the cafeteria at the LEC, you promised you wouldn't be an asshole. Are you being an asshole?"

At the fourteen-minute mark, I swung the Mustang into the parking lot next to Rickie's. My headlights reflected off a black Mercedes-Benz S550 with tinted windows.

"Mike," I said. "I'm at Rickie's."

"You can't talk to me over the phone? You expect me to drive to—"

"Mike, Adam Berenson is at Rickie's, too."

Swenson paused briefly before he asked, "Are you sure?"

"Unless someone else drove his car," I said.

"I'll be there in a few minutes."

"Mike, wear your uniform."

Shows on the main stage upstairs started at seven P.M. on Sundays and Andrew Walesch and his Orchestra were already deep into their second set of Sinatra tunes when I entered Rickie's. Only Adam Berenson wasn't there for the music. He sat alone in a booth in the downstairs lounge. His nephew Tony sat on a stool in front of the bar with a clear view of his uncle. Nina Truhler sat on a stool behind the bar, her elbow propped on top of the bar, her chin resting in her hand. She was the only one of the three wearing a mask.

I was also wearing a mask because the sign on Rickie's front door told me that's what I should do. I took it off, though—both Berenson and Tony watched me do it—when I sat in front of Nina.

"They came in about an hour ago and asked for you," she said. "I told them I had no idea where you were or when you'd be back. They said they'd wait."

"You could have called me."

"To tell you what? That a couple of punks were here waiting for you?"

"I like when you say 'punks.' You sound like Barbara Stanwyck in one of her film noirs."

"How many times have I asked you not to bring your extracurricular activities into my place? Business is iffy enough without having a shoot-out while Andrew is upstairs singing 'One for My Baby (and One More for The Road).'"

"I'll shoo them away," I said.

"Quietly. Please."

I moved from the bar to the booth where Adam Berenson was sitting. I claimed the bench across from him without asking permission. He was drinking what looked like whiskey neat from a squat glass that he rotated one quarter turn at a time in front of him. The soft light from the lamp hanging above the booth reflected off the class ring he wore on his right hand—University of Wisconsin 1978. I had a class ring somewhere, only I hadn't worn it since I joined the cops. Bobby

Dunston had a ring, too, only he took his off when he married Shelby.

"McKenzie," Berenson said. "I've been waiting—"

I couldn't think of a reason to hem and haw with the man, so I cut him off.

"Suzanne Costello," I said.

Berenson paused briefly before he answered.

"Who?" he asked.

"The woman who was working as director of operations for North Country Properties the day David Carrell disappeared. Funny how she disappeared at the same time, yet no one reported it."

"I don't know her."

"Jeanette Carrell says you do."

Berenson paused again.

"Where is she?" he asked.

"You shouldn't have come here to lean on my wife . . ."

"I didn't . . ."

"It was a mistake."

"You're the one making a mistake by involving yourself in my business."

"Have you ever been hit in the face?" I asked.

"Excuse me?"

"Have you ever been punched in the face? I'm sure you've had other people punched, but have you ever been punched in the face?"

"No."

"I have. It's very disorienting."

"Are you threatening me?"

"Mike Tyson; used to be heavyweight champion—he famously said that 'everyone has a plan until they get punched in the face.' You have a plan, don't you? That's why you came here; why you have your nephew sitting at the bar trying to look menacing, although he's really not that much of a thug is he? Well, I'm going to hit you in the face, Berenson, because you involved my wife in your shit when I told you not to. I'm going over to Jeanette Carrell's house on the Circle, where she has hidden evidence that confirms you were not only intimately involved with Suzanne Costello, it proves you had both her and Carrell's husband killed. We'll see how your plan holds up then. Now get the hell out of here before I come across this table and really do punch you in the face."

Berenson took his time because he didn't want to appear worried; didn't want to give the impression that he wasn't still in charge. He slipped out of the booth and adjusted his winter coat.

"You're the one who is going to be hit in the face," he said.

"I've been hit before."

Berenson gestured toward Tony. His nephew set his drink on the bar, slipped off the stool, and made for the door. He joined his uncle there and the two of them stepped out into the night.

This had better work, my inner voice told me.

I left the booth and moved to the bar where Nina was standing.

"Now what?" she asked.

Good question.

A few minutes later, Mike Swenson walked into the bar wearing the dark brown jacket of the Ramsey County Sheriff's Department, his gold five-pointed badge gleaming above his left breast. He paused and glanced around while half the patrons in Rickie's paused and looked at him. He moved to where Nina and I were standing.

"Is Berenson here?" he asked.

"He and his nephew left a few minutes ago," I told him.

"McKenzie, what the hell?"

"Hey, watch your language."

"Yeah, Mike," Nina said. "What the hell?"

Swenson offered his hand and Nina shook it.

"Pleasure to meet you again," he said.

"Likewise."

"But seriously, McKenzie, what the hell?"

"Don't worry, Mike," I said. "I have a plan."

I parked my Mustang in Jeanette Carrell's driveway. It was nine thirty P.M. on a Sunday night and all the houses in the area were well lighted except hers. It made me think that the Ramsey County Sheriff's Department had been careless, advertising that the house was empty.

I left the Mustang and went to the front door. I unlocked it using the key that Mike Swenson had lent me. Once inside, I turned on the hall light, followed by the lights in every room that I entered. I didn't mind that the neighbors would know I was there. I wanted them to know that I was there.

Just off the kitchen, I found the door that opened onto the staircase that led to the basement. I turned on the basement light, too, and climbed down. The basement was finished with carpeting, wall paneling, and furniture. There was a Ping-Pong table, although, for some reason, I couldn't imagine Jeanette Carrell playing the game.

There was another door on the far side. Behind it I was sure I would find a furnace, water heater, washtubs, and a washer and dryer. Across from the door was a large cabinet with carved wood that looked older than the house itself. I took my cell phone from my pocket, propped it against its wall, and opened the door. The cabinet was filled with brown and white cardboard boxes in various sizes all stacked neatly. There was a layer of dust over all of them and I wondered when was the last time Jeanette had opened the boxes.

I started rummaging through them.

In one box, I found a light blue photo album with the words *My Wedding* embossed on the cover; the gift from Danielle Carrell-Mowry that I was told would be there. On the first page Danielle had fixed an invitation—*Jeanette Lee Fitch and David Allen Carrell invite you to celebrate their joyous wedding . . .*

I skipped over the pages with photographs of the wedding itself—Luna/Jeanette/Amanda truly was stunning in her white gown—and settled on those taken during the reception at Columbia Manor. It didn't take long before I found Adam Berenson. Most of the pictures of him also included a woman; I placed her at about forty, approximately five foot four with blond hair. They appeared as if they were together both physically and romantically.

Good evening, Ms. Costello, my inner voice said.

In one photo, though, Berenson was standing alone on the edge of the dance floor and watching Jeanette and David as they hugged each other tight. The expression on his face was of amused surprise.

In that moment, I understood what had happened and why.

I'll be damned. What did Amanda call it? The coincidence of all coincidences; God's idea of a prank?

I set the photo album aside and resumed searching boxes. There was a big one at the bottom sealed with packing tape. It was very heavy; I had to muscle it out of the cabinet.

Behind me I heard the soft thud of footsteps made by someone trying very hard not to make a sound.

Maybe you should have thought this out more carefully.

Despite my growing concern, I pretended I hadn't heard the footsteps and tore the tape from the box; it was old and peeled off easily.

I opened the box.

It was filled to the top with money.

"Wow," I said.

That's why Danielle had seen David and Suzanne leaving Jeanette's house when she arrived to water the plants. It wasn't because they were sleeping together—well, maybe they were, but the real reason they were there was to hide the money.

I pulled a bundle of cash from the box. At least twenty-five bills, all of them fifties.

"That's mine," Adam Berenson said.

I dropped the bundle back into the box and turned my head cautiously. Berenson was standing about five yards behind me. His nephew Tony was standing about three yards behind him. Tony had a gun in his hand that he was aiming more or less in my direction.

"How much is here?" I asked.

"Seven hundred and sixty-eight thousand dollars."

"Wow," I repeated. "So, you want me to help you carry it to your car or what?"

Berenson's reaction made both Tony and me flinch.

"That bitch stole from me!" he shouted. He pounded his chest with his fist three times as if the crime had been committed just thirty seconds ago. "They both stole from me! Me! Carrell created a network of bogus vendors. They sent invoices to North Country and Costello paid them."

"You could have called the police," I said. "Your pal Jerry Empson would have taken care of it for you."

"I would have looked like an idiot. An idiot!"

"I'm just saying, you didn't need to kill them," I said.

"I have a business to run, McKenzie. Do you think people would have taken me seriously if they knew I let those two steal from me? If they knew I had been played?" He pounded his chest again. "Do you think they would have been the last ones to try?"

"So, you killed them. Shot them in the head."

"It's what they had coming."

"I'm surprised you didn't use a tommy gun like they did in the old gangster movies," I said.

"Fuck you."

"You dumped their bodies on Jeanette Carrell's doorstep because you figured the cops would blame her, especially when they discovered she wasn't Jeanette Carrell, am I right?"

Berenson cocked his head like he was surprised I knew that.

"You went to the University of Wisconsin, Class of '78." I pointed at his class ring. "You also told me that you tried to walk onto the baseball team there but they wouldn't have you. Were you a business major?"

His nod was nearly imperceptible; I would have missed it if I hadn't been looking for it.

"Along with Jeanette Lee Fitch. You took classes together, didn't you? I bet your picture is only a page away from hers in the Badger yearbook."

He nodded again.

"Were you the one that Jeanette's sister Daphne claimed seduced Jeanette and then dumped her, ruining her life?"

Berenson's head remained still.

"I bet it came as a huge surprise when a woman claiming to be Jeanette Lee Fitch with a business degree from Wisconsin, class of 1978, married your employee. Being who you are, though, you just slipped that tiny tidbit of information into your pocket until you found a use for it. Tell me, did you ever learn who she really was?"

"You seem to know all the answers, you tell me," Berenson asked.

Actually, we're just guessing.

"I think you did," I said aloud. "That's why you dumped the bodies on June eighth. Only Jeanette was more resourceful than you gave her credit for, disposing of them the way she did and filing a missing persons report. But what the hell, no foul, no harm; am I right?

"You went to little Jerry Empson and told him that there was no need to follow up on the missing persons; that the disappearance of David Carrell *and* Suzanne Costello was a domestic matter. You might even have told him that they stole from you and went on the run together only you didn't want them prosecuted or even found because it would be bad for business, but that's just a guess. What isn't a guess is that Jerry quashed the investigation just like you wanted; told the investigators to let it go.

"Later, when Charles Sainsbury was killed and Jeanette was blamed for killing him, you figured the problem would go away for good. When David's and Suzanne's bodies were discovered on the hill and Jeanette was blamed for that, too, you hoped she would go away for good. As long as Jeanette was in the wind, suspicion would stay off you. Which is why you're so pissed off that I found her. Am I right?"

"You don't know what you're talking about," Berenson told me.

"What part did I get wrong?"

He hesitated before answering.

"I never did know who that woman really was," Berenson said. "I thought she was just a grifter. I expected her to hustle David Carrell and be on her way. I thought it was funny. I was surprised that she didn't take off when we left Carrell's car in the driveway."

That it happened on June eighth really was God's idea of a practical joke. I'll be damned.

"We?" I asked aloud.

Tony must have thought I was accusing him.

"I wasn't even born then," he said.

Berenson shook his head sadly, except I didn't know if it was at Tony or me.

"I knew when we first met that you were too smart for your own good," he said.

"You'd be surprised how many people have told me that."

"I'll be the last. Tony."

"Wait," Tony said.

"Tony," Berenson repeated.

His voice suggested that there was no room for debate.

Tony stepped reluctantly toward me.

"You wanted to be a part of the family, here's your chance to prove your value to the family," Berenson said.

"Tony." I spoke loud enough to be heard across the street and down the block. "Stop waving that gun around. You might hurt someone."

It was the cue Deputy Sergeant Michael Swenson, dressed in full uniform, had been waiting for. He opened the door that led to the laundry room and stepped out. His own piece was in his hand. He brought it up, sliding into a Weaver shooting stance, and set the sights on Tony, aiming center mass.

"Freeze," he said, just like in the movies.

Tony moved his hand as if he intended to swing the gun toward Swenson.

Swenson didn't shoot him, though; probably what I would have done. Instead, he shouted *"Stop!"*

Tony stopped.

He looked at Swenson.

He looked at Berenson.

Back at Swenson.

He released the gun; it bounced harmlessly off the carpet at his feet.

Swenson moved deeper into the room.

Tony turned to look at Berenson again, the expression on his face asking if he had done the right thing.

Berenson shook his head no.

"Move back, move back," Swenson said.

Tony stepped backward until he was flat against the basement wall.

It was only then that Swenson felt safe enough to scoop up Tony's gun and shove it into his pocket.

"You're under arrest," Swenson said. "You have the right to remain silent. Anything you say can and will be used against you in a court of law. You have the right to an attorney. If you cannot afford an attorney, one will be provided for you. Do you understand the rights I have just read to you? With these rights in mind, do you wish to speak to me?"

Berenson smirked.

"You got nothing," he said.

"We got this," I said.

I picked up my cell phone and held it next to my head, screen out, so Berenson could see that my voice recorder was taping every word he said.

"How does it feel?" I asked. "Getting hit in the face, I mean?"

NINETEEN

There was nothing subtle about the Ramsey County Sheriff's Department. Even though it was unnecessary, a posse of deputies arrived on the scene with sirens blaring and light bars flashing. They lured neighbors living on and around the Circle to venture into the cold October night to see what was happening. One of them was Katherine Hixson, who was able to watch the comings and goings from her front steps. There wasn't much to see, though, except for a couple of well-dressed men in handcuffs being driven away in separate cars and a deputy hefting a cardboard box weighing at least fifty pounds into his trunk.

I wasn't coming or going but staying, partly because my car was trapped in Jeanette Carrell's driveway by various Ramsey County vehicles. Mostly, though, it was because I was asked to make a statement to the sergeant supervising the crime scene—not Swenson—and another to the superior officer who replaced him, and finally to an assistant county attorney, who demanded that I meet him in his office the next morning to give my statement yet again, this time on-camera. He wasn't satisfied with my promise that I would email him a copy of my voice recording of Adam Berenson, however, and confiscated my phone.

I was surprised by how much that bothered me; losing my cell phone.

Most of the neighbors had returned to their own homes by the time I left Jeanette Carrell's house except for Hixson, who was still sitting on the steps outside hers. She called to me.

"McKenzie?"

I walked across Carrell's lawn to hers, stopping in front of the steps. She seemed to be shivering beneath the winter coat and boots she wore.

"Ms. Hixson," I said.

"I thought it was you. McKenzie, can you tell me what's going on?"

I didn't think it was a secret so I answered.

"The Ramsey County Sheriff's Department just arrested the man responsible for killing David Carrell and the woman whose body was buried next to his under the gazebo."

Hixson's eyes grew wide.

"It wasn't J. C.?" she asked.

"No."

"What I read in the newspaper . . . I thought . . . What everybody thought . . . Why, McKenzie? If it wasn't J. C., why were they killed?"

"As a wise man once said, the answer to all of your questions is money."

"Money?"

"They were killed for money."

"Are you saying that J. C. was innocent all along?"

Well, not exactly innocent, my inner voice said. *She did bury the bodies.*

"It would seem so," I said aloud.

"And Charles Sainsbury. She didn't kill him, either. McKenzie, I was so sure I saw her that night."

Maybe she did.

"What happened at eleven at night isn't nearly as important as what happened at eleven in the morning," I said.

"I don't know what happened," Hixson said. "I wasn't here. I was at work. My boys were in school. So many people are angry at me even now; even after they dropped the charges against Jeanette. Everyone except Linda Welch. Suddenly, she's my friend and I don't even like the woman."

The enemy of my enemy . . .

"For what it's worth," I said, "I don't believe you did anything wrong. What you told the deputies; even going before the Chippewa Woods HOA and exploding like you did—if someone had drenched my children with a hose, I would have been upset, too."

"Thank you for that, McKenzie."

It's the very least you could do.

After my nine A.M. meeting at the Ramsey County attorney's office located in the Lowry Hotel Building in downtown St. Paul—where gangsters like Bugsy Siegel and Alvin "Creepy" Karpis used to hang out back in the day—I drove to the Circle. I didn't have much of a plan except to interview the same people I had spoken to before Jeanette Carrell had gone on the run, hoping for different answers to the questions I had already asked.

I started with Evan; parking in her driveway. She took me to her backyard and showed me the trees on the hill that had been marked with pink paint.

"I don't know why Sainsbury is cutting them down," she said. "I would think that the people buying the mini-mansions would want a nice, thick forest separating them from the riffraff. 'Course, the mini-mansions are just large holes in the ground right now, still . . ."

"How are the 'circlelites' taking it?" I asked, using the word that Rebecca Westermeyer Sauer had coined.

"About how'd you expect."

"That well, huh?"

"McKenzie, my social media feeds are buzzing, not to mention I've been getting texts about every ten minutes. Rumor has it that the man who really killed David Carrell and the woman they found beneath the gazebo was arrested last night. That you had something to do with it. Katie Hixson, of all people, is practically giddy about it."

"It happened too late last night to make the newspapers. I'm surprised that the TV and radio stations haven't picked it up yet."

"I haven't been watching or listening."

"A man named Adam Berenson committed the crime," I said. "David Carrell and the woman worked for him. They stole from him."

"Really?"

"Yeah."

"J. C. had nothing to do with it?" Evan asked.

If she had, she would have taken the box of cash when she left, my inner voice said.

"No, I don't think so," I said aloud.

"So, she'll come back home now, right?"

Not a chance.

"I don't know," I said.

"Sara is desperate that she come back home. Beth Gilman is still upset, too."

"Is anyone happy that Jeanette's gone?"

"I thought Hixson was, only now I'm not so sure," Evan said. "Linda Welch keeps saying she hopes the deputies catch her and she gets what's coming to her, whatever that is. McKenzie, if J. C. didn't kill her husband and that woman, if she didn't kill Charles Sainsbury, why wouldn't she come home?"

"It's complicated."

"Meaning you know stuff that you won't tell me. I thought we were friends."

"Speaking of friends, what's the gossip on the hill?" I asked.

"No one goes up the hill anymore."

"You know what I mean."

"What do you want to know?"

"About Sainsbury," I said. "What have you heard?"

"Me? Not much. Most people were delighted when they dropped the charges against J. C., but when they discovered the bodies beneath the gazebo, everyone figured that maybe she did do it after all, kill Charles Sainsbury, I mean, and that the county attorney screwed up when he let her go. Although, now . . ."

Evan spread her arms and shrugged, looking as bewildered as I felt.

Rebecca Westermeyer Sauer seemed awfully glad to see me.

"You, you, you," she chanted. "Katie Hixson said you caught the guy who killed J. C.'s husband and the woman they found buried with him."

One never tires of the adulation of the crowd.

"Not exactly," I said.

"But you were there," Katie said.

"I was there."

"You were there when they proved that J. C. didn't kill Charles, too."

"I suppose."

"Are you trying to act humble, McKenzie?"

"No. I doubt I could spell the word if you spotted me all of the consonants."

"You're our hero, you know that, right, me and Rachel's?" she said. "Oh wait, there goes another one."

We were standing inside Rebecca's living room. She pointed through her bay window at Derek Carlson as he jogged past.

"Mr. Pectorally Perfect," Rebecca said. "Although, he is wearing a shirt today."

"It is cold outside," I suggested.

"You'd think he'd want everyone to see his nipples get hard."

Rebecca laughed not so much at her own joke as my reaction to it.

"Did I embarrass you, McKenzie? I'm sorry."

Clearly she wasn't, though, because she continued to try to embarrass me throughout our conversation by making reference to other parts of the anatomy that react to the temperature. Unfortunately, she offered nothing that moved me closer to finding out who killed Sainsbury.

Maybe you were wrong, my inner voice told me. *Maybe the person who killed him doesn't live on the Circle, after all.*

Jennifer Carlson wasn't particularly helpful, either, although she did pour me another spectacular cup of coffee.

She said she was happy to hear that Adam Berenson had been arrested for killing J. C.'s husband; that J. C. was no longer wanted for the crime.

She said she was happy that J. C. wasn't suspected of killing Sainsbury, either, so maybe she'll come home now. She said she'd be happy to see her again.

She also told me that her firm had just announced that it was bringing everyone back to the office starting the first workday of the year, which also made her happy.

Yet at no time did Jennifer smile.

"I'm sorry that Derek isn't here to talk with you," she said. "He went jogging. Again. He jogs a lot. I don't think COVID has anything to do with it, though. What do you think, McKenzie?"

"I think you're right," I said.

My next stop was Linda Welch's house. I was halfway there when I saw Derek Carlson running toward me. He didn't even acknowledge my presence until he was moving past me and a thought apparently occurred to him.

"Hey." He spun toward me, pumping his arms and legs as he jogged in place. "Where are you going? Are you asking questions again? Who are you going to talk to?"

I decided to play him; see how he reacted.

"I was just talking to your wife," I said. "Now I'm going to chat with some other women who live within jogging distance."

He stopped running in place.

"Why?" he asked.

I responded by asking him a question—"Tell me something. How is it possible for you to jog 10-K without getting so much as an ounce of sweat on your shirt and shorts?"

He stared at me for a few beats as if the question had never occurred to him, much less an answer.

"Do you honestly believe Jennifer hasn't noticed?" I asked.

"You already messed up my life once by telling the cops about me and J. C," Derek said. "Don't do anything like that again or I'll mess you up."

I laughed at him—one of those fake laughs that movie villains make before acting villainous.

"Awhile ago someone shot me in the back," I said. "I nearly died. Since then I have gone out of my way not to hurt anyone. In your case, though, I'll gladly make an exception, you lying sack of dog shit."

Derek's response was to turn and jog away. Quickly. For a moment, I thought about running him down, only what would have been the point? Whoever suggested that you could beat sense into someone didn't know what they were talking about.

I knocked on Linda Welch's front door. She pulled it open.

"What did you forget?" She recognized me. "Oh, it's you, McKenzie. I thought you were someone else."

Linda was wearing a long robe cinched tightly at the waist and nothing else that I could see. I flashed on what the Westermeyer sisters had told me three weeks earlier about square pegs and round holes.

"Were you expecting Derek Carlson?" I asked. "I was just talking to him."

"You were?"

Linda closed her eyes and sighed dramatically.

"He told you, didn't he?" she said. "I had the feeling he might, the way he treated me today; the way he spoke to me. Not necessarily you, but someone. I knew it was just a matter of time. I've always known."

Wait. What?

"He didn't tell me everything, though," I said.

"He doesn't know everything."

Linda opened her door wider to allow me to pass. I stepped inside her house; she led me to her living room. She stood in front of me. Every time I had seen her in the past she had appeared angry. Now she seemed tired.

"I suppose after hearing that they found the man who killed Jeanette Carrell's husband, Derek is now thinking that she'll come home and he can go back to fucking her instead of me," Linda said. "So, why should he keep my secrets?"

Careful, careful, careful.

"I'm surprised he kept them this long," I said.

"McKenzie, the texts I've been getting this morning say that you found the killer, is that right?" Linda asked.

"I helped."

"Now you're here to catch Charles Sainsbury's killer, too?"

"I just wanted to hear your side of the story," I said. "I wouldn't trust Derek as far as I could throw him."

"I never trusted him, either. Ah, McKenzie, it's not fair. What happened, it's just not fair."

Oh my God, she's getting ready to confess. Do not screw this up.

"Tell me."

Linda reached behind her, searching for a chair. She found one and sunk into it.

"I don't want to go to jail," she said. "Only I can't keep going on like this. It's been months and I'm just so tired of it."

"Tell me," I repeated.

The words came out so fast it was as if Linda was trying to speak them all in one breath. I let her, not daring to interrupt.

"William—when I first started having my affair with William—he kept telling me how his marriage was a sham and he was going to end it and I didn't believe him and finally he did end it, he left his wife, and I thought, good Lord, he was telling the truth. I was so happy. Then one day—we had a strong wind the day before and a lot of dead branches had come off my trees and I dragged them up the hill to the brush pile near the fire ring. That's what most of us did. Kept a nice supply of wood for fires. He was standing there, looking at the hill like he was saying good-bye to it. He saw me. Charles Sainsbury. He came over and started shouting. He didn't say hello; didn't allow me to say hello. Just started shouting. He said he knew that I was sleeping with William. That I had ruined his marriage. He said he would not tolerate it. He said he would not allow me to disgrace his family name. *Me,* like William was completely innocent in the matter. He said he would break us up even if it meant disinheriting William and putting Bethany in charge of his company. Then he started calling me names. Called me fat. Called me a whore. Called me the same names that my ex-husband had called me before he left to marry a woman fifteen years younger. The branch was in my hand. The tree branch. I hit him. I hit him twice. He fell. I dropped the branch and I walked home. I didn't run. I didn't even look back. I locked myself in my house and I wept and I waited. I didn't know Charles was dead, McKenzie. I thought he'd get up and call the police and they'd come for me. Only they didn't. The next day a deputy knocked on my door and I thought, here we go. Except he didn't arrest me. Instead, he said that Charles had gone missing and wanted to know if I had seen him. I thought it was a trick. I thought; is it possible that Charles got up and wandered off somewhere? Did I hurt his brain like Carson Vaneps's brain was hurt? After the deputy left, I nearly ran up the hill to the brush pile to see if Charles was still there. I didn't, though. Instead, I kept waiting. I waited until Jenny Carlson found Charles's body. Someone had buried him. Then they said it was Jeanette Carrell who had buried him and I thought; why would she do that? She wouldn't have done it to help me. She wouldn't have lifted a finger to help me. She did it for one of her girls, I decided. She must have thought that one of her girls had killed Charles. When the deputies arrested her I thought, it was her own fault. If she hadn't tried to be so clever, if she had left Charles where he laid, none of this would have happened."

"That was your excuse for not coming forward," I said at last.

"It was either her or me, that's the way I saw it."

I dropped the hammer on Linda, surprised that it landed so softly.

"Derek Carlson," I said.

"He saw me walking home while he was jogging his way to Jeanette Carrell's bedroom. It wasn't until they arrested Jeanette that he figured out that I was the one who killed Charles. That's when he decided to blackmail me. I don't know, maybe he was blackmailing Jeanette, too."

"What did he want? Money?"

"No, he didn't want money. He wanted me. He wanted me in any way he could imagine whenever his spirit moved him. He would jog over. Most of the time, he didn't even warn me he was coming. The thing is, McKenzie, I would have let him have me if he had just asked, I was that hard up. I always knew he would betray me, though. It was just a matter of time."

"You could take him down with you," I said. "He knew you committed the crime and took steps to protect you. That makes him a co-conspirator. Also, the blackmail. That's a criminal offense, too."

Now who's a lying sack of dog shit? Derek will never even be arrested, much less see the inside of a jail cell.

"How?" Linda asked. "How can I hurt him?"

Deputy Sergeant Michael Swenson arrived twenty minutes later, only he didn't come alone. He had an ACA with him, along with a camera and recording equipment. They were there to tape Linda's confession in the comfort of her own home at my suggestion.

I thought Linda would fully realize what she was about to do while we waited and go ballistic. Or at least demand to speak to an attorney. Only she remained calm, relaxed, and after they set up their equipment and read her her rights—for the third time!—she began talking.

This time, though, Linda spoke slower, relating her story with much more detail than when she confessed to me. Questions were asked; the ACA asked some of those questions several times in different ways. Linda answered them patiently. When she was finished, she wept; not with fear, but with relief.

Linda was formally taken into custody and the equipment was packed up. I left her house along with Deputy Swenson.

"Just so you know; there was a double homicide in Vadnais Heights last night," he said.

"You're telling me this because . . . ?"

"You seem pretty good at doing my job."

"You're welcome."

JUST SO YOU KNOW

It became obvious long before Adam Berenson's trial began that his very expensive attorneys would be mounting what I knew as a Plan B defense—blame someone else—that others sometimes called a TODDI—The Other Dude Did It.

The Other Dude, of course, was Jeanette Carrell, aka that well-known fugitive bank robber Luna Cifuentes.

This despite the recording I had made. And Mike Swenson's testimony.

This despite a witness named Peter Sarper—Dominic Belden had thought his name was Harper—that Swenson and the Ramsey County CIU had identified.

Sarper had been the assistant director of operations for North Country Properties under Suzanne Costello. He testified that Berenson had come to him two days after she disappeared and told him that he was now the director of operations and if he wanted to keep the job, he and his staff would keep their mouths shut. They would forget that Costello—and David Carrell—had even existed, much less worked for North Country.

According to Sarper, Berenson explained that Costello and Carrell were lovers; that they had conspired to embezzle more than $700,000 from the firm, and they had run off together, probably to the Cayman Islands because that's what embezzlers did. Berenson said that he didn't want anyone to know about this, though, especially the police, because it would be bad for business. Investors would stop trusting both North Country Properties and the Polachek Companies, building developments would evaporate, and everyone, including Sarper, would lose their jobs.

Sarper told Berenson that he would do what he was told because what else was he going to do? However, he had documented the thefts and all of his communications with Berenson from that moment forward "just in case," he told the deputies. Swenson later told me that he was so delighted with the documents, "I almost kissed that old man."

Meanwhile, Linda Welch's much-less-expensive attorney thought he'd try the same tactic, despite her taped confession, which he hoped to get thrown out. After all, Jeanette Carrell had threatened the victim and had been seen burying something on the hill by her next-door neighbor, never mind that Katherine Hixson's testimony was now tainted both by her appearance before the Chippewa Woods HOA and her own reluctance to swear beyond a doubt that she had seen Carrell that night.

I explained all of this to Amanda when she called me using a burner phone from God knows where—"Just to say hello," she said. I was genuinely surprised to hear from her despite what she had told me in Sault Ste. Marie.

After I caught her up, she said, "I never suspected that Linda had killed Charles."

"Who did you suspect? Carson Vaneps?"

"Of course not."

"Was it Sara?"

"McKenzie . . ."

"Kate Hixson did see you that night, didn't she? You found

Sainsbury's body on the hill and decided to bury it because you thought Sara had killed him and you wanted to protect her. Who else would you have risked your own freedom for?"

She paused before answering.

"It's no longer important," she said.

"What's important is that there's a chance that both Berenson and Welch will get off."

"Do you honestly believe that's a possibility?" she asked.

"All it takes is for one juror to have just a flicker of doubt, reasonable or otherwise," I told her.

She paused again, this time for so long that I thought she had hung up.

"Amanda, are you there?" I asked.

"McKenzie, have you ever heard of Rule 11(c)(1)(C) under the Federal Sentencing Guidelines?"

"No."

"That's okay. Alexander Brandt has. I hope to see you soon. Good-bye for now."

See me soon, what the hell does that mean? my inner voice wanted to know. *Good-bye for now?*

I almost called Jeanette Carrell's attorney to ask him. I didn't, though. Instead, he called me a week later.

"Apparently, you are one of the very few people that J. C. trusts," Brandt said.

"Trust me to do what?"

"Protect her."

"Excuse me?"

"Just in case Adam Berenson sends his thugs to rub her out."

There were so many ways to respond to that statement. I chose, "Does your mother know you talk like that?"

Once we began speaking like adults, I was told that, with Brandt's help, Amanda had cut a deal that would finally bring her home. It was complicated because it involved two Ramsey County assistant attorneys, an assistant United States attorney, the U.S. Marshals Service, and a federal judge.

According to Brandt, what it came down to was this— Jeanette Carrell, aka Luna Cifuentes, would surrender to the marshals. She would then enter into a cooperation agreement with all the attorneys involved. She would testify against both Adam Berenson and Linda Welch in their respective cases in a Minnesota court. She would then plead guilty to robbing that bank in Cedar Rapids in federal court. If her testimony was everything that the assistant county attorneys hoped it would be, they would notify the assistant U.S. attorney that Carrell had held up her side of the deal. The AUSA would then recommend that the federal judge sentence Carrell to two years' probation for the bank robbery, plus restitution, meaning she'd have to pay back the money she stole.

I asked Brandt where the protection part came into it. "She'll be in the custody of the U.S. Marshals, won't she?"

"No. As per the agreement, she'll remain under her own recognizance. As long as she appears in court when required to do so, she'll be fine."

"When is all of this going to take place?"

"Starting tomorrow," Brandt said.

"Tomorrow? Geez, thanks for the heads-up."

"The trial dates have not yet been scheduled, although, given the notoriety of the case and insistence by Berenson's attorneys for a speedy and orderly trial, it shouldn't take long. His won't, anyway. Lord knows how long Linda Welch will have to wait in jail before she goes to trial."

"Money talks," I said.

"Doesn't it always? Anyway, J. C. will arrive tomorrow. I don't know exactly when she'll arrive or from where. You'll find her or she'll find you, one or the other. You'll shepherd her to me and I'll walk her through the system. Afterward, she'll appear before the ACAs trying first Berenson's and then Welch's case, give her depositions, and melt away until the trials are scheduled."

"I'll find her or she'll find me?"

"She said you should wait in that fine car of yours and she'll be in touch."

"That woman," I said.

"Isn't she, though?"

I didn't actually wait in my car, however. Instead, I sat in my chair behind my desk in my condominium and stared at my cell phone—my new cell phone. The assistant county attorney never did return my old phone even though it had been nearly six weeks since he confiscated it.

While I waited, I asked Nina if she minded if we put Amanda up in our guest room for a few days. She thought that was fine as long as she moved on by the time Erica came home from Tulane University during Christmas break.

"I'd like to meet her," Nina said.

Finally, the phone rang.

"This is McKenzie," I answered.

"Minneapolis Institute of Art," Amanda's voice said.

"When?"

"As soon as possible."

The institute was eight minutes away from our condominium in downtown Minneapolis. I found a place to park and walked through the glass doors like I was a dues-paying member. I expected to see Amanda waiting for me among the Christmas decorations in the foyer. She wasn't. I hung around for a bit, watching people come and go, reminding myself that she had probably changed her appearance since we last met.

Finally, I decided she must be waiting for me upstairs at one of the exhibits, where it was easier to hide.

I started wandering. Eventually, I found myself in Gallery 355 and standing in front of *Olive Trees*, a painting by Vincent van Gogh. After a few moments, an arm circled my arm and a head rested against my shoulder.

Amanda had allowed her hair to grow out in the past six weeks and had dyed it blond. She looked very much like the old Jeanette Carrell.

"Technically, van Gogh wasn't that great of a painter," she said. "His brushstrokes were so spontaneous. What set him apart, what made him great, were his colors. Yellows and oranges and reds—his world was so bright and bold. Even something as gloomy as *The Potato Eaters* is full of life."

"Is that how you see it, too?" I asked. "The world?"

"No, McKenzie, that's not how I see it."

"What should I call you? Amanda?"

"I've retired Amanda, at least for the time being. You can call me J. C. for now."

"What only your dearest friends call you."

"I think you've earned it."

I escorted J. C. out of the Minneapolis Institute of Arts to my Mustang.

"You're welcome to stay with Nina and me while all this gets sorted out," I said.

"That's very kind of you, except I have a place to stay."

"Where?"

I parked the Mustang in the driveway next to Carson Vaneps's house on the Circle.

"Would you think to look for me here?" J. C. asked.

I didn't get a chance to answer. That's because J. C. opened the door, launched herself out of the car, and dashed across the yard toward Sara Vaneps, who was running toward her. They met in a splendid collision and fell to their knees while hugging each other.

I sat in the car and watched, giving them some privacy. Carson Vaneps appeared in the doorway. I left the car when he left the house.

"Jacey," he said. "There's my girl."

J. C. regained her feet and marched to where Carson was standing. They embraced. I heard J. C. muttering, "My good and kind friend."

"Jacey, I've been thinking," Carson said. "Screw Charles Sainsbury. How 'bout you and me buy the hill? We'll turn it into a private park."

"Yes, Carson, yes. That's a wonderful idea."

"Do you think your young man will mind?"

"No, I don't think he'll mind."

J. C. stayed with the Vaneps for nearly two weeks. During that time I served as chauffer and bodyguard—mostly chauffer. No one came near her.

I drove her to and from her attorney's office, the Ramsey County attorney's office in the Lowry Hotel Building, and the Warren E. Burger Federal Building. I have no idea what was said or by whom; I wasn't allowed in any of the meetings and both J. C. and her attorney, Alexander Brandt, were tight-lipped about it all. I do know that the information J. C. supplied was eventually shared with the attorneys for Linda Welch and Adam Berenson.

As a result, Linda Welch pled guilty to manslaughter in

the second degree and was sentenced to seven years and four months at the Minnesota Correctional Facility in Shakopee.

Adam Berenson also pleaded guilty, only his sentence was stayed. According to news reports, like J. C., he had also entered into a cooperation agreement. Apparently, he had a lot to say about a large number of building developments and the people involved in them and an army of state and federal prosecutors were anxious to hear it.

A typical gangster thing to do, my inner voice suggested. *Honor among thieves my ass.*

Which left me confident that J. C. was now free and clear.

I was mistaken.

The Ramsey County attorney hadn't forgotten how incompetent Carrell had made him appear, this just before an election that he eventually lost! Even though she had upheld her end of the bargain, he ignored the promises made by his own ACAs, went over the head of the assistant U.S. attorney, and a few days before Christmas contacted the federal judge directly—an unusual if not altogether unprecedented move. He informed the judge that the state hadn't required J. C.'s testimony after all; that they would have reached plea agreements with the defendants without her. The AUSA insisted that the court honor J. C.'s deal, anyway. The judge refused. J. C. was now faced with two options. A: she could appear before the judge and take her chances. B: she could withdraw her guilty plea and go to trial.

J. C. chose option C.

I learned about it when Deputy U.S. Marshal Amy DeVries Linabery called and asked me to meet her at the Caribou Coffee shop near the federal building in downtown St. Paul. This time she paid.

"Luna Cifuentes is in the wind," she told me. "She was expected to appear in federal court at nine A.M. this morning. She was a no-show."

That woman.

"Why?" I asked. "What happened?"

DeVries told me about the Ramsey County attorney's machinations.

I challenged his manhood with a long string of expletives.

"You forgot coward," DeVries said. "I had never known an elected official who wasn't terrified of losing their job."

"That, too," I said.

"McKenzie, do you know where Cifuentes is?"

"No."

"Do you know what name she is using?"

"No."

"Do you expect her to reach out to you?"

"No."

"If she does, will you contact me?"

"No."

"Okay," DeVries said.

"Okay?"

"Cifuentes kept her part of the deal. She surrendered to the marshals. She pleaded guilty. She paid restitution. She testified against the bad guys. The only reason she's in the wind now is because of the bruised ego of the coward that the good voters of Ramsey County were smart enough to kick out of office."

"Makes me wish I still lived there," I said.

"My point—the case is on my desk, only I will not be looking for her that hard. If you hear from Cifuentes, you might tell her I said so."

That afternoon, Sara Vaneps called.

"J. C. left," Sara told me. "She left in the middle of the night. She just . . ."

"Walked away," I said.

"She left a note," Sara said. "She wrote: *Carson is gone. Your grandfather is gone. It's time to put him in an assisted living facility; use the money your family received from selling the Circle to pay for it. It's time for you to live your own life. Live it as the strong and beautiful woman you are.*"

"That sounds like good advice, Sara," I said.

"J. C. didn't even say good-bye."

"Maybe I can help with that."

Evangeline had scheduled the party between Christmas and New Year's, hosting the Plot Whores Book Club and as many of J. C.'s girls as we could find, at her home on the Circle, although, I was told, they didn't call it that anymore.

A lot had changed since William Sainsbury had sent his excavator up the hill.

Jennifer Carlson had been promoted, given an office with windows, and kicked her husband Derek to the curb—all on the same day.

Katherine Hixson had been welcomed back to the fold.

Rachel Westermeyer Wright bought her daughter a blood python.

"God help me," she said.

And a dozen mini-mansions on the hill were now looking down into the rear windows and backyards of the houses that surrounded them. Many of the women were considering moving.

"McKenzie," Bethany Gilman said. "Evan said that you're responsible for this little get-together. Is that right?"

"Yes."

"What's going on?" Rebecca Westermeyer Sauer wanted to know.

"A friend asked me to do her a favor," I said.

"J. C.?" Sara asked.

I took a sip of the maple-flavored bourbon that Evan had poured for me.

"Let me tell you a story," I said. "Some of it might be true. Some of it not so much. I'll leave that for you to decide. The story is about a woman named Amanda, who lived her entire life in the hard, hard wind . . ."